Dear Reader,

I often think this is [the most romantic month of the]
calendar: the start of [the year which] holds, Valentine's Day, Spring brides and lots of beautiful flowers. Well, I hope I can make this particular season even more romantic for you with this month's selection of books for you to enjoy.

Last year we were able to announce popular author Margaret Pargeter's return to writing and this month we are thrilled to welcome much loved romance writer Mary Wibberley to the *Scarlet* family. Mary's heroine finds herself involved in *The Most Dangerous Game*, when she falls in love with her bodyguard. In *Craven's Bride*, by talented author Danielle Shaw, the last thing Max views Alison as is a potential wife! Award-winning Julia Wild tantalizes readers as they share a *Blue Silk Promise* with her amnesiac hero. And finally we are delighted to welcome yet another exiting new author, Lisa Andrews, to the *Scarlet* list with an intriguing and *Dangerous Deception*.

As always, I hope that you will enjoy all of these titles which I have chosen especially for you, but if there is a theme we haven't covered, or if you'd like, say, to see more exotic settings or more American authors on our list, why not write to me and I'll do my best to include *your* request over the coming months.

Till next month,

Sally Cooper

SALLY COOPER,
Editor-in-Chief – *Scarlet*

About the Author

Lisa Andrews has always been an avid reader and, at university, couldn't believe that someone was actually paying her to read books! Unfortunately, studying the classics had a counter-effect on her, because she knew she could never write so well, so she didn't even try. Twenty years later, Lisa was working in a bookstore over Christmas, when the manager gave her a romance novel. She read it, decided *she* was going to write a romance and was hooked! The author says she becomes easily bored in jobs, but, with romance writing 'at last I've found the perfect career.'

Lisa lives with her husband and their two teenage children in Wales. They've lived in quite a few places in Britain, but returned to Wales for the quality of life and for the magnificient beaches nearby. Lisa remembers 'we tried our hand at self-sufficiency for a while, but when the fox kept eating the chickens, the pigeons ate the cabbages and the birds stripped the fruit bushes, we gave it up as a bad job!'

Other *Scarlet* titles available this month:
BLUE SILK PROMISE – Julia Wild
THE MOST DANGEROUS GAME – Mary Wibberley
CRAVEN'S BRIDE – Danielle Shaw

LISA ANDREWS

DANGEROUS DECEPTION

SCARLET

Enquiries to:
Robinson Publishing Ltd
7 Kensington Church Court
London W8 4SP

First published in the UK by Scarlet, 1998

Copyright © Linda Steel 1998
Cover photography by Colin Thomas

The right of Linda Steel to be identified as author
of this work has been asserted by her in accordance
with the Copyright, Designs and Patents Act 1988.

All rights reserved. No part of this publication
may be reproduced in any form or by any means
without the prior written permission of the publisher.

This book is sold subject to the condition that it shall
not, by way of trade or otherwise, be lent, re-sold,
hired out or otherwise circulated in any form of binding
or cover other than that in which it is published and
without a similar condition including this condition being
imposed on the subsequent purchaser.

A copy of the British Library Cataloguing in
Publication data is available from the British Library

ISBN 1–85487–866–2

Printed and bound in the EC

10 9 8 7 6 5 4 3 2 1

CHAPTER 1

Emma fingered the personal alarm that she kept in the pocket of her uniform. If the dark, arrogant man who was watching her like a hawk pounced, she'd let it rip, penthouse suite or no penthouse suite!

She'd complained to her friends about feeling invisible as she cleaned up after the rich and famous who frequented this top London hotel, but to be regarded this closely was infinitely worse.

As he stirred his coffee she stole a cautious glance at his hard uncompromising features. He was about thirty, she guessed. Raven-black hair swept straight back from his face gave him a gangster-like appearance, but this was contradicted by a roman nose which lent him an almost patrician air. He was handsome, she supposed, in a brooding continental type of way, but there was a ruthless edge to his countenance that made her nervous. The way he had been coldly analysing her for the past twenty minutes gave her the shivers.

As if to dispute this, dark brown eyes flickered up suddenly and met her deep blue ones, and the most expressive, perfectly formed mouth she had ever seen twisted into a slow lazy smile.

What was it about these Latins? Did they think it was bad luck for a woman to cross their path and not try to charm her?

Arriving at the conclusion that the man must be a high-ranking member of the Mafia, because of his looks, expensive clothes and the cost of the apartment, Emma hurriedly completed her tasks. It would be a relief to leave and no longer be subjected to that intense appraising gaze.

Suddenly hearing him speaking Spanish as he picked up the telephone and asked another man to come in made her smile. She really shouldn't be so quick to make judgements about people, she realized, but even if he wasn't an Italian mobster she certainly wasn't going to hang around and wait for his friend. One hot-blooded Spaniard was bad enough.

'Where are you going?' She was halfway to the door and freedom when a deep, resonant voice stopped her in her tracks.

'I've finished now, sir.' She turned back defiantly. She had left the room spotless. What more did he want from her, and why on earth should he sound angry that she was leaving?

'Clean the television screen please; it appears

2

streaky.' An elegantly clad arm peremptorily indicated the corner of the room.

Emma snatched up her spray-bottle and cloth and flashed him a look of contempt. To her astonishment, as she turned back to the television she was certain she saw his lips curling in amusement.

She couldn't take much more of this, she decided, taking her anger out on the television screen. It had seemed such an ideal way of paying off her overdraft – free accommodation, free food and tips. But the reality had been different. She accepted the hard work, but found the superior attitude of some of the guests difficult to stomach. Some of them seemed to think she should feel privileged to clear up their mess and clean their loos. If she was ever rich she'd –

'What do you think, Ramón?' The authoritative tones of the man cut through her reverie. Emma hadn't heard the door open and she looked up to see another man studying her curiously. If the first man had reminded her of a gangster, the second was an older, seedier, almost thirties version of the type.

Despite her earlier resolution, she took an instant dislike to short, fat, balding, supercilious Ramón, and kept her finger purposefully on her alarm as she walked back across the room.

'Amanda?' Ramón regarded her with a puzzled expression.

'No. Not Amanda,' continued the younger man in his native tongue, 'but quite an amazing likeness, don't you think?'

Ramón nodded and his eyes swept over her body with a coarseness that made her feel sick. 'This one is bigger on top,' was his verdict.

'Just a moment,' said the first man, restraining her with long slender fingers.

'Please sit down. I have a business proposition for you.'

This was the final straw. Emma's fine porcelain skin flared with colour and she spat out her words, 'I'm sure the floor manager can accommodate your needs, *sir*. I don't do things like that!'

To her shocked surprise, the man threw back his head and roared with laughter. 'You insult me, *guapa*,' he said when he had recovered his self-possession. 'I believe it is demeaning to both parties to pay for sexual services. Now sit down!'

The brown eyes seemed to be boring into her skull. He was obviously not used to being denied anything, but Emma remained standing. She had cleaned his room, fulfilled her contract; she didn't have to take this.

'No. I'm not interested,' she snapped, pushing past him to the door which was now blocked by the flabby bulk of Ramón.

Panic swept over her and she stepped back, holding aloft her personal alarm. 'L . . . Let me go, or this will make such a racket that everyone

4

in the hotel will come running.'

'Allow the lady to leave, Ramón,' said the man, standing up and moving to one side.

Emma glanced at the face towering above her, but it had adopted a mild expression and his stance was non-threatening. She hurried past, congratulating herself that she'd thought to take precautions against occurrences such as this, and made once again for the door.

Gripping the handle, with freedom almost in sight, Emma gasped as the younger man, who had approached silently behind her, pulled the alarm quickly away from her.

Laughter rang in her ears as she began to shake, and her face, always pale, became deathly white.

'Shut up, Ramón!' The command was uttered and Ramón became silent. 'Do not be afraid,' he added to her in a tone gentler than any she could have imagined him adopting. 'I am not going to hurt you. I only wish to talk to you.'

She sat down, defeated, in the chair indicated for her presence, and stared at her hands, which were still trembling.

'I believe the coffee is still drinkable,' continued the man in the same soothing manner. 'May I pour you a cup?'

'If you like,' she answered flatly. 'Milk, one sugar.'

He handed her the cup and she sipped the warm liquid gratefully. He'd made it sweeter than she'd asked, but it tasted good and she felt her spirit revive. It was right to be cautious, but sometimes her imagination got the better of her. If he'd had designs on her body, she didn't think she'd still be sitting here drinking his coffee.

'That is better,' he said as she drained the cup. 'I thought you were going to faint. Now try one of these croissants. They're very good.' He pushed the tray towards her and refilled her cup.

What was he playing at? He probably knew as well as she did that if the management knew she was sitting here eating a guest's breakfast she'd be sacked. But she was hungry, and with the time she'd already spent in his room there was no way she'd get her break this morning.

She looked up – the dark face regarding her was inscrutable – but as she tore a croissant apart she witnessed a flicker of triumph in his eyes. He sat back now, totally at ease, on the other side of the table and opened his wallet.

'This is my fiancée – correction, *was* my fiancée.' He handed her a crumpled photograph, and she noticed that the gentle note in his voice had now vanished.

Emma gazed at the photo. It showed the man in a dinner suit with a blonde sophisticated woman on his arm. The woman's dress was elegant and expensive and her hair was shorter, but the face was the exact image of her own. They could have been twins.

'You see, this is my only interest in you.'

'So?' she answered ungraciously, flicking the photograph back across the table.

The man's eyes narrowed and she felt a shiver creep down her spine. It was a mistake to think he was capable of kindness just because she was eating his food. Laboratory technicians probably gave their rats a good last dinner before dissecting them.

'So,' he continued equably, and she felt instinctively the effort it cost him to maintain his mild manner, 'I am not, as you say, the type of person to look a gift horse in the mouth. I am meant to be travelling to Sevilla on Saturday in order that my grandfather, who does not have long to live, can meet my future wife. Unfortunately I proved hasty in notifying him of my marriage plans. Amanda gave me back my ring on Friday night and the engagement is cancelled. I intended to travel alone on Saturday and explain everything, but I know that this will upset the old man. He was delighted that, after a misspent youth, I had finally decided to settle down. You will accompany me instead. I will pay you to act the part of my fiancée.'

Emma gave a hollow laugh. 'You're joking,' she said, amazed at the gall of the man.

'Completely serious,' he replied, eyeing her coldly.

'You'd be taking a risk, wouldn't you? What if I told the old man the truth?'

'You would not do that. Believe me, you

7

would regret it.' His lips compressed in an effort to control his patience.

'A threat?' She was almost beginning to enjoy taunting him now that she was more secure of his motives.

'A promise,' he stated, his lips twisted in a cruel smile that made her uneasy.

'I think it would be difficult for me to pretend to be in love with you,' she muttered, but he ignored her.

'I will pay you five hundred pounds to accompany me for a week to Sevilla plus suitable clothes which will cost considerably more than that. My lawyer will draw up a business contract, and naturally I will pay for the services of a lawyer of your own choosing.'

Emma stared into her empty coffee cup. Why did it have to be Spain where he lived? Anywhere else and she would have dismissed his ridiculous suggestion out of hand. But he was offering her what seemed the only solution to her problems. She'd given up hope of being able to pay off her overdraft and visit Spain before her final year at university began in October. Language students were expected to spend most of the summer in their chosen country. If she failed to go she'd be at a definite disadvantage when it came to taking her finals next year.

'There will be a bonus for you if you acquit yourself well,' continued the deep velvety voice, correctly interpreting her silence as weakness.

Emma despised the man for his money, and herself for even considering his offer. 'Do you always get what you want?' she flashed, not attempting to conceal her feelings.

His head tipped back slightly as he registered the hate in her eyes, but he answered softly, 'Everyone has a price.'

And this is mine, she pondered, dropping her gaze. How contemptible he must believe me. 'I don't think so,' she said, shaking her head.

'I believe I know what's worrying you. Ramón, fetch the manager.'

'Blackmail?'

'Hardly,' he replied with a sardonic smile.

Uncomfortable under the dark, penetrating gaze he was subjecting her to, she turned her attention to the last remaining croissant. She may as well make the most of it, she decided, popping it into her mouth. If the manager was on his way up then there was every likelihood that she'd shortly be on the way out. In this hotel the guest was king. Any member of staff who forgot it was quickly reminded of the fact when they saw their belongings scattered on the pavement outside.

'You have not had breakfast?' he asked, as she picked up the coffee pot and shook it to see if there was any left.

'You mean do I always eat like a pig?' she challenged, pouring herself another cup.

'That is not what I asked,' he said, though his

eyes were glinting with amusement.

'May as well have.' Emma shrugged. She was used to it. Her friends were always moaning how unfair it was that she could stuff her face and remain so slim. Maybe if they'd pushed a vacuum cleaner over miles of carpet week after week they'd realize how hungry it made you.

'Are you going to answer my question – have you had breakfast?'

Emma scowled at him. What difference did it make? 'Yes, I've had breakfast, but it didn't taste as good as this. They should get an award for recycling in this place. They save everything that the guests leave and serve it up for the staff the next day.' It was only a rumour, but tasting this man's croissant she was convinced of it. They never tasted this soft and buttery in the staff restaurant.

She took another sip of coffee and considered. Yes, it had a different, more luxurious taste. 'They even warm up your leftover coffee as well,' she informed him, 'so do us all a favour and try not to slurp any of it back into the pot, would you?'

The man's face puckered with distaste, and Emma stifled a giggle. What was the matter with her? She wasn't normally this antagonistic, but there was something about this arrogant stranger's attitude that made her want to provoke him.

Stranger? It struck her that although he'd

asked her to travel to Spain with him, he hadn't as yet volunteered his identity. He was quick enough to ask her questions.

'Who are you, by the way?' she enquired.

'I am Luis García Quevedo.'

'Course you are, she thought, unable to hide her amusement at the pride in his voice when he pronounced his name. He obviously thought it should mean something, but she still didn't have a clue who he was.

'You find this amusing?'

'No. The name suits you.' She couldn't have dreamed up a more arrogant title herself.

He picked up a piece of notepaper and began writing, and she finished off her coffee. It was unfortunate that the Spanish had a tendency to spoil their male children completely. They even referred to their baby boys as 'the little king' and treated them accordingly. It was small wonder that some of them grew up to be overbearing despots like Luis García Quevedo.

Eventually there was a knock on the door and the man whom the staff referred to as 'God' entered the suite.

Emma hastily wiped the last remaining croissant crumbs from her fingers and stood up.

'There is a problem with this girl, Mr Quevedo?' enquired the manager, looking down his nose at her.

'No. No problem, Mr Carter,' replied Luis,

the corners of his mouth twitching imperceptibly into a smile.

'Cartwright,' said the manager, and when Luis raised a quizzical eyebrow he reiterated, 'Cartwright. My name is Cartwright, not Carter.'

'I do beg your pardon, Mr Cartwright,' said Luis, and she knew for certain that he'd been aware of the fact all along. Why on earth should he want to intimidate the manager? The man was being obsequious enough in his presence already, she thought, viewing him with distaste.

'I wish to ask a favour of you, Mr Cartwright,' said Luis, pausing as the man assured him that if it was in his power etc. etc. 'I wish to take this young lady away with me on business for a week. However, I believe she is concerned about employment prospects on her return. Would it be possible for her job to remain open?'

'No problem whatsoever.' The manager smiled his assent.

'And would you be so kind as to recommend a lawyer to her?'

The manager left on a tide of assurances, and Luis turned his attention back to Emma. 'I trust that is satisfactory?'

'I haven't agreed to come with you,' she said, though the idea of being able to visit Spain and finish work at the hotel was becoming more and more appealing.

'You have not said that you will not,' he

pointed out in his rather formal English, which was also rather appealing.

'Why did you call the manager Carter?' she asked, changing the subject and giving herself more time to think.

'A simple mistake.'

'You knew his name was Cartwright.'

'Did I?'

'You know you did.'

A smile deepened into a broad grin over the man's face, and she was caught by the contrast of white, even teeth against his mahogany-tanned skin. 'Actually I did it for you, *guapa*,' he said, chucking her under the chin. 'It amused me to see the look you gave him when he immediately jumped to the conclusion that you were to blame for his having being summoned.'

Despite herself, Emma began to laugh, and as his brown eyes twinkled, sharing the joke, she found herself thinking that he was almost human when he loosened up a little.

'My terms are acceptable, then?' he enquired, bringing her back down to earth.

'If I come with you, I want to stay in Spain for a while after the week is over.'

'Why?' He regarded her suspiciously.

'Why not? Wouldn't you rate it as a country worth visiting?' she asked sweetly, deliberately goading him.

His lips contracted into a tight line, but he

refused to take the bait. 'What about your job?' he demanded.

She shrugged. 'One word from you and old Cartwright would turn cartwheels. I don't think he's going to lose any sleep about me going AWOL for a few extra weeks.'

'AWOL?' he murmured, frowning.

'Absent without leave,' she explained. He spoke English much better than she could speak Spanish. It was quite satisfying finding something he didn't understand. 'Besides,' she added, 'after a week with you I reckon I'll deserve a holiday.'

He laughed. It wasn't the reaction she expected, and for some reason it annoyed her. 'You may stay in Spain,' he conceded, 'but you cannot remain in Sevilla. You may go to Madrid, Barcelona, somewhere far enough away. I shall arrange a ticket for you at the appropriate time.'

'And my ticket home?'

He gave a curt nod. She knew she was pushing it a bit far asking for it, but she needed to know exactly where she stood. Having to fork out for the fare home would make a great deal of difference as to how long she could afford to stay in Spain.

'That is all, then? It is settled?' He was growing impatient, but there was one more question she needed to ask. She took a deep breath.

'I'm to act as your fiancée?'

'That is what I said.'

'You also said you didn't pay for sexual services.' She dropped her head in an effort to hide the flush of colour sweeping upwards.

'Exactly,' said Luis. 'Your duties end at the bedroom door unless you persuade me otherwise.'

Emma looked up quickly, but his face was inscrutable and she couldn't decide whether he was joking or not. Did women usually try and seduce him? It was a whole different world from the one she was used to, but she was probably safer with him than with most. Her inferior status, in his eyes, would prevent him thinking of her as a sexual partner. He was employing her to do a job as he would employ a cook, a gardener, or a maid. That was how he saw her - as hired help. She couldn't imagine a man as arrogant as Quevedo ever demeaning himself by consorting with the lower orders of society. Whoever this Amanda person was it was a pretty safe bet that she hadn't been working as a chambermaid when they'd met.

'You appear to have reached some conclusion,' he prompted.

Emma trailed her finger along the back of a chair and tried to shake off the strange feeling of foreboding that gripped her stomach. What was she afraid of? It was a business contract, for goodness' sake. If she didn't take it she'd be stuck here for the rest of the summer.

15

She raised her head and gazed enquiringly at the man. He gazed levelly back, passing the 'shifty character' test.

'All right,' she murmured. Until she signed anything she was free to change her mind, and her solicitor would tell her if there was anything dodgy about the contract. If there was then Luis Quevedo wouldn't see her for dust, and he'd be visiting Sevilla without his fake fiancée.

'Excellent. I will arrange for my secretary to take you shopping, and also to the hairdresser.'

'Hairdresser?'

'Yes. Amanda's hair is lighter than yours. You need to have splashes of brightness inserted.'

'You mean highlights?'

'I believe that is what they are called, yes. The condition would also be improved by cutting.' He fingered the dry wisps escaping from her ponytail.

Emma shrugged away. Cheek! Not everyone could afford to visit the hairdresser every couple of weeks, though she couldn't imagine him even doing that. He would lift up the phone and one would come rushing to do his bidding.

'Let me see that photo again,' she demanded.

He opened his wallet and handed it over. The woman's hair hung sleek and shiny in a perfectly shaped bob. Emma smiled to herself. It would be rather exciting having a complete change of image.

'OK . . . I wouldn't mind looking like that,'

she answered magnanimously, handing it back.

The irony appeared to be lost on Ramón, but Luis laughed. 'That is most sporting of you.'

'I've just realized. You've never asked me my name.'

Luis shrugged. 'It is not important. I shall call you Amanda; it is less complicated.'

'No way! You can call me by another woman's name when we land in Spain, as part of the bargain. Not before and not after.'

He looked surprised at her outburst and studied her for several moments before replying, 'As you wish. What is your name?'

'Emma.'

'Emma,' he repeated, rolling the syllables over his tongue. She thought she'd never heard it said so seductively, but she was still too cross with him to appreciate it fully.

'This name also suits you, but I will not think it such a good one if I forget and pronounce it in front of my grandfather.'

'You're too soft, Luis,' said Ramón, conversing as ever in his native tongue. 'She'd have given in.'

Luis raised his eyebrows in dispute. 'In this matter I believe she would have been stubborn. It is only a small concession, worth doing if it makes her happy.'

'Happy! Who gives a damn about her happiness? You're kitting her out and paying her probably a month's wages just to come on holiday with you. The stupid girl should be ecstatic.'

'Do not call her that!' Luis flashed.

'All I'm saying is that she'll think you're weak and try to get away with other things now.'

Luis sighed. 'What is there to get away with? She will play her part in front of my grandfather; she is not stupid. The visit is only scheduled for a week after all. Besides, you have often accused me of being weak in matters concerning women.'

'Not with ones of her sort.'

'What exactly is her sort, Ramón?'

'Do you really want me to spell it out?' Ramón sneered. 'The girl's a chambermaid, for heaven's sake. All she's got going for her is a pretty face and big —'

Luis barked out a reply but Emma missed it. All she could hear was the roar in her ears as blood pounded around her system. She might have a habit of jumping to conclusions about people, but in this case she'd been spot on. Ramón was every bit as obnoxious as her first impression of him.

Since the beginning of this exchange, Emma had turned to look out of the window in case her expression gave her away. It was as well she had, because the men would need only one look at her face to know that she could understand every word they'd been saying. She'd kept quiet about knowing Spanish because she needed to be sure that Luis wasn't trying to trick her and she wanted to find out as much information as possible about him. And she wouldn't do that by becoming angry and failing to listen to them.

Emma turned her attention back to the discussion. She glanced quickly across at the men. Luis looked flushed and angry, and Ramón appeared to be backing away from him. 'I've been like a father to you, Luis,' he protested.

'No!' The denial boomed through the air, and Emma started with the ferocity of it. Luis didn't appear to notice. He was glaring at Ramón, but continued in a more controlled voice. 'You have been a faithful and loyal employee for many years, Ramón. For that I indulge you and make allowances, but you never replaced my father.'

Quevedo certainly didn't pull any punches, thought Emma, as she studied the cowed Ramón with satisfaction. There probably weren't that many people who would cross him lightly either.

But could she trust him? She gazed at the arrogant demeanour of the man and gave a wry smile. Yes, she thought she could. To Luis García Quevedo she was a nothing. A chambermaid. A servant. He wouldn't have given her a second glance if she hadn't resembled his girlfriend.

Oh yes, she'd be safe all right. He wouldn't demean himself by touching her with the tip of one manicured fingernail unless she 'persuaded him otherwise'. And she could never in her wildest imaginings find someone as overbearing and insensitive as Quevedo the least bit attractive.

'We have been discussing some of the arrangements, Emma,' lied Luis, his face softening as he addressed her. 'You will meet Moira, my secretary, in the foyer tomorrow at ten o'clock to go shopping. She will also make arrangements for you to see the lawyer, and on Saturday you will meet me in the hotel foyer at half past nine in the morning. If you have any questions in the meantime, you obviously know where to contact me. We have a deal, yes?' He smiled and held out his hand.

Emma hesitated. 'Do I have to spend any time alone with him?' She jerked her head in Ramón's direction. If he announced that Ramón was to be her minder for the week then the deal was most definitely off.

Luis frowned. She waited for him to ask whether she could understand Spanish, and she was going to admit it. Would he look embarrassed when he knew that she'd understood what they had been talking about? 'Why do you ask?' he said instead.

Because I couldn't stand to be in the slimy little toad's company one minute more than I have to, she thought. 'I just like to know exactly where I stand,' she said.

Luis shook his head. 'I don't envisage you spending any time alone with Ramón.'

'I suppose we have a deal, then.' She held out

20

her hand and he shook it firmly.

'This is a list of clothing requirements. Please ensure that Moira has it.' He handed the notepaper on which he'd been writing to Ramón.

'Underwear?' queried Ramón, reading down the list.

'Yes, underwear,' replied Luis curtly.

'Your grandfather won't see that.'

'You are a philistine, Ramón. All the items on this list are to be purchased or I expect to know why not.'

'It's your money, Luis.'

'Do not forget it.' He escorted Emma to the door and again shook her hand.

'Until Saturday,' he said, switching easily from one language to another.

'Until Saturday,' she murmured, then found herself once more in the corridor with only her cleaning trolley for company. What a morning it had been! Emma leaned against the trolley and took in several much needed breaths of air. She couldn't wait to ring her best friend Kate and tell her all about it. Kate would accuse her of being a wimp with regard to Ramón, of course. Emma's face creased into a grin as she thought how her friend would have handled the situation. Faster than lightning one heavy boot would have located Ramón's most sensitive area, the Spaniard would have hit the deck, and his fat little frame would probably still be writhing around on the carpet at this very moment.

The picture was sweet. Emma retained it in her mind as long as possible. What a worm that man was. He had obviously taken as great a dislike to her as she had to him. Or perhaps he hated women of 'her sort', full stop.

CHAPTER 2

At half past nine that Saturday, Emma paraded about the hotel foyer, delighting in the curious stares of the staff who recognized her. The nearest she'd ever come to designer clothes before was on the other side of a plate-glass window. It had never entered her head that one day she might actually wear something similar.

She'd needed quite a bit of courage to walk into the first store. The assistants seemed intimidating, the atmosphere rarefied, and the prices ridiculous. But Luis's secretary was quite a formidable woman herself. She understood the power her boss's gold card wielded in these establishments. To Emma's amazement she was fitted with a new wardrobe in less time than she'd normally have spent browsing in the High Street at home.

In the afternoon they'd visited a hairdresser who boasted a three-month waiting list. Miraculously, after a private word with Moira, he found that a client had only just cancelled and he was able to give Emma his exclusive attention.

A vibrant, more confident version of herself emerged from his salon two hours later. Her muddy-blonde straggly hair had been transformed into a well conditioned, expertly cut, highlighted bob, which suited the shape of her face to perfection.

Now that she'd agreed to the trip and there was no turning back, Emma could hardly contain her excitement. Her eyes shone and her skin glowed, drawing appreciative glances to her. She was like a child at Christmas, cocooned in her own bright bubble of happiness.

'You are on time. Good,' a deep masculine voice boomed behind her, and she twirled round, giving Luis a dazzling smile which reflected her inner emotions.

There was an unmistakable flicker of surprise in the dark brown eyes that surveyed her, but he made no comment on her appearance, which deflated her slightly. She had been feeling like Cinderella. Did he intend her not to forget that she was, in reality, only Cinders? As soon as he turned away she pulled a face at his back. Maybe it was childish but it made her feel better.

Even dressed casually, as Luis was today, in a white polo shirt and dark grey chinos, there was an air of authority about the man, and the staff rushed to do his bidding. Their baggage disap-

24

peared as if by magic, and the manager escorted him personally out of the hotel.

As soon as they were seated in the back of the chauffeur-driven limousine that was to take them to Heathrow, Luis clicked open his briefcase and forgot, or chose to ignore, her presence completely.

'What do you think, then?' she asked, unwilling to be dismissed so easily.

'About what?' he enquired infuriatingly, not lifting his head from his work.

'About me. My transformation?'

A slow smile played on his lips and he considered his words for a moment before answering, 'You were beautiful before, *guapa*. The hairstyle and clothes simply embellish this.'

He immediately returned to his papers, leaving her to reflect whether she had been given a compliment or, more importantly, whether he had meant it to be one. He must think she was attractive otherwise he wouldn't have called her *guapa*, which meant beauty in Spanish. However, on previous visits she'd found Spanish men to be liberal with their compliments, so perhaps it meant nothing. He certainly didn't give the impression of being over-enthralled by her presence.

Shortly before they arrived at Heathrow, Luis slipped his papers back into their briefcase, dug into his pocket, and produced a dark blue velvet ring box. 'Let us hope that this fits,' he said,

25

taking her left hand and slipping the engagement ring on to the third finger.

Emma gazed at the enormous ruby and diamond creation in horror. 'I hope I don't get mugged,' she said.

'Is it likely to fall off?' asked Luis.

Emma gave the ring an experimental tug. 'It's a bit loose but, no, it won't drop off.'

'Good.'

Emma continued to stare at the ring. To her mind it was grotesque, and about as subtle as walking around in a T-shirt with 'Rich Bitch' emblazoned on the front.

The deep, mellow voice of Luis intruded into her thoughts. 'Do you like it?' he asked.

'I think it's awful.' She looked challengingly into the dark brown eyes surveying her closely. 'But it does proclaim a certain message, don't you think?'

'It was not my choice,' said Luis, and turned to look out of the window. For a second Emma glimpsed the emotion he was trying to hide. Surely it wasn't pain? Had this Amanda woman dumped him and he was devastated by it? A tinge of regret seeped into Emma's romantically biased heart. Maybe she should make allowances for his behaviour in the circumstances.

'It's not so bad once you get used to it,' she attempted in a conciliatory tone when he turned back to her.

A sardonic smile played on his lips. 'I must be

sure to convey your sentiments to the jeweller when I return the ring,' he said sarcastically.

Emma glared at him, her decision about making allowances for his behaviour instantly reversed. After all, it was a girl's prerogative to change her mind.

'You are Amanda Fortescue,' he intoned dully. 'You are twenty-five, your parents are divorced, and you live with your mother in Chelsea, London.'

'I'm only twenty,' muttered Emma, but he ignored her and continued.

'Your father owns a women's magazine where you hold the post of Beauty Editor.'

'Beauty Editor! How the hell am I supposed to swing that?' she gasped.

'You are a woman, you are beautiful, I imagine that you know about make-up – it should not be so difficult.'

'Oh yeah? And I suppose I could be a gynaecologist if I put my mind to it, because as a woman I'm blessed with all the necessary equipment?'

Luis pursed his lips and thrust his hands into the pockets of his chinos. 'Listen, Emma,' he said coldly. 'My grandfather is an old man who knows that he is dying. All he wants is to be reassured that his grandson, who has disappointed him until now, is finally ready to settle down with the woman he loves. It is twenty-seven years since my grandmother died so I can

27

safely say that he knows little about women's beauty products and probably cares even less. If he asks about your work it will be purely out of politeness. You may be as vague as you choose, and if you change the subject I am sure that he will be heartily relieved.'

'You could have hired yourself a performing monkey really,' muttered Emma, scuffing the leather upholstery with her toe.

The car slowed down and came to a halt outside the airport. Emma would have liked to ask Luis about his relationship with Amanda, but there would probably be an opportunity later.

'We will be meeting Ramón here,' he said, as the chauffeur opened the door for him.

'Prince Charming?' she groaned. When Ramón hadn't shown up at the hotel Emma had begun to hope that Mr Personality was staying behind in Britain.

Luis turned her face towards his and she had an odd sensation of dizziness as his hot breath fanned her cheek. 'You will advise me if Ramón does not always treat you with respect. Do you understand?'

She nodded and followed him into the main hall. Ramón appeared from nowhere and attached himself to them. He chatted pleasantly to Luis, but as soon as his boss turned away he took the opportunity of scowling at her. Emma smiled sweetly back. She didn't know what

28

Ramón's problem was, or why he'd taken such a dislike to her, but she wasn't going to let it bother her. Let him twist his face all he liked; there were more exciting things around here than him.

One of them was the VIP departure lounge. Emma tried to gaze around nonchalantly as though she travelled from Heathrow in such style several times a month. The stupid grin that crept over her face as she recognized one person after another betrayed her, however. She'd been cleaning up after people like these for the past month, but she'd been invisible. Now they actually seemed to notice her presence.

She longed to go over to the rock star who was smiling at her and ask for his autograph, but thought that it would annoy Luis. However, when she went to the bar for a coffee and he followed her, she decided to throw caution to the winds and ask him to autograph her book. Her cheeks flamed scarlet when she glanced down and saw the particularly graphic message he'd added to his name and phone number.

'You'll be lucky.' She snapped the book shut then hurried back to her seat, pursued by his loud, mocking laughter. He'd been her idol since she was fourteen. There were still posters of him on her bedroom wall at home. The first thing she'd do when she visited her mum again would be to rip them down.

Luis gave her a hard stare as she sat down again, but refrained from commenting on the incident. Their flight was called shortly afterwards, but thankfully the musician made no move to board it.

Air travel was still a novelty to Emma. Holidays had been limited to caravans or holiday camps when she was young. Her father had abandoned her mother before his child had been born and had vanished without trace. Consequently, money had always been tight in the Blackmore household. She'd never been abroad until she went to university, where it was a necessary part of her course that she should spend some time in Spain. Student flights had never been like this, though.

She fastened her seat belt and gazed around the first-class cabin, revelling in the amount of leg space she had. Palaces for the rich and cattle trucks for the poor, she reflected grimly. No doubt next time she was in a plane it would be of the latter variety.

The exit closed with a pneumatic hiss, a safety video flickered on to the screen in front of her, and the plane began to taxi down the runway. All thoughts were blotted out with the prospect of what was coming next. Take-off was the part of flying she enjoyed most. To her mind, there were few sensations that could equal it.

'Is this the first time that you have flown?' enquired Luis.

As she looked into dark eyes twinkling with amusement, Emma realized that the glee she'd felt when the plane surged into the air had been audible.

'No, of course not.' She tossed her head with embarrassment and stared out of the window.

'Would you care for an aperitif before lunch?' The enquiry came from a smartly dressed, smiling flight attendant, who appeared as soon as the seat belt light went out.

Luis shook his head and raised a quizzical eyebrow at Emma.

'Mmm, yes, a dry sherry, please.'

'Any particular brand, madam?'

'Oh . . . Quevedo would be nice, thank you.'

She caught a strange expression in Luis's eyes as he glanced towards her. 'What's the matter? Don't you want me to drink?'

'You may eat or drink whatever you choose,' he said, returning to the papers he'd fished out of his briefcase the moment he'd sat down.

The flight attendant returned with her drink, and as Emma twirled the golden liquid around in the glass she recalled where sherry originated.

'This sherry has the same name as you,' she said hesitantly.

Luis glanced up from his work and nodded in an off-hand manner. 'Yes. We will soon be staying in the place where it is produced.'

Emma uttered an unladylike word and threw herself back into her seat, much to the amusement of Ramón opposite, who had been listening intently to her discovery.

'I had visions of meeting a nice cosy little grandfather,' she hissed at Luis when she regained her equilibrium, 'not the mogul of an international empire.'

He seemed surprised by her outburst. 'My grandfather is not an ogre. In fact I guarantee that he will be most courteous to you. There is no reason to be annoyed or afraid.'

That was all very well for him to say, she thought grimly as she polished off her sherry. He'd been brought up to believe that everyone else in life was inferior; she couldn't imagine him being afraid of anyone.

When the flight attendant arrived with a tray of champagne she took a glass, and by the time she had drained that her spirits began to revive. It proved impossible to concentrate on her book, however; the letters had developed a strange habit of moving around the page. She snapped it closed and laid it to one side.

'*Hard Times*?' said Luis quizzically, picking up the tatty paperback. He leafed through the pages and glanced at the title page where the musician had scrawled his message. 'Not a very subtle man, this. You like him?' His tone was pure contempt.

'I like his music,' she answered defiantly.

'You will phone him on your return to England?'

Emma shrugged. 'Maybe.' She wouldn't touch the ageing rock star with a surgical glove now, but she wasn't about to admit that to Luis.

With a look that was more expressive than words, he gave her back the book and returned to his work.

Out of the corner of her eye, Emma saw a flight attendant bearing yet more glasses of champagne. Dared she have another one? She felt like a child who had just inherited a sweet shop. It was amazing stuff, completely unlike the odd glass of sparkling wine she'd tasted at Christmas. Luis had said she could eat or drink anything she wanted, Emma reasoned, and she accepted another glass while he asked for a mineral water.

The meal that followed was delicious: smoked salmon mousse, chicken breast in a light creamy sauce and fresh fruit salad. She was feeling very mellow and sociable and wished that Luis would make conversation, but it was like sitting next to a robot; as soon as he had finished eating he returned to his large file of papers, underlining and circling great chunks of print. If she really had been his fiancée she would have had something to say about it. Instead, she decided to stretch her legs and go to the washroom.

On her return a shiny package was sitting on her seat. 'What's this?' she asked, picking it up and shaking it.

'A freebie, I believe is the word. Samples of

toiletries that the airline sells. You have accepted everything else that has been offered. I believe you would have been disappointed to miss these.'

'Thank you,' she mumbled, fighting the flush of embarrassment that crept over her face. Damn him! What did it matter what he thought of her? She opened the package and carefully examined the pots and phials inside. He was right. She would have been disappointed to miss out on it.

Her reaction to the package appeared to interest Luis. For once, he put down his pen and watched her closely.

'Oh, this is really lovely,' she declared, dabbing some perfume on her wrist and wafting it under his nose. 'What do you think?'

'Very nice,' he agreed, inhaling the fragrance and reaching over to examine the phial from which it came.

Moments later a flight attendant arrived. 'Would you like to purchase any duty free goods?' he enquired.

Emma shook her head. She'd buy something for her mother on the return journey, after she'd been paid.

'A bottle of *Pas de Jour*,' said Luis.

It was the same perfume she'd liked, and the fact amused her. What type of woman would he give it to? Even duty free the perfume was wildly expensive.

It would have to be someone special. Or

perhaps he'd keep it in his bedroom on the off chance. As she conjured up different scenarios and different women Emma was forced to turn her head away to hide the grin that was slowly spreading over her features.

'Don't you want it?' he said softly.

Her head spun round and she saw that he was holding out the box of perfume to her. 'Oh!' she said, flustered. 'I wasn't hinting . . . I didn't expect you to – '

'I know you didn't, but it is always a pleasure to give perfume to a beautiful woman.' His smile reached his eyes, and she felt a warm tingle of response deep within her.

Gosh, he's smooth, she thought, taking the bottle out of its box and running her fingers over its many faceted surface. It was the 100ml size. The cost of it would have paid the food bill for Emma and her friends for a fortnight.

'Thank you.' She smiled back, touched by the gift. She possessed a suitcase of expensive clothes he'd bought her, but they were part of the deception he was practising on his grandfather. This was something else, something he had no reason to do.

Warning bells clanged in her brain. She'd better be careful otherwise she could end up liking him. That was the last thing she wanted. She didn't intend ending up as just another notch on any man's bedhead, not even someone as rich and powerful as Quevedo.

'Little Miss Innocent,' sneered Ramón from across the aisle. 'I tell you, Luis. That one is not as naive as she seems.'

'Shut up, Ramón,' he said irritably, 'at least she does not bore me as you are beginning to.' He threw down his file, stretched out his long legs, and lay back in his seat, closing his eyes.

Emma resisted the urge to poke out her tongue at Ramón and settled for another glass of champagne. The rest of the flight passed hazily; she must have dropped to sleep, for now people seemed to be disembarking.

'Time to go.' Luis offered her his hand when she showed no inclination to move.

She stood up slowly, but gripped Luis tightly when the cabin spun round and hit her in the face. 'I'm going to be sick,' she gasped, beads of perspiration standing out on her forehead. She raced unsteadily up the aisle and just managed to lock the washroom door behind her before it was too late.

There was only Luis left in the cabin when she re-emerged. He was leaning, stony-faced against the exit, and he flashed her a contemptuous look as she walked towards him. 'You will limit your alcohol intake at my grandfather's,' he hissed. 'If you attempt to sabotage my plans you will be sorry.'

Tears of shame pricked her eyes and emptied down her cheeks as he towered above her and gripped her shoulders harshly.

'Answer me if you understand what I am saying,' he growled, his rage gaining momentum.

'I'm sorry,' she sobbed, 'it's the first time I've tasted champagne. I didn't realize it would have that effect.'

'All right.' He released her and handed her a carefully pressed handkerchief. 'There is no need to cry. At least it happened here. There is no harm done as long as you have learned your lesson.'

Emma nodded, rubbed her eyes, and blew her nose noisily on the handkerchief, which smelt subtly of him.

'Come, then. Unless you have a need to be sick again?'

'No, there's nothing left,' she said, taking the hand that he proffered. She was feeling a little delicate.

Would you like a cup of coffee or something to settle your stomach before we leave the airport?' he asked when they rejoined Ramón.

'Yes, please.'

'I know what she does want,' muttered Ramón.

'Take our luggage to the car, Ramón,' said Luis, ignoring him. 'We'll meet you there.'

They left a disgruntled Ramón at baggage retrieval. Maybe the bloke did have some use after all, she smiled to herself, following Luis into the main foyer of San Pablo airport.

'Sit,' he said, indicating an empty seat at the bar.

He'll be telling me to come to heel next, she thought, as she obeyed his instructions and watched his lean, elegant figure threading its way through the tables and chairs to reach the counter.

Emma sniffed the air. Yes. It was unmistakable – that aroma of being in a foreign country – the mixture of ground coffee, pungent cigarette smoke, alcohol and air-conditioning.

Excitement stirred inside her again. She couldn't wait to see outside. She'd never been this far south before. Tales of old Andalucía and its Moorish conquerors filled her brain. Would there be any sign left of the invaders in the architecture of Sevilla? Was Granada and its magnificent palace of the Alhambra too far away to visit?

'You are looking better,' remarked Luis, arriving with a tray of coffee and biscuits.

Emma nodded and pounced greedily on the biscuits.

'You attack your food like someone who has not eaten for days,' he sighed. 'Please do not act thus in my grandfather's house.'

Emma giggled. 'I'm not a fool, Luis.'

'I hope not, Amanda.'

She glared at him for a second for using that name, then realized he was perfectly within his rights. She also realized that she hadn't asked him any more about her. 'Tell me about Amanda,' she said, seizing the moment.

Luis's face took on a more guarded expression than usual. 'What is there to tell? I have given you the same details I relayed to Grandfather. I don't wish to confuse you by overloading your brain with information.'

Emma stared at him as he calmly tore the end off a packet of sugar and tipped the contents into his coffee. The bloke was truly amazing. He should write a book: *How To Insult People Without Really Trying*. It would be a bestseller.

'I had a brain scan once,' she began. That got his attention. His head jerked up and his eyes widened with surprise. 'They gave me the bad news first – yes, it was as they feared, my brain was the size of a pea, but the good news was that it was of the marrowfat variety and not a *petit pois*.'

Luis frowned and continued to gaze at her. 'I didn't mean to imply . . .' he murmured, then bent to stir his coffee.

Not much you didn't, thought Emma, sipping her own coffee and savouring the rich continental taste. 'Why did you and Amanda split up, then?'

Luis didn't look up. He continued stirring his coffee, staring hypnotically at the mini whirlpool he'd created in the cup. 'I really don't think that is any of your concern,' he said eventually.

That's put me in my place again, thought Emma, gazing at him with renewed dislike. So what was the big deal? Why wouldn't he tell her the reason for their break-up? Emma twiddled the ruby and diamond monstrosity around her finger and pondered. Why would someone who craved a ring like this give it back? Emma then put herself in Amanda's position. If she was engaged to a man, what would cause her to break it off?

She picked up another biscuit and chewed it thoughtfully. She could think of only one reason – infidelity. What was the betting that poor old Amanda had called round one day and found Luis in the arms of another woman? She eyed him coldly as he finished his coffee and replaced the cup carefully in its saucer. Yeah, she'd bet that was what had happened. He was arrogant enough to believe that he would never get caught, and he was too arrogant to admit what he'd done to her.

'Shall we . . .' Luis looked up, but the smile on his face froze as he registered the expression on hers.

'You really must learn to hide your feelings, *chica*,' he said. 'Your opinion of me is written in capital letters across your face. This does not affect me personally, but I do not wish others to be aware of it.'

'Oh, don't worry, Luis,' she snapped, 'I'll be so loving towards you in front of your grandfather it'll make you want to puke.'

He regarded her with surprise for a second,

then gave a low chuckle. 'I do believe that I might enjoy this week after all.' He rose to his feet and extended his hand in silent command that it was now time to go.

A silver-grey Rolls-Royce was waiting for them on the tarmac and Emma had only a momentary impression of the sizzling heat outside before entering its air-conditioned interior. She gazed in fascination at the cobalt-blue sky of Sevilla as the car purred out of the airport and southwards to their destination.

Dared she now disclose to Luis that she could speak Spanish or would she have to keep up the pretence for the week? She should have admitted it sooner, once she was certain of his motives for bringing her to Sevilla, but the time had never seemed to be right. She now felt guilty, but the longer it continued the more difficult it became to tell the truth. The two men were now discussing business figures and strategies, which she was certain were for their ears alone.

Her decision was postponed when they stopped before tall wrought-iron gates topped with an arch. These swung open after a moment and the car progressed through carefully manicured grounds, finally coming to a halt before a huge white villa.

Emma gazed in awe at the magnificent house with its traditional wrought-iron balconies, and black grilles on the windows. She was aware that Luis was studying her reaction to his family home, but she didn't mind how impressed he thought her. She'd never dreamed that she'd ever stay in so beautiful a place, and she could hardly contain her delight. As soon as the chauffeur opened the door for her, she rushed to one of the flower beds surrounding the house, and knelt to inhale the wonderful fragrance emitted from the profusion of plants and bushes.

An elderly woman dressed completely in black emerged from the main entrance. She was almost as wide as she was tall, and as she waddled her way towards them Emma wondered who she was. Her thoughts were thrown into confusion when she reached Luis and immediately threw her arms around him. Her embrace was returned with enthusiasm. Luis bent down, and a smile of genuine warmth and affection melted his stern features.

She was obviously someone important. Good grief, it must be his mother! That was why she was in black of course: Luis's father was dead; she was a widow. Trust Luis not to tell her anything about her existence. What was wrong with the man? Did he think she was going to sell his life story to a lifestyle magazine? She'd have to get her camera out. That would get him worried.

Eventually the woman seemed satisfied that she'd hugged the stuffing out of her son, and turned her attention to Emma. She smiled back nervously. The Spanish were a demonstrative race, but Mrs Quevedo seemed more demonstrative than most. A quick peck on the cheek like Emma's mother favoured wouldn't be her style at all.

'Welcome to the Villa Quevedo, Señorita Amanda.' The woman took Emma's hand and squeezed it warmly between both her own. 'I hope your stay with us will be a happy one.'

She glanced at Luis, then reverted to Spanish. 'Your grandfather is resting at the moment. I'll tell him you're here the moment he wakes.' Then with a last huge grin at both of them she trotted back to the house. Ramón, Emma noticed, was ignored completely.

'She speaks English very well,' said Emma.

'No, she doesn't.' Luis started to laugh. He took her hand and led her towards the main entrance. 'That's her party piece, I think is the expression. She welcomes all English visitors in this way, then panics when they answer her.'

Emma smiled back. 'She's very nice, your mother.'

'What are you talking about?' All traces of merriment instantly vanished from his face. 'My mother died when I was ten.'

'Then who . . . ?' Emma pointed vaguely after the unknown woman.

'That is María, our housekeeper. Hardly a striking family resemblance, I think you'd agree.'

They entered the villa. At first it seemed

43

gloomy, but Emma realized it was only because of the contrast with the brilliant sunshine outside. She had a fleeting glimpse of a grand entrance hall lined with paintings and antiques, before being whisked up a marble and wrought-iron staircase to the floor above.

She felt a complete idiot over the mistake with María, and was only grateful she hadn't addressed her as Señora Quevedo in front of Ramón. It would have made his day. 'It might have been your mother,' she muttered. 'How was I supposed to know who she was? You haven't told me a thing about your family.'

Luis sighed, then shot her a look that suggested he was growing weary of being accompanied by a moron. 'Be assured that if I was bringing you to Sevilla to meet my mother it would have crossed my mind to mention it.'

He paused before a heavy wooden door, beautifully carved like all the others they'd passed. 'This is our room,' he said, walking in and throwing open the shutters that led out to the balcony.

Emma's reply froze on her lips, and she remained standing in the doorway. The room was large, accommodating a great deal of furniture, but all she could see was a huge double bed which seemed to dominate everything else . . .

CHAPTER 3

'What on earth are you doing standing there? Come in!' Luis strode across the room and pulled her inside.

'Our room?' said Emma quietly.

'Yes,' he answered irritably.

'But this is Spain.'

He sighed with exasperation. 'Exactly what decade do you think you are in, Amanda? My grandfather is well aware that I would not choose a bride without first testing her suitability.'

'You promised, Luis.' Her voice quavered as she realized how foolish she'd been to trust him.

'Yes. You have my word. This does not change anything.' He indicated the bed with long slender fingers. 'For goodness' sake stop acting like a virgin, Amanda. I did not contrive the whole thing just to take my pleasure of you.'

Emma flushed scarlet. How had he known? Had her behaviour towards him been so gauche?

By the time she realized he'd only been using a figure of speech it was too late.

'Well. Well.' He ran his fingers mockingly over her hot cheeks. 'Does this mean what I think it means? It never occurred to me.'

'What difference does it make?' she challenged, hating him.

'A small difference. Come out here.'

Emma gasped in awe at the vista from the balcony, but she hadn't been led outside to admire the view.

'What I need to determine,' said Luis, whose strong arms suddenly encircled her waist and pulled her towards him, 'is whether I may embrace you in public without you behaving like an ice-maiden.'

One hand slid up her back, coming to rest at the nape of her neck, while firm, warm lips descended to meet her own. Her body stiffened but she forced herself to relax. After all, she knew that this meant nothing to him; he was simply conducting an experiment.

It was strange how her mind had blotted out the possibility of physical contact between them when she had agreed to act the part of his fiancée. Ironic also that, after years of parrying men's attentions while she waited for the right man to love, she was allowing herself to be used by this man in exchange for his money. What on earth did that make her?

She must stop thinking like this, she told

46

herself sternly. Actors and actresses kiss and nobody condemns it as immoral. This was exactly the same. She was simply playing a part. It wasn't important. A week from now she'd be history; he'd have forgotten all about her.

That was it. It was easier to relax if she thought about it logically like that. She might detest Luis for what he was, but she didn't want him to think she was frigid. Why that should matter she couldn't explain. Other men had hurled that accusation at her when she wouldn't sleep with them, and she'd blithely insulted them back. But he was different. For some unfathomable reason, she knew it would hurt her deeply if Luis reacted the same way as them.

Emma released a long, slow sigh. Whatever else Luis might be guilty of, she couldn't accuse him of being a lousy kisser. She thought back to the last time she'd been held in a man's arms. Why did it seem to take years of experience before they grasped the simple fact that kissing was supposed to be an act of affection and not akin to a tackle on a rugby field?

Luis's fingers played gently over her neck, sending a tingle of excitement coursing down her spine. Oh, yes, he was an expert in such matters all right. It was as well that she hated him and was immune to his tricks. Nevertheless, it did feel pleasant being close to him like this. In some strange way she felt that he was compensating her for his obnoxious behaviour the rest of the time. For the first time since she'd met him she felt that she was actually in harmony with him.

But how much longer did he intend this kiss to continue? Surely she'd convinced him by now?

She became aware of Luis's tongue flicking gently across her lips in an attempt to tease open the pearly white fortress behind. That was his first mistake. Blokes had thrust their tongue into her mouth before when she had been unprepared and she'd found the experience quite revolting. Did they really think that allowing girls to sample their five pints of lager and chicken vindaloo second-hand was a turn-on? No, thank you. This time she was ready, and she kept her teeth clamped securely closed.

The heat on the balcony was becoming oppressive. Her body felt languid, and she twined her arms around Luis's neck in order to support herself. That was better. She still felt a little dizzy, but there were so many things out here that could contribute to that. There was the fierce Andalucían sun above, that beat down mercilessly on anyone foolish enough not to shelter from its rays. There was the intoxicating scent of bougainvillaea cascading down the walls, the heady perfume of pelargoniums wafting upwards from the pots crammed into the corner, and nearer still the aroma of musky aftershave and warm male.

Her body felt so heavy. She was aware that she

was leaning against Luis and that if he removed his support she would fall down, but her legs seemed incapable of taking her weight at the moment.

Luis's eyes were closed. How different he looked like this. His harsh features had softened and he looked almost beautiful. And why had she imagined that his hair would feel coarse to the touch? It was the texture of silk. Running her fingers through it, and on to the soft down at the nape of his neck, reminded her of the wonderful sensation of stroking a puppy.

The giddiness had passed and she was feeling extremely mellow. She was just thinking how beautiful his long, curved eyelashes were when his tongue brushed against hers. Involuntarily, she cried out at the spark of electricity that surged through her being.

He released her immediately and stepped back, his dark eyes glittering with triumph. Her body had betrayed her and she hadn't consciously been aware of it happening.

'You'll do,' he murmured insolently as she gasped for air.

'You're an arrogant conceited chauvinist pig!' It was blindingly obvious now that he'd meant to prolong the kiss until she showed some reaction to it. She'd simply represented an amusing challenge to him.

'And you are rather sweet,' he replied, stroking gently down her cheek with long, sensitive fingers.

He walked back into the room, stripped off his polo shirt and threw it on the bed. While the blood was pounding in her ears as she wondered what he was going to do next, he walked into the *ensuite* bathroom and began washing himself.

From her vantage point on the balcony she had a good view of his body. It was surprisingly muscular for someone as lean as he was. She had been aware of the strength in his arms as they had lain uncovered next to hers in the plane, and again just now as they pressed her close to him, but to witness that the rest of his frame was just as powerful was something of a shock.

Luis opened one of the wardrobe doors, extracted a clean shirt, then kicked it shut. 'I'll send up one of the maids to unpack. Tell her what you would like to eat and drink and she will bring it for you. You may as well have some time to yourself. I have quite a lot of business to discuss with my grandfather, and I will tell him that you are tired after travelling.'

'Won't he think that's rude?'

'Not at all. I'll tell him I insisted you rest. I will come up to change for dinner at about half past eight.' He left her on the balcony and walked out of the room without a backward glance.

Emma walked into the bathroom and splashed her face with cold water. She looked strange: her eyes seemed a little vacant and her body felt weird, as though she'd beamed here via a science fiction transporter and her molecules had reassembled in the wrong order. She'd have to be more careful with the sun in future; she'd always been sensitive to it.

Returning to the bedroom, Emma gazed around at her surroundings. The furniture was dark, intricately carved wood, very heavy, very Spanish, and very masculine. She'd expected Luis's room to be lavish in its opulence but it had an almost monastic simplicity. The only hint that its owner wasn't your average monk were the paintings that adorned the white walls; they probably cost more than most people could hope to earn in a lifetime.

Emma continued her inspection. The floor was a creamy marble, sensible in this climate for its coolness. Its starkness was relieved by a scattering of richly patterned rugs. There were no curtains at the windows, only shutters, and the duvet on the bed was of white cotton. She stroked the material between her fingers – good quality but simple.

A wave of irritation swept over her. This was ridiculous. Why should she feel irritated just because she couldn't find fault with Quevedo's room? She gnawed at her bottom lip and gazed around again. Yes, she had to admit it, she actually liked it.

And what about the man himself? Her heart fluttered strangely against her ribcage as she thought about the way he'd kissed her. That was something else she couldn't find fault with. Men were usually so arrogant when they discovered you were a virgin. 'Come with me, darling, and I'll show you what you've been missing,' was a familiar response, or else they tried to shame you into it by calling you frigid or gay.

It was the type of response she would have expected from a man as insensitive as Luis Quevedo, but she was totally wrong. His kiss had been long, slow and tender. There had been no pressure, no cajolement, just perfection. It was painful to acknowledge, but it was the truth. If the man wasn't so completely full of himself she'd probably be totally besotted with him by now. Whoever ran this universe was definitely fond of sick jokes.

Emma went back on to the balcony, dragged a chair into a shaded corner and sat down. Why was she still a virgin? She'd tried to explain it once to Kate. 'You like all types of apples,' she'd said, 'but what you really want is a Red Delicious. You go into a fruit shop and the man says, "No, I haven't got any Red Delicious, but I've got plenty of Granny Smiths, Cox's Orange Pippins, Golden Delicious, Russets and McIntosh Reds." They all look good, but what you really want is a Red Delicious so you don't buy any.'

'You're cracked,' Kate had said. 'Variety is the spice of life.'

Emma's stomach rumbled and she smiled. It

was thinking about food that did it. So was Luis a Red Delicious? She trailed her finger over a vibrant purple head of bougainvillaea and considered. Maybe there were parts of him that were all right, but he'd definitely been left lying in the fruit bowl too long. You'd sink your teeth in, expecting crisp juicy flesh, and get a mouthful of mush and maggots instead. The thought cheered her. Her defences would need to be on red alert this week to counter this alarming physical attraction which had sprung to life with a kiss.

What was she going to do for the rest of the day? She'd have liked to have met his grandfather and got that ordeal over with. Despite Luis's assurances that his grandfather would like her, she was nervous about meeting him. What on earth would he make of her? She was hardly high-society material like the other women he must have brought home over the years. As head of Quevedo's, and an astute businessman, he'd probably see straight through the sham.

A tap on the bedroom door interrupted Emma as she was picturing the scene where Luis's grandfather lost his temper and threw her out of the villa. The knock was so gentle that she thought she must have imagined it, but as she tentatively opened the door a maid in a neat blue dress was standing there.

Emma smiled and stepped back for her to enter. The girl was beautiful: sleek black hair swept back in a single plait down her back, huge dark eyes, and a wonderful olive complexion. She looked about sixteen, but had the serenity of a Madonna.

'Señor Luis asked me to unpack,' she said softly, turning to bring in one of the cases that had been left outside the room.

Emma rushed to help her with the other one, then realized by the look on the girl's face that she'd done the wrong thing. She was supposed to be Luis Quevedo's fiancée. The woman he'd choose to marry wouldn't risk snagging a fingernail by doing physical work of any kind. Though it felt completely wrong, she'd have to sit idly by while this girl hung up all her clothes for her.

'Do you speak English?' she asked, to mask her blunder.

The girl smiled more widely. Apparently she didn't. Emma wanted to ask her about the villa and its occupants, but she could hardly start speaking Spanish to the maid when she hadn't said a word yet to Luis about understanding the language.

Humming quietly to herself, the maid transferred Emma's clothes from suitcase to wardrobe, pausing every now and again to exclaim how beautiful and magnificent they all were. Emma had to return to the balcony to hide her amusement. No wonder Luis had insisted she leave behind all her own clothes in England. The maid would probably never have recovered from the shock if she'd unpacked the ancient jeans and T-shirts stored away in her case at the hotel.

'It is finished, *señorita*.' The girl appeared on the balcony ten minutes later. 'May I bring you something to eat?' She accompanied the request with unmistakable sign language.

'Mmm, yes. Cheese and tomato roll?' asked Emma hopefully.

The girl shrugged her shoulders expressively, and Emma repeated the request.

The girl shook her head. She didn't have a clue. Emma was at a loss. What could she do? Draw it? No, she was absolutely hopeless at drawing. Oh, to hell with it, they could be here till Christmas. '*Bocadillo . . . queso . . . tomate*,' she said in an atrocious accent. It wasn't beyond possibility that she might know a few words of Spanish.

The girl beamed at her and returned shortly afterwards with two rolls bursting with cheese and tomato, a jug of freshly squeezed orange juice, and a pot of coffee.

'Wonderful!' said Emma, inspecting the tray. 'Thanks . . . oh, I don't know your name.'

The girl smiled at her politely.

'*Nombre*?' asked Emma.

'Teresa,' she answered shyly.

'I'm Emm . . .' She stopped, horror-struck at what she'd almost said. She was no good at lying. She was bound to give the game away before the week was over.

'I'm . . . erm . . . Amanda,' she said again, holding out her hand.

Teresa looked surprised, but took her hand. 'Señorita Amanda,' she murmured, then with a final dazzling smile walked over to the door.

Emma watched her go with relief. She didn't think Teresa had guessed she was an impostor. Probably thought she was dealing with a typically mad Englishwoman. Still, she must be more careful in future.

'Amanda, Amanda, Amanda,' she repeated, drumming the name into her skull. How she hated that woman's name now, but she couldn't afford to forget that was who she was for the next week.

Eating a cheese roll cheered her up. She walked around the room munching while she idly opened drawers and cupboards. She salved her conscience by not actually disturbing any of the contents, but her resolve weakened when she opened Luis's sock drawer.

'Oh,' she gasped, spluttering bits of bread and cheese over the neatly arranged socks. Who, except perhaps a prince of the realm would have their socks lined up in colour-coordinated rows? The devil in her ached to mix them all up, but she managed to control herself because she didn't want Teresa to be blamed.

She wandered back on to the balcony and looked out over the garden. It would be fun to explore outside, but she was supposed to be

resting. Resting! What did they think she was?
An invalid? She prowled restlessly around the
room. She just wasn't used to inactivity. She
poured herself a cup of coffee, then decided to
take a shower. That was an experience. The
water shot out through various jets positioned
in the wall of the shower cubicle. It left her
feeling like a building that had been sand-
blasted. She'd use the bath next time, or maybe
she'd ask Luis how to turn the dratted thing
down.

By the time she'd finished in the bathroom
and dried her hair it was half past six. The heat
in the bedroom was sweltering. She should have
closed the shutters, she supposed. That would
have made it cooler, but she was loath to blot out
the magnificent view of hillside, vines and flowers that surrounded the house. Instead, she
dressed in a peach silk teddy, and kept a wrap
handy in case anyone should knock on the door.

Right – *Hard Times*! If she didn't achieve
anything else this week she'd finish her book,
and if Luis planned on leaving her alone for great
chunks of the day she might even have a stab at
writing her essay on it. She poured herself a glass
of juice, and settled down on the bed to read.

It was no use. Maybe she should have brought
a steamy saga with her instead. Her brain refused
to concentrate, and her mind wandered. Eventually the excitement of the last few days
caught up with her; the heat in the room was

making her drowsy, and she drifted away.

It was a delightful dream: she lay on the soft sand at the edge of a clear blue ocean, warm waves lapping over her body, their undulating rhythm washing away all her cares.

Who was this man leaning over her as she surfaced from sleep? She gazed at Luis, her eyes soft with slumber, for several seconds before recalling who he was.

'Good evening, Sleeping Beauty.' His tone was light, but there was something about his face, his eyes especially, which disturbed her. Why was her body tingling so much? She glanced down and encountered her nipples straining against the silken material of her teddy.

Luis's eyes were staring brazenly at her and she glared angrily into their brown depths. Had he touched her while she'd been asleep? She wasn't certain so she couldn't accuse him. Her body did feel strange, but perhaps it was the after-effects of her amazingly sensual dream. She snatched up her wrap and covered herself from his gaze.

'It is warm in here.' Luis rose from the bed and began to discard his clothing into a heap on the floor. 'My grandfather will not have air-conditioning installed. He believes it is detrimental to health. As he is already eighty-three, who knows? Perhaps he is right.' He strode into the bathroom, and a few moments later she heard the blast of water in the shower.

Half past eight, she noted, glancing at her watch, and she walked out on the balcony to breathe in the cooler evening air and clear her head.

'Much as I admire your choice of clothing, I really do think that you should change for dinner,' taunted Luis, whose bathrobe-clothed figure had approached silently behind her.

'I was waiting for you to finish in the bathroom,' she said, pushing past him. By the time she re-emerged, Luis was wearing a dinner suit and was flicking through some business papers.

'You're incredibly messy,' she said, defying her brain to register how attractive he looked. 'Don't you ever put the tops back on bottles or pick anything up?' Whoever was responsible for the military neatness of his drawers and wardrobe it certainly wasn't him.

'You are supposed to be my fiancée; not my wife,' he answered shortly, and returned to his work.

Summarily dismissed, she opened her wardrobe and hesitated between two dresses.

'We will be dressed quite formally as it is the first night,' he said, not looking up. 'May I suggest the blue dress? I believe it should look quite spectacular.'

Emma resisted the impulse to choose the other one, took down the turquoise dress, picked up clean underwear, and made her way back to the bathroom.

She surveyed herself in the full-length mirror there, and was gripped by the same excitement she'd felt when first trying on the dress. It was amazing to think she could look as regal as this. The silk dress fell in gentle folds to the ground from a bustier top that flattered and enhanced her bosom. She felt like a princess on her way to a premiere. Perhaps she would be able to carry off this charade after all.

'Superb,' said Luis, his breath expelled in a rush at the sight of her entrance.

'It's smashing, isn't it?' She had intended to look haughtily down her nose at him, but his reaction to the dress had been gratifying.

'Smashing,' he agreed, his tone mocking her choice of words, but she refused to be intimidated by him and opened a small jewellery case that she'd brought with her.

'I regret this is something that I overlooked.' His breath was warm on her neck as he reached over and picked up a row of pearls that were not too obviously fake. He fastened them around her neck and she clipped on some matching drop earrings, pleased with the overall effect.

'A woman any man would wish to marry,' he murmured as he led her downstairs.

Emma took a deep breath as Luis pushed open the door to a drawing room and she caught sight of eight people already assembled there: Ramón was part of the company, she noted glumly; there were three couples and an elderly man sitting on a hard high-backed chair, who must be Luis's grandfather.

Conversation ceased as they entered the room, and the elderly man's head swivelled like everybody else's to inspect her. Nervousness turned to compassion, however, as he immediately struggled to his feet. He stood for a few moments gripping the chair-back, his face reflecting the pain this effort cost him. He then strode determinedly towards them.

'Ah. I knew she would have to be special, Luis.' He took her hand, raised it to his lips in a chivalrous gesture, and smiled warmly.

Emma was immediately won over. She had expected Don Rafael Quevedo to be arrogant like his grandson. Perhaps he had been in his youth, but here among his friends and relations there was no trace of it – he was a kind and charming host. He wasn't as tall as Luis, but considering his age and infirmity he had a very upright bearing. His eyes, in a mahogany leather face, reminded her of his grandson's, but they twinkled and shone with humour much more. With his silvery-grey hair, he was her exact idea of what a grandfather should be.

'Doesn't your grandfather speak English?' she whispered to Luis after Don Rafael had introduced her to three of his friends and their wives.

'Unfortunately not. I will translate for you. He wishes you to try a very rare *fino* that he has had brought from the *bodega* especially for you.'

'Yes, I understand.' Her mind was made up. This was her last chance for confession. It would be such a pity to miss the opportunity of conversing freely with the lovely man who was still holding her hand so warmly.

'Thank you, Don Rafael,' she said in his native tongue, 'it would be an honour to try the sherry.' Out of the corner of her eye she had the satisfaction of seeing Luis's jaw drop visibly. Ramón, who was sitting in the corner of the room, appeared to jump up like a jack-in-the-box.

'Please call me Grandfather, as Luis does. After all you will soon be family.' He patted her arm kindly. 'Now where did you learn Spanish? Luis didn't tell me you could speak our language.'

'It was a surprise for this visit. I've been taking lessons.'

'Well, you've certainly surprised him, *niña*,' chuckled the old man, enjoying his grandson's discomfiture. 'Perhaps he and Ramón have been discussing matters in front of you that they shouldn't?' he enquired shrewdly.

'Of course not, Grandfather.' Luis flashed her a warning glance, then took her hand and squeezed it harshly before she could answer. 'Amanda is a constant source of surprise and delight to me.'

The arrival of a maid with the treasured bottle of *fino* allowed Luis to change the subject. He poured glasses for everyone, then began a heated discussion of its merits with an elderly man who she gathered was a rival producer.

'I expect you're bored to tears with all this discussion of grapes and harvest and yield.' Don Rafael refilled her glass and seemed amused.

'Oh, no! I'm really interested!' she said, and his smile grew wider.

Emma winced inwardly. Her nervousness was making her act a little too gushing. He probably thought she was totally insincere.

'I shall ask you the same question at the end of the week,' he chuckled.

María appeared opportunely to announce that dinner was ready, and they went into the dining room. Don Rafael insisted that Emma should sit beside him. 'I am enjoying speaking to you so much, my dear. It is a wonderful surprise of yours. How long have you been taking lessons?'

'Oh, they've been very intensive,' she replied, evading the question. 'I'd taken the subject at school so I knew all the basics.'

'You must care for my grandson a great deal to make such an effort.'

'Yes, *Abuelo*. I love him very much.' She smiled over at Luis. Honestly, he could try a bit harder. It was almost cracking his face to smile back.

The arrival of their *gazpacho* distracted her attention from him. It looked delicious and she automatically reached for her spoon, changing her action at the last minute to pick up her glass of water and take a sip. Only Luis seemed to notice her near blunder. He stared hard at her, his lips twisted in a supercilious smile. She gave him a sickly sweet smile in return and he looked away. It was all right for him, but years of school dinners had taken their toll on her. Only those who gobbled their food up quickest stood any chance of seconds.

'The Goya I told you about will be auctioned at Christie's in three weeks' time, Grandfather. I asked Henry to send you a catalogue,' said Luis as they finished their soup.

'Was that really a Goya I noticed hanging in your entrance hall?' she asked Don Rafael, and Luis almost choked on his wine.

'Indeed, yes,' smiled his grandfather, 'a total madman, but also a complete genius. I adore him. I've two more paintings that you won't have seen yet. It will be my pleasure to show you them tomorrow.'

It was a stroke of luck that history of art had been Emma's third subject during her first year at university. The set books had been cripplingly expensive but they'd turned out to be an investment. If she hadn't studied them she'd never have been able to speak knowledgeably about Goya, or about Picasso when the conversation turned to him.

It was a mystery to her why Luis appeared so stony faced. Why were he and Ramón exchanging so many glances? Surely he would wish his girlfriend to appear intelligent in front of his grandfather? Don Rafael seemed happy enough about it. It was Luis's fault for not priming her if there were certain subjects he didn't want discussed.

'Have you read any of our literature, Amanda?'

Emma could almost feel Luis and Ramón holding their breath. She didn't want to push her credibility too far so she answered, 'Only in translation, *Abuelo*.'

'Of course. What have you read?'

'*Don Quijote* and some of the plays of Lorca. I enjoyed those so I tried some of his poems, but I'm afraid they don't lend themselves very well to translation. I'll look forward to reading them in the original.'

The evening passed quickly. Emma sparkled and thoroughly enjoyed herself. Don Rafael was an interesting, lively companion, but his grandson seemed to slip into a deeper, darker humour as the night progressed. Emma had controlled her alcohol intake, as requested, but she noticed that he was drinking heavily. She saw his grandfather regarding him strangely more than once.

'I apologize for monopolizing your beautiful lady all evening, Luis. Forgive me. I may only have this week to enjoy her company, and you have the rest of your life,' he said, when everyone had gone and they were left alone.

One part of that was true, she thought sadly.

Luis muttered something about a headache and feeling tired, and swept her out of the room.

'You're hurting me, Luis,' she said, as she was almost frog-marched up the stairs.

His only answer was a dark, penetrating glare, and she felt his grip on her arm tighten even more.

CHAPTER 4

'Now, miss, you are going to tell me exactly who the hell you are.' Luis's voice was almost a growl as he kicked the bedroom door closed behind them.

'You know who I am.' Her heart was thudding, but she tried not to show Luis how afraid she was. All the pretence had dropped from his face and she was confronted by a look of sheer hatred.

'Oh, yes, I forgot,' he said sarcastically, 'a chambermaid who speaks Spanish almost fluently, who reads Dickens, and has a fair knowledge of Spanish painting and literature. Is this a speciality of the Northminster hotel chain?'

'You believe everyone who works in a hotel to be essentially a moron, then, do you?' she spat back.

His face grew darker and he advanced towards her. She automatically flinched, thinking that he was going to hit her, but his hand came round her throat and gripped her by the chin.

'Oh, you're very good. You had me fooled,' he hissed into her face. 'A woman who pretends to be a virgin but who lies scantily clad on the bed, feigning sleep, when I return; a woman who responds and moans so seductively to my caress when I can't resist the impulse to touch her; a woman who uses the time waiting for her flight at Heathrow to enlarge her list of clients. I know what you are now – you are a very accomplished *puta*.'

The word sounded no more pleasant in Spanish than its English counterpart, and Emma angrily brought her hand up to slap him. 'I despise you!' she shouted. 'You knew I'd never been with a man and yet you touched me like that when I was asleep.'

'Outraged innocence?' he snarled, grabbing her arm and pushing her away. 'I think not.' He picked up her handbag and emptied the contents on the table.

'What are you doing?'

'With the information in here,' he said, holding up her passport, 'Ramón will be able to find out for me by tomorrow, maybe the next day, everything I need to know about you.'

'Anything that you find out about me I'd have told you freely if only you'd asked. But you weren't interested. I was nothing to you – a menial – to be used for your convenience.'

'Well, I am interested now,' he snarled, pushing her into an armchair and sitting down opposite her.

'I'm almost in my final year at university,' she began, finding it difficult to think clearly with so much animosity directed at her. 'I'm studying a joint honours course in English and Spanish. I was working in the hotel to pay off my overdraft. I can't manage on my grant. There are so many books I need to buy, and there's only my mum at home, who doesn't have any money. You were the answer to my prayers: my overdraft will be paid off and I've also managed to come to Spain and practise my Spanish.'

'You have proof of any of this?' His expression was one of pure disbelief.

'I didn't realize I would need it,' she snapped. Why on earth should she be made to feel a criminal just because she'd acted differently from his expectations of her?

'Then I shall keep this.' He pocketed her passport. 'With so many priceless antiques and paintings around, you must understand that we cannot afford to take any risks.'

Emma turned haughtily away from him. She longed to take another swipe at that arrogant countenance, but knew she stood no chance of beating his reflexes. Let him think what he liked; once he'd had her checked out he'd have to apologize.

Apologize! Who was she kidding? She bet he'd never apologized for anything in his life. She scooped up the contents of her handbag and replaced them inside. Just who the hell did he think he was, tipping everything out and taking her passport? 'Do you always behave like a spoiled brat when things don't go exactly your way?' she flashed. 'Or is it just with women? You were born too late, Luis. You'd have had a whale of a time in Franco's day. Women knew their place then. Subserviency ruled OK.'

'Will you be quiet?' Luis's eyes sparked angrily, but Emma ignored their warning.

'You'd have been one of those men who voted against education for women,' she continued, 'but it's happened. It's official: women have brains too. Some of us, God forbid, can even manage a second language, and some of us –' she glanced pointedly at the ring on her finger '– want more from their men than someone who's only good at tossing money in our direction.'

'Shut up!' Something inside Luis seemed to snap. He leaped from his chair with the suddenness of a panther, and the next moment towered threateningly over her. She backed away, but retreat was blocked by the wall and she came to a halt.

'You know nothing about me,' he hissed, 'yet you make these wild assumptions.'

'And that's the pot calling the kettle black if ever it did,' retorted Emma. 'Just why did it upset you so much when you realized I could speak Spanish? It wasn't because of what you and Ramón were saying about me, although it should have been. It was because I wasn't the nice simple chambermaid you thought you were getting. I'd have told you I spoke Spanish if you'd asked me, but you weren't interested. You couldn't be bothered to find out. You didn't even want to know my name. All you wanted was a little doll you could dress up and parade in front of your grandfather. You had to pay for a new one because you'd messed up with the first!'

His face darkened and she noticed a vein on his temple begin to pulsate as she spoke. 'So you thought you'd pay me back? You listened to confidential company information, and then you made me look a fool in front of my grandfather and his friends. Whatever your motives were, and don't think you've convinced me with your little tale, I believe you deserve to be taught a lesson.'

Luis forced her against the wall and began kissing her harshly, his teeth catching on the soft flesh of her lips as his mouth ground roughly over hers. Emma tried to push him away but his body was as hard and as unyielding as rock. She opened her mouth to protest but he seized the opportunity to thrust his tongue inside. Emma tasted the alcohol and she remembered how much he'd drunk that evening. She had to stop him. Without thinking, she raised her arm and gouged her fingernails into his neck.

He gave a cry of pain and staggered back, but

before she could break free he'd grabbed her arms and pinioned them above her head.

'Well, well.' He smiled sardonically. 'It didn't take much before you showed your true colours.'

'What did you expect? That I'd just stand here meekly and let you do what you want?'

'You should know. You seem to know everything else about me – how I think, how I feel – so tell me, *guapa*, what is it that I am going to do now?'

Emma tried to pull her hands away but they were held in an iron grip. 'You're going to let me go and never touch me again,' she said, making a valiant effort to control the quaver in her voice.

He shook his head slowly and the dark orbs of his eyes glowered menacingly in the soft light. 'Wrong,' he said. 'You see, you really don't know that much about me after all.' His head lowered, and as his lips began their onslaught on hers the hand that wasn't gripping her own tightly above her head stroked insolently down her body.

'No,' she gasped. She fought desperately and tried to bring up her knee to incapacitate him, but he was standing too close, his legs were pressed firmly against her own, and she was powerless.

His kiss became more demanding, any subtlety of technique that had been evident earlier in the day vanished without trace. Emma grew more and more frightened as Luis's breath grew hot and rapid and an unmistakable hard mass pressed threateningly against her stomach. Her struggles, she realized, had aroused him.

Emma's body became rigid as it prepared itself for the inevitable. Tears poured down her cheeks and every fibre of her being ached with the threat of violation.

'Please, Luis,' she pleaded to the man who hardly seemed human to her any more. 'Whatever I said, whatever I did, I don't deserve this. Nobody deserves this as a punishment.'

'What?' The grip on her hands yielded and he stepped away, but remained staring at her as though she'd beamed into the room from outer space. He raised a hand and probed gently at the dampness on her cheeks, and then he swore softly to himself.

'Go and get ready for bed,' he said wearily, and then he flung open the shutters and walked outside.

Locking the door behind her, Emma turned the bath taps on full then immersed herself in the warm depths. Gaining no comfort there, and having drained the reservoir of her tears, she wrapped herself in a bathrobe, knotted the belt firmly around her waist, and came out again. Luis was still on the balcony, his tall frame hunched over the wrought-iron railing.

'Let me go home tomorrow,' she said, standing well back from him. 'I'll say that my father is ill.'

'Not out here.' He grabbed her arm and pulled her back into the bedroom, closing the shutters behind him. He threw himself into an armchair and raked his fingers through his hair. 'You said you had no father,' he stated.

'That's why I don't mind saying he's ill. Please, Luis, I can't carry on this pretence. I'm terrified of you.'

'*Dios*! Amanda, you don't seriously believe that I would have hurt you, do you?' His eyes lifted to hers but fluttered away again.

'You put on a pretty good act.'

'Don't you think that I would at least have attempted to take off your clothes or my own if it had been my intention to . . . ?'

'Not necessarily.' Emma's cheeks stung with humiliation. Had she really so totally misread the situation?

'You infuriated me so much with your talk of dolls and the way you taunted me over the break-up of my engagement.'

'I can't help it if you've got a guilty conscience.'

'I beg your pardon?'

'Well, isn't that why you wouldn't tell me why you and Amanda split up?'

He stared at her for several long seconds. 'No,' he said.

'Oh, well, of course I believe you,' she muttered, moving away.

He reached out a hand to restrain her. 'Do you

tell everyone everything about your life?'

Emma shrugged him away. 'If they ask, yes. Why not? I've got nothing to hide.'

He considered this for a moment, then up-turned his palm in a gesture of defeat. 'I thought I had it in my power to give Amanda everything she wanted, but I was wrong. She left me for a Scottish duke who could give a title to her and her unborn children.'

Emma turned away from his probing gaze. Her taunt about some women wanting more from him than his money had obviously hit a different nerve from the one she'd intended. 'But that doesn't excuse the way you turned on me,' she flared.

Luis shook his head. 'For once we are in agreement.'

And that, she supposed, was the nearest to an apology she was going to get. 'I can't stay here. I've got to go. What are you going to tell Don Rafael?'

'Nothing, because you won't be leaving. I swear to you that however much you provoke me in future I shall not lay one finger on you. We have an agreement, Amanda. You must play the part of my fiancée, for which you appear to have a natural talent, until next Saturday. I shall then put you on a plane to whatever destination you wish, and our business will be concluded.'

'And if I refuse?'

'Then I shall be angry, but Grandfather will

be devastated. The last time I saw him so animated was before his illness. That was because of you, in case you didn't realize.'

'You're a complete swine, Luis.'

Luis accepted the statement with a curt nod. Perhaps he thought it was a compliment. 'I shall go and brush my teeth,' he said, rising from the chair.

As soon as the door was closed behind him, Emma hurriedly pulled on a nightgown and climbed into bed. This week was going to be pure hell, but Luis was a good judge of character, he knew she would stick it out. She couldn't intentionally hurt the lovely old man who'd welcomed her into his home with such evident pleasure. How the two of them had ever come to be related was beyond her.

Poor old Don Rafael. Would Luis eventually tell him that they'd broken up if he lived longer than the doctors predicted? Emma suppressed a shudder. She knew it was Luis's business and not hers, but before she left she'd make sure he was aware that shocks like that could kill old people.

The bathroom door opened and Luis walked over to the bed. He picked up a glass of water from the bedside table, took a sip, and then casually untied his bathrobe and allowed it to fall to the floor.

Emma's body stiffened and her heart began to thud against her ribs. He was naked! Despite her alarm, her eyes slipped lower until they encountered a minuscule pair of white briefs.

'*Buenas noches, guapa,*' he murmured, climbing into bed and switching off the light, apparently unaware of the havoc he'd just caused.

Emma didn't reply. She lay as stiff as a corpse in the blackness. The bed was immense. She could easily avoid touching him, but she couldn't fool her brain into thinking he wasn't there. In the darkness it was all too easy to recall her emotions when she'd thought he was going to hurt her. She turned over and clung to the edge of the bed in an effort to control her body, which had begun to shake.

It was no use. Her trembling vibrated through the frame and the whole bed began to quiver.

'What is it?' Luis whispered.

'Nothing. I'm all right,' she hissed, and clung harder.

She heard him sigh as he rolled over, and his hand gently reached out and stroked down her back. Her body stopped shaking and instantly became rigid.

'Emma,' he soothed, and repeated her name several times as he massaged gently down her spine. He seemed to know instinctively that the use of her own name, more than anything, would cause her to relax.

'That's better,' the velvet-smooth tone encouraged her. 'I won't hurt you again, I promise. You must learn to trust me. Now come here.'

Emma cried out in protest as his strong arms lifted her and wedged her tightly against his side.

'Shh,' he said, as his arm nestled her head close against his chest and her brain resonated with the slow thud of his heart. 'I don't hold you in order to take advantage of you. It is merely comfort because I regret what has happened.'

'Don't tell me I'm getting an apology,' she said bitterly.

'Yes. I'm sorry, Emma. I went too far. You made me so angry, and I thought you were a different, harder type of woman. I've become too accustomed to the breed, I'm afraid. You must forgive me.'

Must she? There was no must about it. He couldn't even apologize like a normal person. One was supposed to ask for forgiveness, not demand it.

'I was terrified,' she said, her voice breaking into a sob.

'I'm truly sorry, *chica*. I understand your animosity. You are right to despise me for my lack of control, but you have my word that it will not happen again. Now go to sleep.' He kissed her lightly on the cheek. 'You'll feel better in the morning, and I shall try to make amends to you.'

Emma gave a token struggle. Luis's grip on her was firm but not threatening, and she felt her trembling begin to lessen. He'd promised not to hurt her again and she had to believe him. But go to sleep? He was mad if he thought she could sleep almost on top of him like this.

The deep musky fragrance of his aftershave tickled her nostrils. She wondered which brand he used. She'd never smelt it before, probably because nobody she'd ever met could have afforded it. Whatever it was it was incredibly nice. She'd have to sniff at the bottles in the bathroom and find out, then when she got back to Britain she might be able to cadge a sample from the perfume counter at one of the big stores.

Emma closed her eyes. Ten minutes later, the musky perfume, the rhythmic stroking of her hair and the hypnotic thud of Luis's heart had combined to relax and float her into blissful oblivion.

CHAPTER 5

Emma awoke to the sound of Luis singing in the bathroom. He could have closed the door, she thought, but apart from irritation at his thoughtlessness, she realized that she no longer felt any great animosity towards him. One cuddle, an apology, and her name spoken after he had said that he wouldn't, and she had forgiven him liberties that no man should ever have taken with her. It was she who was mad, she told herself in amazement as she propped herself up on the pillows until the bathroom was free.

'Ah, you are awake.' Luis entered the bedroom already dressed in jodhpurs and a loose, open-necked white shirt. 'May I say, *guapa*, that it was most pleasant to have you snuggled against me in sleep last night.' He sat down on the bed and smiled easily at her. 'The quivering has now stopped?' He reached out and touched her arm. 'Good. Now go and get ready. We're going riding.'

Emma's heart sank. The brand new jodhpurs purchased in London had been stashed at the bottom of her case and she'd hoped, ostrich-like, that they would stay there.

'Yes, master,' she muttered, making no attempt to move.

A broad grin spread over Luis's features. 'You may call me Luis,' he advised her. 'Perhaps after the wedding master may be more appropriate.'

She pulled a face at him but he continued smiling. Morning people were so irritating. Didn't they realize that lesser mortals needed three cups of tea and two slices of toast before they could be expected to be sociable?

'Come on, Amanda, we're already late. We shall have less than an hour before breakfast at this rate.'

A deep rumble of her stomach answered him. 'I can't go riding without any breakfast,' she wailed. 'I'll be sick.' She knew she was acting like a wimp; maybe he'd go without her.

'You can pick up a roll on the way past the kitchen; that should keep you going,' he said, then without further ado he ripped the duvet back.

'You're such a bully!' she hissed, scurrying into the bathroom. On her return a tray containing two freshly baked rolls, a pot of butter, a pot of jam, and a glass of orange juice was sitting on her bedside table.

'Please be quick,' said Luis, who was sitting in

an armchair, his attention absorbed by one of the ubiquitous files that were never far from him. 'Mornings and evenings are the only pleasant times to be out of doors during summer here.'

Emma tore open a roll and breathed in its wonderful yeasty aroma. 'I'll be quick,' she said, spreading it thickly with butter and watching with satisfaction as it turned molten. 'I didn't come first in the annual pie-eating competition for nothing.'

'I beg your pardon?' Luis glanced up quizzically from his file.

'A joke,' said Emma, wiping crumbs from her mouth with the back of her hand. 'Wouldn't expect you to understand.'

'Ah,' said Luis, without curiosity, and returned to his work.

He became animated again as he led her into the stables. Each horse was greeted by name and patted fondly, and he seemed completely unaware that she was trailing miserably behind him. The horses here bore no relation to those in the riding school that she'd attended briefly as a horse-mad girl of eleven. In exchange for mucking out the stables the owners had given her the odd lesson, but she realized now that the horses there must have been refugees from the knacker's yard. The sleek thoroughbreds here would probably go on strike rather than share their stables with them.

'I think I should tell you that I'm pretty

hopeless at riding,' she said, all hopes of bluffing her way through the situation vanishing as she took in the sheer height of the brutes before her. It grieved her to admit to any shortcomings in front of Luis, but it was either that or hanging on for dear life while one of these monsters sensed her incompetence and took the opportunity of galloping off into the next province.

'How hopeless?' Luis stopped burrowing his head into a horse's neck and turned to her with a frown.

In her mind, Emma could see herself as a girl, trotting round and round a churned-up field. It was difficult to decide who had been the most bored: the older girl leading her or her geriatric mount.

She glared at the groom, who'd never taken his eyes off her bottom since she'd entered the stables, then turned back to Luis. 'I can trot and I can canter, but I never got round to galloping.' The fact had never bothered her before, but as she registered the disbelief in Luis's eyes she felt a total failure.

'And I've never been skiing, yachting, scuba diving, to Ascot, or to the Paris fashion shows either,' she challenged. As she spoke she knew how infantile it sounded. What on earth was it about the man that made her act this way? But once she'd said it she couldn't un-say it, so she glared at him defiantly.

He met her gaze levelly, but she saw the corner

of his lips twitch into a smile. 'I knew that if I kept searching I'd find something that we had in common,' he said.

She raised her eyebrows in silent question.

'I haven't been to the Paris fashion shows either,' he replied, and they both started to laugh. The tension was dispelled, and Emma made a mental note to try and keep her mouth shut in future.

'You have the most beautiful laugh I have ever heard,' he said, momentarily brushing her cheek with the palm of his hand. He was about to turn away again when he saw the fire that blazed where he'd touched. It glowed even more brightly as he remained staring at her in surprise.

Emma turned away and tried to control her emotions. It must be the incident last night that had unsettled her, that was making her over-sensitive to his actions. Whatever it was, this week with Luis was turning into a roller coaster ride – all highs and lows and very little coasting.

'Miguel! Saddle Estrella!' It was a relief when he moved away and barked out the instruction.

The groom lifted his eyes from her posterior and she saw them widen with surprise. '*Es para niños, señor*,' he said, laughing.

'Do as I ask.' Luis's tone brooked no argument. The man nodded and hurried away.

'He said that the horse was only for children,' said Emma, envisaging a Shetland pony that was

84

kept especially for visiting toddlers. Why hadn't she said straight away this morning that she couldn't ride and saved herself further humiliation?

Luis shrugged. 'That is because she is the most reliable mount that we have. A bomb could explode beside her and she would not throw you. She is a little slow perhaps, but try her today while you are nervous and choose a more lively mount tomorrow.'

Emma wasn't convinced that Luis wasn't taking the opportunity of making a fool of her until Estrella was led into the yard.

'Aren't you gorgeous,' she cried, reaching up to stroke the white star-shaped mark on the horse's head which had obviously earned her name.

Luis smiled, took a packet of mints out of his pocket, and gave the horse one. 'You're not so bad for your age, are you, girl?' he said, patting her head as she crunched greedily. He gave the packet to Emma. 'She runs on these, Amanda. If she shows signs of slowing down give her one and it should keep her going for another five minutes.'

Emma started to laugh, but the groom shook his head. '*Es verdad, señorita*, you will win no prizes on this one.'

Emma took his hand to steady herself as she climbed up on Estrella's back. She still felt as though she were perched on top of a skyscraper and was grateful for the reassurance of Estrella's trustworthiness. 'I'll be happy to get back in one piece,' she said, only half joking.

The groom smiled back. 'Oh, she'll get you back safe, *señorita*, though it might be dark by then.'

'Saddle Hierro, Miguel!' Luis's voice wiped the smile off the man's face.

'It is done, *señor*,' he said, hurrying off to fetch him.

Now she was going to get a lecture about fraternizing with the hired hands, thought Emma, but Luis turned back to her with a smile.

'Comfortable?' he enquired, and she nodded. 'You hold the reins thus,' he said, demonstrating.

'Oh. Right. I remember now.' She threaded the leather through her fingers as he showed her. He bent to adjust her stirrup, and she felt quite touched as he fussed around making sure that everything was in order.

The closeness of the moment was shattered, however, as she caught sight of the horse Miguel was leading back into the yard. She received such a shock that her mouth dropped open and a colourful expletive left it and echoed round the stables.

'Sorry,' she murmured, as Luis frowned at her and Miguel grinned. He was holding on with difficulty to the most enormous black stallion she had ever seen.

'It's one of the four horses of the Apocalypse,' she gasped, as Miguel failed in his task and the animal reared impatiently into the air.

Luis grabbed the reins, brought the beast under control, and immediately mounted. The horse's powerful physique and glossy coat, almost blue in lustre, were testament to its pedigree and to the excellent care and grooming it received. The brute was an aristocrat, equally as arrogant as its owner, and she had to admit that together they made an impressive sight.

'We'll head over in that direction.' Luis pointed to a well-worn track that seemed to stretch to infinity. 'I'll have to give Hierro his head and leave you for a while otherwise he'll be impossible to control. I'll come back when he's quieter. I won't be long. You'll be fine.'

Already the horse seemed restless and agitated and was pulling fiercely at its reins. The instant Luis kicked with his heels it was off like a bullet, leaving Emma coughing with the dust left in its wake.

'We don't mind, do we, old girl?' She patted her trusty steed, who didn't appear to have noticed the rapid departure of its stablemate, and urged it out of the yard. Once she adjusted to the unaccustomed motion, Emma relaxed and began to enjoy herself. The warm breeze rippling through her hair was exhilarating, and the scent of rosemary and wild lavender floated upwards as it was crushed under Estrella's hooves.

Like a beach pony travelling the same stretch of sand every day of the summer, Estrella seemed to know exactly where she was going. Emma soon gave up all pretence of guiding her and gazed around at her surroundings instead. The track they were following seemed timeless. On both sides of her she could see vineyards planted in regimented lines, and behind her was the impressive splendour of the villa presiding over everything.

There were no signs of the twentieth century here; Don Rafael's grandfather could have trodden this path and it would have looked exactly the same. The continuity of life cheered her. She took a deep breath, exhaled, and felt at peace with nature. Certain things remained in your mind for ever. She knew this moment in Andalucía would be one of them.

The thunder of hooves and a cloud of dust announced Luis's return. Caught up in her reflective mood, Emma had almost forgotten about him. She popped another mint into Estrella's mouth and smiled at him happily. He might be the most infuriating male she'd ever met, but she could forgive him a lot for giving her an experience such as this.

'I came to apologize.' He looked taken aback by her friendly greeting. 'It hadn't occurred to me that you might not be able to ride, that you wouldn't want to come with me. It was meant to be a treat.'

'It's a lovely treat,' she said, then started to laugh at the look of perplexity that shadowed his face.

'What you said about being hopeless . . . this was not true?' he asked. You seem at ease now . . . your posture . . . you have a natural stance.'

Emma felt a surge of pride at his praise, and her smile broadened. 'It was true,' she confessed. 'I haven't been on a horse since I was eleven.'

'*Dios!* I should cut my throat.'

At his look of utter incredulity that anyone should be deprived of riding for so many years Emma started to giggle. He stared at her, smiling, until she recalled what he'd said earlier about her laugh, and she stopped abruptly.

'You're incredibly lucky having all this.' She waved her hand in a broad sweep, hoping he wouldn't notice her embarrassment.

He nodded his agreement then leaned over to her. 'And you, *señorita*, are incredibly beautiful.'

Once again her cheeks flamed, but Luis didn't seem to notice. He spurred Hierro into a gallop and became a distant speck on the horizon. She wished he would keep his personal remarks to himself; he was much easier to deal with when he was being sarcastic and superior than when he was being nice. Of course, that was it! How stupid she was! That was the reason for his compliments. It was because of what had happened last night. He'd said that he was going to make it up to her so that was why he was saying such things. He didn't really mean them; it was just his way of making amends.

Emma sighed with relief. It was as well that she understood him or else she might have made a fool of herself. She took two mints out of the packet and tried to bribe Estrella to canter. Maybe she should ask for a more lively horse tomorrow. It would be really something if she could learn to gallop. She wondered if he was telling the truth when he said that she had a natural stance.

'Gosh, I'm starving. All that fresh air and exercise, I'm not used to it.' Emma helped herself to another slice of tortilla under the benevolent eye of Don Rafael, who was encouraging her to eat as much as she wanted. They were sitting on the east terrace that overlooked the main vineyard. Although Don Rafael could no longer undertake his daily inspection of the vines he said that he could tell a great deal by viewing them from a distance, and that was why he liked to sit here.

'It is so rare today to see a woman who enjoys her food instead of picking at it as though it were poisoned.'

Emma hesitated. Was Luis's grandfather saying in a roundabout way that she was greedy? She met his warm open gaze, decided not, and placed a slice of melon on her plate. If enjoying her food was the main criterion that Don Rafael sought in a granddaughter-in-law then she could beat the competition hands down.

Emma glanced across at Luis, who smiled back at her. His mood was mellow and she was enjoying it as long as it lasted. They'd returned to their room for a quick shower after riding and she'd noticed that her passport had been returned to her bag. Now that she knew why Luis was being nice to her she found it easy to relax with him and it seemed natural being bright and bubbly with his grandfather. She sensed immediately Don Rafael's deep attachment to his land. It seemed to please him when she asked him questions, and she could have stayed talking to him all day when María came and announced that it was time for his rest.

'Do you really want to visit the *bodega* and learn about sherry production or was all that simply for Grandfather's benefit?' drawled Luis in an amused voice when the old man had gone.

Emma flushed. It hurt to realize that Luis thought she'd been play-acting for the last couple of hours. 'I'd like to go some time, whenever it's convenient,' she said.

'No time like the present,' he said, standing up. We shan't bother Carlos. I shall drive. I have a small car that I use sometimes.'

'I'll just go to the loo first,' she said, and saw him wince. Didn't his usual girlfriends admit to normal bodily functions? She'd have to remember to say she was going to powder her nose next time. Did people really say such things? She thought of some of the cruder expressions her friends used, and smiled. Luis would probably faint away if he heard them.

'I will meet you at the main entrance,' he said, breaking into her thoughts and striding off.

When Emma hurried down the main steps and saw Luis's small car – a blood-red Porsche – she fell about laughing. 'Don't tell me, you've a sticker in the back saying "My other car is a Mini",' she spluttered.

Luis looked bemused, which only served to increase her hilarity. 'You haven't a clue what I'm going on about, have you?' she asked.

Luis admitted he did not, and they were some way to Jerez de la Frontera before she managed to explain. 'You see, most people that say they've got a small car mean it and, what's more, it's usually clapped out, and sometimes they think it's funny to have a sticker in the back saying, "My other car's a Porsche".'

Luis smiled politely, and Emma decided to change the subject. He did have a sense of humour, she'd seen flashes of it, but it was almost as if he didn't like other people to know about its existence. 'Did you love Amanda?' she asked. The question came out more bluntly than she'd intended; it had been revolving in her brain ever since last night and was determined to get out.

Luis flashed her a look and then returned his

gaze to the road. His fingers, she noticed, were gripping the steering wheel fiercely.

'Well, did you?' she persisted, when it became obvious that he wasn't going to answer.

He sighed. 'You remind me of a puppy I had when I was a boy. If it could get into one of the downstairs rooms and seize a cushion it wouldn't stop until it had every last piece of stuffing out of it.'

'What was its name?' she asked, and he started to laugh.

'Tell me that you are like this with everybody, that you haven't singled me out especially to provoke.'

Emma smiled. 'You haven't answered my question yet.'

'His name was Pícaro. He was a true rogue, nobody could control him,' he said, grinning.

'My first question.'

Luis's face grew serious. 'Amanda – beauty without flaw,' he murmured, almost to himself. 'She seemed to be everything I wanted from a wife. The time was right and she was willing. We had even decided on a name for our first-born child. And, no, you may not know the answer to that one.'

They continued for a while in silence. Emma sensed Luis's hurt, but she couldn't help feeling that he'd had a lucky escape. For once in her life she kept her mouth shut and resisted the impulse to tell him so.

'So, *guapa*, I have answered your question. Will you answer mine?'

Emma started. For the past few minutes she'd been speculating to herself what Amanda's version of events would be. 'You haven't answered my question,' she said. 'I asked you about love.'

'Love.' Luis rapped the steering wheel with the back of his hand. 'How can one truly and honestly put hand to heart and swear that one is in love? How does one know?'

Emma started to laugh. 'Thanks, Luis, you've answered my question brilliantly.'

He stared at her. 'What do you mean?'

Emma shook her head. 'I'm not saying. You'd only say I was trying to provoke you again, and in answer to your question I don't do it intentionally, well, most of the time I don't, it just happens.'

Luis took a moment to digest this. 'I wish to know how I answered your question and why you laughed.'

'No, you don't. You'd take offence if I told you.'

'No, I will not.'

Emma shrugged. 'If you have to stop and ask yourself if you're in love then it's a sure sign you're not.'

'And madam is an expert in such matters, is she?' he flared.

'I told you you'd take offence,' she said, and turned and looked out of the window.

They came to the outskirts of Jerez, and Emma sat up in her seat with excitement. Every other building they passed seemed to be a *bodega* advertising sherry tasting and tours. 'There're loads of them,' she said. 'I wonder how many barrels they've got hoarded away in there.'

Luis slowed down to turn right into the grounds of a huge whitewashed building with his family name emblazoned on the side. 'At any one time in Jerez there are over one million barrels maturing in the cellars.'

'That's some party.'

He smiled in answer. Apparently she was forgiven.

'So why is the *bodega* in Jerez when you grow the grapes in Sevilla?' she asked.

His sable-brown eyes crinkled at the edges as he smiled, and she sensed his pleasure in finally discussing a subject that was close to his heart. 'It is to comply with the *denominacion* regulations,' he said, and went on to explain that there was only a certain area of Spain, known as the sherry triangle, where conditions were right for the growth of the *flor* on top of the wine. This was a yeasty type substance that was essential for the production of the finest sherry.

As he spoke his features came alive, the sternness dropped from his expression, and his eyes sparkled. Emma was fascinated by the transformation and kept asking him questions. Sherry production was a subject she'd never given a second thought to, but by the time they'd toured the *bodega* and he'd insisted on her tasting the wine in its various stages of storage, Luis had managed to transmit a great deal of his own enthusiasm to her.

He took her for a late lunch in a beautiful restaurant situated in the woods in Jerez. 'It must be wonderful to have a job that you love,' she said, as they were eating. 'I've had some absolutely awful jobs in factories, shops and pubs, but I suppose in a way they've been good. If I ever get fed up of writing essays I think of being stuck in the jam factory or clearing up after other people for the rest of my life. It works every time and spurs me on to get a good degree and a decent job at the end of it.'

Luis twirled the stem of his glass between his fingers and nodded thoughtfully.

Encouraged by the harmony she felt with him at the moment, she continued. 'I owe it to my mum as well. I'm all she's got, and she's given up so much so I could go to university. She's desperate for me to have the opportunities she's missed in life, and I won't let her down. It's the least I can do.'

Luis studied her for several moments before replying, 'When I pay you at the end of the week for your services I shall add a bonus.'

'What?' It took a moment for the full impact of his words to register. When it did it hurt more than if he'd reached across and struck her. She slammed her glass on to the table and a red stain spread outwards from it across the pristine white tablecloth.

'Is that what you think? Do you really believe I've been telling you about my life, hoping I might wheedle some more money out of you? "Payment for my services"? Such a revealing choice of words, wouldn't you agree? Thanks, Luis. Thanks a bunch for reminding me that you consider me a *puta*, a prostitute, whatever you like to call it.'

She stormed out of the restaurant. It was small consolation when she glanced back to notice that Luis's cheeks were glowing like the imitation coals of her mum's electric fire. How she hated that man! Nobody had ever humiliated her like he had. Why hadn't she learned her lesson the first time instead of coming back for more?

Outside the restaurant, even though it was almost four o'clock, the afternoon sun was still blisteringly hot. Emma headed for the shade of a tree and leaned her body against its trunk. Slowly she felt her anger dissipate. It wasn't really Luis's fault. She was to blame for forgetting what type of man he was. They were worlds apart. How could she ever have been so stupid as to think he could understand what drove her? That even in this day and age she felt the slur of her illegitimate birth and was determined to rise above it. Perhaps he'd meant to be kind with the offer of his money. She'd try to give him the benefit of the doubt, though in fact it had been the greatest insult of all.

'I am so sorry.' Emma felt the touch of a hand on her shoulder and she stiffened. 'I wished only to help you, but it seems that we are fated to misunderstand each other.'

'Oh, I think I understand you all right, Luis,' she murmured, not looking at him.

He gripped her chin between his thumb and index finger and forced it gently upwards. 'I don't think you do, *señorita*,' he whispered, and her stomach performed a perfect somersault as it registered the tenderness in his eyes. She was sure he meant to kiss her and self-preservation made her pull away.

What game was he playing? She glanced at him again and saw that the tenderness had vanished and annoyance had taken its place. She'd been right to pull away from him. It was too easy for him to manipulate her; she wasn't an inflatable doll he could amuse himself with for a week before he decided that she wasn't quite what he wanted and returned her to the shop.

'At least tell me that you forgive me,' he said eventually. 'I swear it wasn't my intention to hurt you.' He turned on her a 'little-boy-lost' look that was so far removed from his habitual stern expression that she acquiesced.

They walked back to the car and, smiling, he took her hand and kissed it. 'You are stimulating company,' he said as he opened the passenger door for her.

Emma climbed in, her thoughts in confusion. Just who was the real Luis Quevedo? He seemed to switch easily from one character to another until he hit on the one that best suited his purpose.

CHAPTER 6

'I'm afraid Carmelita will be dining with us this evening,' said Luis, as he rejoined her at half past eight that night.

Emma put down her hairbrush and watched as Luis unselfconsciously stripped off his clothes and flung them into the corner of the room before walking into the bathroom. His tone had sounded ominous. Who was Carmelita? And why should Luis be 'afraid' that she was dining with them? It was a strange thing to say.

She picked up her brush and finished brushing her hair. She'd ask Luis who this mystery person was when he came back into the bedroom, but she had the strongest of feelings that she wouldn't like his answer. The current state of affairs between them was too wonderful to last, she supposed.

Since the fracas in the restaurant, Luis had almost fallen over himself being nice to her. He'd made her laugh as he described some of the more eccentric characters of the sherry community while they drove slowly back to the villa. They'd found Don Rafael relaxing in the inner courtyard and spent an hour with him before he took another nap, then Luis left her to her own devices while he caught up on some work.

Emma had wandered around the grounds for a while and then into the kitchen. María had seemed glad to see her and had shown her how to make paella the Sevillana way. This didn't seem much different from the paella she'd eaten in other parts of Spain, but Emma kept her thoughts to herself. María obviously believed *Paella Sevillana* to be better than any other region's, and was delighted when Emma tasted it and had to agree. María hadn't mentioned any other dinner guests though.

'You look exceptionally beautiful tonight, Amanda.' Luis shot her a dazzling smile as he towelled dry his dark hair.

She returned it with a scowl.

'What did I say?' His eyebrows lifted in astonishment. 'Don't you like compliments?'

Of course she liked compliments. Who didn't? 'It's that name,' she ground out. 'I can't stand it.'

The good humour vanished from his face. 'I am afraid that's your problem.' He reached into his wardrobe for a shirt. 'Amanda is the name of the woman I told Grandfather I would marry.

101

He may be frail, but he still has all his mental faculties, I think you would agree. And I think you would also concede that if I became confused and called you by another woman's name in front of him he might be a little suspicious. Amanda you must remain, in private as well as in public. It is only for a week. Is it so much to ask?'

Emma shook her head. He was right, of course. The last thing she wanted was for Don Rafael to find out about their deception. 'I'm sorry. I'm being stupid.' She gazed up at him through long golden lashes. 'I'll try not to let the name grate on me so much.' She wondered if the name irritated her because she was in some way jealous of the woman, then immediately dismissed the idea.

Luis smiled. 'You are not stupid, *chica*. A little over-sensitive, perhaps, but I shall attempt to keep the use of Amanda to a minimum. I expect I should also resent it if I had to answer by the name of Archibald for a fixed period.'

Emma giggled, and his dark eyes twinkled.

'Talking about names,' she murmured. 'Carmelita?'

'Ah, yes.' His expression hardened. He turned away and proceeded to put on his trousers. 'Tell me, *chica*, is there anywhere in Sevilla that it would most please you to visit?'

Emma stared at his back in surprise. This was an abrupt change of subject. 'It's not in Sevilla,' she said, seizing the chance, 'but I'd really like to see the Alhambra.'

He turned to her with a frown. 'That would take a full day. Granada is at least two hundred and fifty kilometres away.'

Emma shrugged. 'You were the one who asked.'

He threaded a red silk tie through the collar of his shirt. Emma could almost hear his brain ticking.

'You do realize the place will be swarming with tourists at this time of year?' he said eventually.

She shrugged again. 'It might be the only chance I get to go.'

'If I take a day off to accompany you then I shall have to leave you alone more on other days so that I can catch up on my work.'

'Oh, for goodness' sake!' she snapped, irritated at his excuses. 'If you don't want to go, why don't you just come straight out and say it?'

His full lips curved into a smile. 'We shall visit the Alhambra on Tuesday,' he said.

'Wow! Great! Thanks, Luis.' She leapt up and brushed her lips against his cheek. For some reason this seemed to embarrass him, and he stepped away from her.

'Carmelita is Ramón's sister,' he said. 'She is a model, and often visits the villa between assignments. I was not aware that she was coming this week.'

'I see.' Emma looked up at him, but he refused to meet her gaze. Whoever or whatever the woman was, Emma realized she'd just been handed the star prize of the Alhambra on account of it. She picked up her bottle of *Pas de Jour* from the dressing table and sprayed herself liberally while she thought about it. At the very least it would mean both Ramón and his sister glaring at her through dinner as if she'd just crawled out of a sewer. Somehow she had a feeling that there was more to it than that.

'Does she know I'm not really your fiancée?' she asked.

Luis shook his head. 'No one knows apart from Ramón. He has strict instructions to tell no one, not even his sister.'

'That's something at any rate.'

'Are you ready to go down?' He opened the door and offered her his arm.

'Hang on a minute.' She raced across to the chest of drawers and took out a guide book of Southern Spain that she'd brought with her. A few moments poring over the magnificent photographs of pools and fountains, courtyards and gardens of the Alhambra palace fortified her.

'OK.' She snapped the book shut and took his arm.

'May I ask what you were doing?' he said as they went downstairs.

'Whenever I was little and I had to have an

injection or something nasty my mum would always have a treat waiting for me afterwards. I was reminding myself of my treat before I went down for the injection.'

Luis burst out laughing. He stopped at the bottom of the stairs and turned her to face him. 'I am growing quite fond of you, *guapa*,' he said, stroking gently down her cheek with the back of his hand.

Emma pulled away. His touch did ridiculous things to her stomach. 'Like a pet hamster, you mean?' she countered, to cover her confusion.

He was still laughing when he pushed open the door to the drawing room, but sobered up quickly enough when the raven-haired beauty that was talking to Don Rafael swept down on him like a hawk.

'Darling! How wonderful!' Scarlet-clad arms with matching scarlet talons at the end of them fastened themselves around Luis's neck. 'It's so good to be here again. You wouldn't believe how much I miss you all when I'm away.'

'It's good to see you also, Carmelita.' Luis detached her hands from around his neck, but retained them in his own for longer than was necessary.

This is Amanda, my fiancée.' He turned to Emma with a smile. The woman seemed to have difficulty swallowing before stepping forward and giving the air on each side of Emma's cheeks a perfunctory kiss.

'Charmed, I'm sure,' she said, turning back to Luis and linking arms with him. 'Now, you wicked man, you must tell me everything that's happened since I saw you last.'

Emma watched them cross the room and caught the eye of Ramón, who was sneering at her from the corner. She marshalled her defences and shot him a syrupy smile. It felled him instantly and he looked away. Don Rafael beckoned to her; her face creased into a genuine smile of pleasure, and she walked over to him.

So Carmelita was just as obnoxious as her brother. Emma expected little less of someone who'd inhabited the same womb as Ramón, but her behaviour still irritated. Emma's female instinct told her that Carmelita and Luis had been lovers at some stage, and the knowledge rankled.

She sat down next to Don Rafael and tried to shake off the unsettling feeling of jealousy that gnawed at her. It was ridiculous. At the end of this week Luis Quevedo would cease to exist for her. She had to remember that. Who he chose to entertain in his bedroom was no concern of hers.

It wasn't only Emma who was more distracted than usual. Don Rafael also seemed in a world of his own. She followed the old man's gaze and realized why: Carmelita and Luis were seated together on a sofa and she was leaning over him whispering in his ear. From the raptness of Luis's expression, Carmelita must have been divulging to him the secret of eternal life at the very least.

'She's an incredibly beautiful woman,' said Emma, when Don Rafael sighed and turned his attention back to her.

He smiled sadly. 'Her father was a good man,' was all he said.

Emma racked her brains for conversation that would divert his attention away from the couple on the sofa. It was a relief when María appeared to tell them dinner was ready.

'I hadn't realized that you were engaged, darling,' purred Carmelita as soon as they sat down.

'It was announced in the newspapers.' Luis raised a quizzical eyebrow at her.

'It doesn't seem to have prevented you from appearing in the gossip columns with monotonous regularity.'

Emma hid a smile. The woman was certainly a bitch of the highest order. Luis deserved all he got by messing with her. She turned to him with interest to see how he would wriggle out of the situation. Amusement turned to pity, however, as she intercepted the look of disappointment which Don Rafael flashed at him.

She took a sip of wine and her brain whirred into action. 'These people will stoop to anything,' she said in a confiding tone to Carmelita. 'Two weeks ago we attended a friend's party and Luis kissed her to wish her happy birthday.

I couldn't believe it when I saw the papers a few days later. The place where I had been standing had been blotted out, and Catherine was reported as being his new girlfriend.'

'Unbelievable.' Carmelita smiled with saccharine sweetness across the table. 'Who would credit it?' she said, raising her finely plucked eyebrows at Ramón.

Across the table, Luis grinned, and raised his glass to her in salute.

Emma smiled back, but though she'd won the initial skirmish for Don Rafael, she had a feeling the battle wasn't over yet.

She was right. The next attack wasn't long in coming.

'And what about that photograph of you and Cerise Lawton in that French magazine?' Carmelita enquired, while she rearranged the paella on her plate instead of eating it. 'One could say that you and Cerise seemed extremely attached to each other.'

Silence reigned. Carmelita looked smug, Ramón was twitching with the effort of controlling his laughter, and Don Rafael was glaring at his grandson, who appeared to be finding the label on the bottle of wine in front of him absorbing.

Emma hadn't a clue what the photograph contained but she could make an educated guess; the reputation of the actress in question was legendary. She crossed her fingers and took a deep breath.

'That was a very old photograph, Carmelita.' She smiled across the table as insincerely as Ramón's sister had smiled at her. 'I expect Ms Lawton needs all the money she can get now that the television company have decided not to screen any more episodes of *Jetsetters*.'

'Strange. I could have sworn it was this season's designer wear she was almost wearing,' replied Carmelita, but her words were drowned by a sudden attack of coughing by Luis.

On the surface, Don Rafael seemed content with these explanations, but as the evening progressed, and the woman continued a barrage of snide remarks to her and sexual innuendoes towards Luis, he seemed to look sadder and older.

Emma seethed inwardly. Why couldn't Luis tell the woman to shut her mouth? Couldn't he see how much she was upsetting his grandfather?

She turned to him for support as Carmelita came out with another outrageous comment, but his face was a blank and it dawned on her that he was no longer listening. His attention was absorbed by the woman's outer shell, which was encased in a red satin gown that barely skimmed the top of her nipples. Perhaps, like Emma, he'd been expecting all evening that one would pop out.

He was destined to be disappointed, however.

Carmelita's breasts were shyer than their owner and behaved themselves significantly better.

'I'll retire now, if you don't mind, Don Rafael,' Carmelita announced as soon as dessert was over. 'Jet lag catching up with me.' She yawned theatrically.

Don Rafael nodded his assent. He looked exhausted, and seemed as pleased as Emma was that the evening had broken up early.

'I shall also take my leave of you,' he said, rising with difficulty and walking stiffly out of the room.

Ramón smugly wished them goodnight and followed him.

Luis reached across the table, picked up a bottle of brandy and offered her some. When she refused he poured himself a glass, leaned back in his chair and sipped it.

Emma glared at him. She felt like a bottle of lemonade shaken to the second before explosion. It was a wonder that he didn't shrivel up and expire with all the bad thoughts that were being beamed in his direction. If he had, in reality, been her fiancé he wouldn't have known what hit him at this moment.

She turned away and tried to slow her breathing as she'd been shown in the meditation class she and Kate had attended for a laugh one afternoon. Her anger was inappropriate. She wasn't Luis's fiancée, so her personal feelings were unimportant, but she'd damn well make sure he realized how much he'd upset his grandfather.

Luis glanced at his watch, finished what was left in his glass, and stood up. 'You were amazing tonight, Amanda.' He slipped his arm around her waist and guided her out of the room. 'You'll have to consider a career in public relations when you graduate. I've never seen anyone think so quickly in a tight situation.'

'It would have been a lot easier if you'd backed me up occasionally instead of staring at your girlfriend's mammary glands all evening.'

He chucked her under the chin. 'Jealous, little one?' he taunted.

The meditation technique wasn't working. She had a strong urge to head butt him, but realized in time that it wouldn't be karmically correct.

'Don't be ridiculous!' She pulled away from him. 'I don't give a damn what you do, but your grandfather does. You should have kept Carmelita in order. She would have shut up if you'd told her to.'

Luis shrugged. 'Carmelita is Carmelita. She's always like that. Nobody takes any notice.' They reached their room. He opened the door then stood back to allow her to enter first.

'Well, your grandfather did.' Emma stormed in, threw her evening bag on to the bedside table, and turned to face him. 'For goodness' sake, Luis, didn't you see his face? Are you

111

really that insensitive? He seemed to age ten years and sink into himself while he was watching you.'

'You exaggerate, Amanda.' Luis stood with his back to the shutters and glared at her.

'Amanda! I'm not Amanda! And thank God for that!'

'Really?' Luis's lip curled with derision. 'You surprise me. You seem to enjoy playing the part well enough.'

Emma's resolution to keep a lid on her temper was forgotten as she registered the supercilious expression on Luis's face.

'Surprised, are you?' She tore off her earrings and flung them into their case. 'Well, stand by to be gobsmacked. I'm pleased I'm not your fiancée. If that's the way you used to carry on in front of her then it's no wonder she decided to take off with someone else. And get this: I wouldn't marry you if you were the last reptile crawling on this earth.'

'Are you completely finished?' Luis's teeth were clenched so tightly that the veins on his neck threatened to explode.

'Not quite. You look down on me, don't you, Luis? You think I'm some stupid working-class little girl who'll never amount to anything, but I'll tell you something, I'm a lot more fortunate than you. When I marry it'll be love. My husband will have eyes only for me, and even if we end up living in a hovel we'll be happy. Oh,

you'll get married. There'll never be any short-
age of takers for the post of Señora Quevedo, but
it'll be your money they're after, Luis. It sure as
hell won't be your personality.'

There was a deathly silence. As the seconds
ticked away, Emma had ample time to reflect
that her words had been well over the top. Even
his behaviour tonight did not warrant such a
personal attack on him. Apologize, her brain
urged her. She stared at Luis, whose body
was rigid with repressed anger, and remained
mute.

There was a movement. Luis walked towards
her. Emma closed her eyes. If anyone could ever
be said to deserve a good slap then she acknowledged that she did. A draught swirled across her
face. She opened her eyes. It was the movement
of air as Luis closed the bedroom door behind
him.

'Damn.' Emma collapsed on to the bed, her
heart booming like a disco beat. What had she
done now? All she'd wanted was to make Luis
aware that his behaviour was hurting his grandfather, but she couldn't stop there, could she?
No, she had to get personal, and who the hell was
she to tell him that his wife wouldn't love him?
She was a total cow.

Emma gnawed at her thumbnail. It was strong
and curved, because she didn't normally bite her
nails, but she continued until she'd weakened
the edge and it split. With a strange surge of

satisfaction she tore it across then stared glumly at the ragged edge it left behind.

What a mess she'd made of it, and she wasn't thinking about her nail. There was no way that Luis would want her to carry on the pretence after what she'd said to him. Even if he had the hide of a rhino, which she considered likely, those words had hit their mark. He'd either confess everything to his grandfather tomorrow or make some excuse why she had to leave. Either way Don Rafael would be upset, and it would be all her fault.

Wearily, she took off her clothes and got ready for bed.

And where was Luis now? Emma didn't need three guesses to know that he would head straight for the guest wing and into the ample and all too willing arms of Carmelita.

And was that her doing too? Emma brushed her teeth so vigorously that the gums bled and a trail of pinky foam splattered into the basin. She rinsed her mouth and walked back into the bedroom. No, she decided, as she gathered the crisp cotton duvet over her. That had probably been his intention all along. That was why he'd been so distracted at dinner, and that was why Carmelita had retired to bed early: she needed time to prepare for the arrival of Superstud.

Emma flung back the covers and went over to switch on the fan that Luis had had brought up when she mentioned how warm it was at night.

Damned heat! No wonder it made you do and say things you wouldn't normally dream of. She climbed back into bed and tossed about restlessly.

It was a long night.

CHAPTER 7

The cheerful greetings of two gardeners under her window the next morning woke Emma. She sat up in bed, rubbing the sleep from her eyes. She felt exhausted. It seemed only minutes ago that she'd finally dropped to sleep. A quick glance around the room confirmed that Luis hadn't returned during the night, and a glance at her watch confirmed that it was twenty to ten.

'Grief!' Emma leapt out of bed and raced to the bathroom. She was in no hurry to face her doom, but she didn't want Luis to think that she was skulking in her room, too frightened to face the inevitable confrontation with him.

Lack of sleep had turned her eyes into two pink marshmallows, but a quick sandblast in the shower should sort them out. She hesitated over what to wear, and chose a pretty floral skirt and lilac silk camisole. Before she left the room she draped a navy jacket over her arm. Be prepared: she hadn't been a Girl Guide for nothing. If a couple of security guards pounced and bundled her off to the airport on Luis's orders then those clothes should suffice for her journey back to Britain.

The villa seemed unnaturally quiet as Emma walked along the corridor, her bravado of the previous night sadly lacking. As she made her way downstairs the distant hum of a vacuum cleaner reminded her of her fate for the rest of the summer. It wasn't so bad, she decided. It was an honest occupation. She'd had a couple of days of intensive Spanish which had improved her accent and vocabulary enormously. It would have to do. She regretted with all her heart how her departure would affect Don Rafael, but it was out of her hands. She could only hope that it would be achieved with as little unpleasantness as possible.

Unchallenged, Emma reached the terrace where the Quevedos took breakfast. Don Rafael was still sitting there reading a newspaper. Emma scanned his face for any sign of disillusionment but, although he looked more tired than usual, he greeted her as warmly.

'You do not ride with Luis this morning, Amanda?' he asked, after he had signalled to a maid to bring fresh coffee.

'Er, I'm afraid I slept in.'

Don Rafael nodded his approval. 'Our guests always seem to sleep soundly here,' he beamed. 'I'm sure Luis will be riding again later and you can accompany him then.'

Emma picked up a slice of watermelon. 'Did you see Luis this morning?' she attempted lightly.

Don Rafael chuckled. 'There was a time, my dear, when I would have beaten your future husband to the stables, but that time is long past. I am generally still eating breakfast when he returns.'

Emma sighed. So Luis hadn't had a chance to say anything to his grandfather yet. She listened to the old man's friendly chatter and felt awful. What on earth would his opinion of her be when Luis apprised him of her true reason for being there?

Half an hour later, with a full stomach and the caffeine from two cups of coffee humming through her system, Emma was feeling slightly better. They had discussed the weather in Britain, the forthcoming elections in Spain, and Holy Week in Sevilla which she must be sure not to miss. Nothing had been mentioned about the previous evening with Carmelita, she noted.

Emma was beginning to wonder if the reason Luis hadn't yet appeared was because he was still in Carmelita's bed, when they were suddenly deafened by the thunder of hooves. 'He rides extremely well, don't you think?' said Don Rafael, turning to her with a proud smile.

Luis reined in the evil-looking horse as it approached the terrace, and it towered above them, churning up the lawn and flowers with its powerful hooves.

Emma glanced up at Luis. His eyes stared mockingly back. He knew she was frightened of his horse. Was that why he was allowing it to pound restlessly in front of her and cover her with the warmth of its breath? Did he hope that she'd run screaming from the terrace like a hysterical female so that he could have revenge and a good laugh at the same time?

Her heart was thudding with terror, but she was damned if she was going to allow herself to be intimidated. She took some lumps of sugar from the breakfast tray, placed them on the palm of her hand, and offered them to the stallion.

'Careful, *niña*,' warned Don Rafael, 'he has a temper to match his spirit.'

Remembering what the staff at the riding school did all those years ago, she talked softly to the horse while she gingerly stroked its head. Hot breath flared out of its nostrils as it devoured the sugar. When it had finished it butted her other hand to see whether she was hiding any more titbits, then nestled into her shoulder.

Don Rafael burst out laughing. 'We'll have to employ female grooms, Luis. Your male grooms must treat Hierro too harshly; that's why he bites them.'

Luis dismounted from the animal's back and handed the reins to a groom. 'I do not think it would make any difference, *Abuelo*. It is simply

Amanda. She expects perfection from the male of the species and they react accordingly.'

Emma stiffened as Luis strode towards her, but evidently he'd decided to maintain the charade for the moment. He pulled her towards him and kissed her soundly on the lips, then threw himself into an armchair.

Emma poured him a cup of coffee, silently cursing her shaking hands as she gave it to him. He took it with a murmur of thanks, placed it on the table, then stretched languidly in the chair and closed his eyes.

Despite everything, her attention was caught by the lean, powerful physique of the man. The closely fitting jodhpurs and T-shirt he was wearing accentuated the tightly packed muscles underneath. Hierro wasn't the only magnificent animal she'd seen that morning, she decided.

Luis's habit of lounging in a chair might have seemed slovenly with any other man, but with him it simply appeared elegant. Her gaze lingered on his long, surprisingly sensitive fingers before being drawn upwards to ponder the perfection of such wide sensual lips.

How had she ever thought that Luis was only averagely handsome, and how had she had the temerity to tell him that women would never love him? If physical beauty was what they sought then they'd be queuing up in droves. She gave a sigh and was disconcerted when his lips, which she was still gazing at, twitched and then curved at the corners. Hastily, she glanced at his eyes, and was dismayed when she registered by their sardonic twinkle that he knew she'd been watching him for the past few minutes.

Luis picked up his coffee and began sipping it. She turned her attention back to Don Rafael, but was unable to concentrate fully on his conversation because of the knowledge of two mocking dark eyes burning into her back.

'Let us go for a walk, Amanda.' Luis rose, draped an arm around her shoulders, and led her across the lawn towards an avenue of lime trees. This was it. At least her misery would soon be over and she'd know whether he planned to retaliate or not.

'It is always so refreshingly cool in here,' he said, gazing up into the canopy formed by the trees.

Emma tensed. They were now out of sight of Don Rafael, but the confrontation still hadn't come. Why couldn't he get on with it?

At last Luis made his move, but it wasn't what she expected. Leaning against a tree, he pulled her towards him. Caught off guard, she stumbled and her body fell heavily against his. Smiling, he lifted her gently up and began kissing her with feather-like pressure around her mouth.

'You have such a delicate beauty.' He ran his fingers through the blonde, silken strands of her hair, lifting them up to the mottled light and allowing them to fall gently back down.

What game was he playing now? Warm, fleshy lips pressed more urgently against hers, and his moist tongue probed at her defences. The experience sent a wave of anticipation churning through her stomach, but she fought it ruthlessly and succeeded in keeping her teeth clamped closed and her body as stiff and unyielding as board.

'I see that you still despise me,' he said, releasing her. 'I have just been with Carmelita.'

So that explained his good mood. Just as she'd thought, he'd spent the night in Carmelita's bed, but how dared he attempt to kiss her after coming straight from that woman! She wiped the back of her hand across her mouth, trying to remove every last trace of him.

'If you want to make a mockery out of this week, then it appears there's little I can do to prevent you! Thank God it's just a week. I couldn't stand it any longer watching you hurt your grandfather the way you do.' She pushed past him, but he caught her arm and prevented her from leaving.

'You make too many assumptions, *chica*. I went riding with Carmelita to tell her that my fiancée's bed was more exciting than hers, and to ask her to leave.'

Emma impersonated a goldfish for several seconds before finding the presence of mind to close her mouth. 'What on earth did she say?' she gasped.

Luis shot her a rueful glance. 'Many things. Which was why I waited until we were far from the house.'

'You did this because of what I said last night?'

'Obviously. Why else should I make an enemy of a very desirable woman and upset Ramón?'

'I'm sorry, Luis. I didn't mean – '

He silenced her with a peremptory wave of his hand. 'Of course you meant what you said. From the little I've learned of you over the last few days, I know that you do not say things just because you like the sound of your own voice.'

'I went too far. It was none of my business.'

Luis frowned. 'I could have throttled you last night, but I'm pleased now that you said what you did. No one has ever spoken to me like that before, and it made me reassess my life. I lay awake for hours thinking about the man I'd become, before realizing I didn't like this selfish person very much either.'

'I'm sorry.' Emma stared at her fingernails in embarrassment. 'I was angry that you'd upset Don Rafael. I shouldn't have said all the other things. I'm sure you'll get married and be blissfully happy. Like you say, I'm too quick to make assumptions. I should keep my nose out when I know nothing about you.'

Luis took her hand and rubbed it absentmindedly against his chin. He mustn't have shaved that morning and the bristles rasped on her soft skin. 'I'd like to tell you something about my life if you'd care to listen,' he murmured.

'You don't have to,' she said, fixing him with her clear blue gaze.

'Perhaps that's why I want to.' He pulled her down to sit with him on a stone bench.

'My parents were killed in a helicopter crash when I was ten,' he began. 'I've been told that I was headstrong as a child and I see now that I became uncontrollable after their death. I had a succession of personal tutors whom I mostly ran rings around, and I more or less did as I pleased. Grandfather then seemed a stern, remote figure; Ramón, in effect, took the place of my father.

'Not an ideal childhood,' she said softly.

Luis shrugged. 'I'm not angling for sympathy,' he smiled. 'I could ride whenever I wished, and I was denied nothing that money could buy. As I grew older and began to show an interest in the company, Grandfather's attitude towards me changed. He patiently shared all his knowledge of the sherry business, appointed me director at an early age, and allowed me to learn by making my own mistakes. I owe him a great deal, and I love him very much. I wouldn't hurt him intentionally for the world. You were right to be angry last night. Carmelita's behaviour was no different from usual, but I see now that mine should have been.'

'Thanks for telling me about yourself, Luis. I appreciate it.' On the spur of the moment she reached up and brushed her lips against his. When he dropped the arrogant veneer, which he habitually wore for public scrutiny, she liked him a lot better. She hadn't imagined that there was a hope in heaven of him forgiving her for last night, but she'd been completely wrong. What you saw wasn't always what you got with Luis Quevedo, she realized.

'You no longer hate me, then?' He stood up and pulled her towards him.

'No.'

'Thank God for that. I don't think I could take any more home truths just yet.' His brown eyes glowed warmly as he bent to kiss her.

For the first time since she'd met Luis she responded to the person hidden inside him – to the ten-year-old boy who'd been devastated by the death of his parents, who'd survived as best he could in the world of privileged neglect he'd been thrust into. The physical attraction she already felt for him deepened with his revelations.

At the first tentative flick of his tongue against her lips, her mouth opened of its own volition. When his tongue asked no further invitation and began to explore deep inside, a sensation which she'd never before experienced crept downwards from her stomach to her lower limbs. She didn't want the kiss to end and this overpowering sensation to stop, and when Luis broke away she felt devastated. Without thinking she wound her arms around his neck, pressed herself close, and asked him to kiss her again.

The sable eyes looked at her strangely and his lips appeared as though they were trying to formulate words, but thankfully they gave up, and she gave a low moan of satisfaction as they bent to do her bidding.

Men had kissed her before; she wasn't that inexperienced. But she'd never before asked them to, and she had certainly never kissed them back as she did now with Luis. His lips and tongue were so warm and velvety, and his mouth so exciting that she could happily have spent the rest of eternity exploring them. When their tongues met in mutual investigation she felt a corresponding tremor deep within her.

'It's so nice,' she whispered, her fingers playing through his thick, jet hair and on to the soft silky down of his neck.

'Mmm.' His hands slipped under her camisole and moved smoothly upwards. One hand shifted her slightly sideways, and the other found her breast, which was already straining against its lace constraint in anticipation of his touch.

'Luis,' she gasped, as his fingers reached inside and encircled the tender bud, beginning a massage that was sweet torture to her. Her

hands slipped inside his T-shirt, needing to feel
the warm naked flesh underneath, and she
found herself clutching wildly at his firm,
muscular back as his kiss became more and
more insistent . . .

'*Perdóname*,' he groaned. She felt his hands
leave her and take her own gently away from him.
'I was so close to forgetting my promise to you.'

Dazed, Emma slumped down on to the bench.
She'd experienced the roller coaster ride of all
time. She was hooked; as soon as she got her
breath back she'd be queuing up for another go.

What a time for Luis to discover a new code of
morals! She rested her head against the stone
support of the seat and came face to face with the
swollen evidence of Luis's arousal, clearly visible through the thin, tight material of his trousers.

Luis was watching her closely. He smiled as
her eyes widened in surprise.

'You see what your femininity does to me?'
His voice was deep and husky, and his eyes
appeared like two dark caverns gleaming at her.

'Perhaps I would marry you after all,' she
joked to hide her embarrassment.

'Perhaps if I'd done what I wished more than
anything else to do, I may have been compelled
to ask you.'

He bent down and cupped his hands around
her face, adding more seriously, 'I envy the man
on whom you choose to bestow your precious

gift, *chica*, but be careful who you kiss in such a manner as this. You are a beautiful flower, ripe to be plucked. Only remember: flowers once picked are easily crushed.'

'You are nice after all, Luis.' She smiled at him, touched by his words.

'No, I'm not,' he said firmly. 'You are a good influence on me, and I find that I care for your good opinion. Now we should go back. I have work to do.' He held out his hand, pulled her to her feet, and they walked slowly back to the villa.

Emma's head was spinning and every over-stimulated nerve-end of her body ached. Was this how men had felt in the past when she'd rejected them? She felt a wave of sympathy flood over her. Life was certainly a whole lot simpler when you were immune to the opposite sex.

As they entered the villa, Luis tipped up her face to look at him. 'Cheer up,' he smiled. 'We're going to the Alhambra tomorrow. When Grandfather learns of it and when he hears that Carmelita is no longer our guest it will make him very happy. He will believe that I truly love you above all others.'

Emma twisted her face in the semblance of a smile, then sighed. In a few days she'd managed to make Luis aware of his selfishness. A week probably wasn't long enough to tackle his insensitivity.

CHAPTER 8

For once, Emma needed no encouragement to jump out of bed. Luis had announced that he would forgo his riding that morning, and even though he'd said it with a slightly martyred expression she'd been touched by his sacrifice. She dressed with lightning speed and shuffled impatiently at the door while Luis followed at a more leisurely pace.

'It will not disappear if we are one minute late,' he said, grinning, as she opened the door the second he was ready.

'It's all right for you. I bet you've been loads of times.'

Luis started to laugh. 'One of my tutors discovered that I had never been on a train and he used this fact to control me. In exchange for my good behaviour we would travel from Sevilla to Granada by train. It must have represented a day's holiday to him and I suppose he told Grandfather that he was broadening my mind and teaching me about my country's past.' He chucked her under the chin and smiled. 'It is some years since I visited the Alhambra but we shall not need a guide to show us around.'

'You're going to be really bored, aren't you?' Emma felt a tiny prick of conscience. She was quick enough to accuse Luis of being selfish. It wasn't too pleasant to realize she could be guilty of it.

Luis's grin grew wider. 'Bored? How could it be possible when I have you for company?'

Emma followed him along the upstairs corridor. He called out a cheery greeting to Teresa, who was retrieving sheets from a linen cupboard. At the top of the staircase he eased his bottom on to the wrought-iron banister then hurtled down like a schoolboy.

'One of these days you'll crack your head open and then what will I do?' she heard a woman's voice admonish from below.

'Then, my dear María, you may do what you have been waiting these past twenty years or more to do and tell me that you told me so.'

There was a burst of laughter and Emma stared down the stairs in astonishment. Was that really Luis she'd seen careering downwards or had the bodysnatchers got to him in the middle of the night? She glanced across at Teresa, to see what she thought of her employer's actions, but the girl hadn't moved.

'Are you all right, Teresa?' she asked gently. There was something about the girl's posture and general demeanour that said she wasn't.

'Yes, *señorita*, thank you.' Teresa gathered up the sheets and with a stiff smile walked briskly away. Emma watched her go then went down to join Luis.

'I thought you'd got lost.' He draped his arm around her shoulder and led her out on to the terrace.

'What's wrong with Teresa?' she asked.

Luis broke open a bread roll and smiled. 'Teresa? This is her first job. She is so shy. One must be so careful not to alarm her. She will come out of her shell in time.'

'No, I don't mean that, I mean just now. She seemed upset. I'm sure she's been crying.'

Luis frowned, took a large gulp of his coffee, and stood up. 'I shall ask María.'

Emma finished her breakfast and poured herself another cup of coffee. There was no sign of Don Rafael and Luis still hadn't returned. She decided to go in search of him. She found him in the kitchen, with Teresa clutching desperately at his shirt and crying. María was fussing around her like a mother hen.

'Enrique will take you immediately and you must stay until your mother is perfectly better. We shall miss you, of course, but we shall manage. You are not to worry, Teresa, your job is safe and María will send you a cheque

131

every week.' Luis patted her shoulder gently as he spoke.

'Come now, Teresita.' María prised her off Luis as soon as she saw Emma. 'The *señores* are waiting to leave.'

'There's no rush,' said Emma, but María smiled and led the sobbing Teresa away.

'That girl has soaked me.' Luis pointed without rancour to a large damp patch on his shirt.

'Trouble at home?' asked Emma.

Luis nodded. 'Her mother has to go into hospital and there is no one to look after the little ones, but the silly girl was too frightened to tell me. Am I such an ogre?' He shook his head with disbelief. 'Thank you, *chica*. Because of you Teresa will be with her mother in time for lunch.'

'That's because of you,' she murmured, but he grabbed her hand and pulled her towards the main entrance.

'And if we don't hurry we'll be lucky to reach Granada before lunch.'

'You haven't had your breakfast,' she protested, as they walked down to the waiting Rolls.

Luis shrugged. 'María has packed some food for us. I doubt I shall starve.'

As soon as they were seated in the back of the car, the chauffeur pressed the accelerator and gravel chippings shot backwards like machine-gun fire. Emma leaned back in her seat and smiled. Carlos drove everywhere as though he should have been there yesterday. She'd bet that he'd give anything to get behind the wheel of Luis's 'little' car rather than being saddled with this monster.

'Happy?' Luis broke into her thoughts with a warm smile.

'Mmm. I'm really looking forward to it. You were really nice with Teresa, by the way.'

'Nice?' Luis looked perplexed.

'Yeah, you know, what you did, sending her home like that and paying her wages.'

'What else would I have done?'

Emma stared at him. He seemed genuinely surprised that she should comment on it or think that there was anything out of the ordinary in his actions. He was a strange man. They definitely broke the mould when they made him.

'I hope her mum'll be OK,' she said, turning away to look out of the window. They hurtled along the N334, catching tantalizing glimpses of pretty villages where whitewashed houses clung to the hillside or perched precariously on top of it. She gazed out with rapt attention. How different this area was from the coast around Benidorm and Alicante where she'd attended summer school last year.

'One of these days when I've passed my driving test I'm going to come back and explore all around here properly,' she announced.

Luis's dark eyes melted to the consistency of hot chocolate as he smiled at her. 'That you will, *guapa*,' he murmured.

Emma's stomach fluttered strangely. When was Luis going to tire of the role of Mr Nice-guy? Her immunity to the Quevedo charm was dangerously low. She wished he would pick up one of the files that he'd brought with him and not opened. It was unnerving how attentive he was being. As they passed through towns he seemed to delight in telling her their history and any anecdotes associated with them.

'We shall stop shortly.' Just after the town of Loja, Carlos turned sharply right and the Rolls bumped alarmingly along a dirt track until it came to a clearing beside a river.

'Lovely.' Emma jumped out of the car as soon as it stopped, slipped off her sandals, and wriggled her toes in the river. There was something about running water that she could never resist.

'Let us see what María has packed for us,' called Luis. He spread a large rug under a tree while Carlos unloaded a coolbox from the boot of the car.

'A picnic!' Emma came racing back and helped to unpack the vast amount of food that María had managed to cram into one coolbox. 'Chilled soup,' she said, unscrewing the lid of a dumpy vacuum flask and sniffing the contents. 'Serrano ham.' She placed it on a plate beside the cheese. '*Yemas*.' Emma waved away a wasp that was immediately attracted to the sweets that María bought from a convent in Sevilla.

As Luis poured chilled wine into crystal glasses, Emma surveyed the spread-out food with satisfaction. Even she would have difficulty making inroads into that lot. 'I've never had a proper picnic before,' she said excitedly, as Luis handed her a glass and raised his own to her.

'And what is a "proper" picnic?' His eyes crinkled with amusement.

'Well it certainly isn't the carrier bag of egg sandwiches, crisps, and pop we usually take to the beach,' she said, sitting down expectantly on the rug.

'Ah.' Luis handed her a plate, then gestured to Carlos that he should help himself.

Twenty minutes later she lay back on the grass, content. 'That was good,' she murmured. 'You don't mind if I take María with me when I leave, do you?'

There was no answer. After a while she opened her eyes and found Luis staring at her, seemingly fascinated. She realized the rather provocative position her body had adopted, and sat up immediately. 'I'll just have a quick paddle before we go,' she said, when the dark eyes showed no inclination of moving.

On her return, everything had been cleared away. 'That was great, Luis, thanks.' Emma indicated the spot where they'd been sitting.

'I'm pleased that you enjoyed it.' Luis smiled warmly. 'I thought originally of reserving a table for lunch in the parador in the Alhambra's grounds. You would like it there. It is an old Franciscan convent built by Ferdinand and Isabella after they reconquered Granada. It is quite beautiful, but it is always so busy, and it would have taken a large chunk of our day. Perhaps another time.'

Emma's head shot up to stare at him. Another time? What was he talking about? She stared at his back, however, as he climbed into the Rolls. Carlos was at the other side, holding the door open for her, and she hurried round. How stupid she was: the words had obviously been said for Carlos's benefit. She had to hand it to Luis – he was a master at pretence – he hadn't slipped up once in public.

'All that food's made me sleepy,' she said, as she sat down next to him in the back seat.

'Then rest.' He patted his shoulder to invite her to lean against him. 'You haven't much time. We shall be there in half an hour.'

'No, it's all right,' she said, ignoring her heart, which was screaming at her to shut up and do as she was told. It was unnerving enough that he'd been nice to her for two days; physical contact would definitely have finished her off.

It wasn't long before they saw the hills of Granada and then they were there, climbing upwards from the town to the massive *Puerta de las Granadas* gateway where the car halted. Luis shrugged on a stone-coloured linen jacket,

136

placed a mobile phone in his pocket, and bade farewell to Carlos.

'What will he do all day?' she asked, as the car disappeared down the hill.

'He will purchase a newspaper, find a bar that subscribes to satellite television, and then watch sports all day, no doubt,' answered Luis, grinning.

'That would drive me round the bend.'

Luis shrugged. 'Each to his own.' He offered her his hand as they walked through the gateway but Emma affected not to notice, and he thrust it into his trouser pocket. They took the left hand path and walked through some woods to the main entrance.

'Uh oh,' she said, as she took in the busloads of tourists waiting to purchase their tickets. 'I suppose you did warn me.'

Luis smiled. 'Come in the winter next time. Just before Christmas is wonderful. Now, *chica*, do you wish to wander around absorbing the atmosphere or do you want me to tell you about what you are seeing?'

'I'd like a running commentary if you can be bothered.'

'Unfortunately I left my umbrella at home but I shall try to do my best without it,' he said, poking gentle fun at the tour guides ahead of them. 'So if madam would care to glance upwards . . .'

Emma looked up obediently at the magnificent gateway of the *Puerta de Justicia*.

'Can you see the outstretched hand above the arch?'

She nodded.

'The five fingers represent the five precepts of Islam: prayer, fasting, alms-giving, pilgrimage, and the oneness of God.'

'Oh, right.' Emma knew exactly what they meant. Since she'd known she was coming here she'd spent every free moment studying her guide book, but she wasn't about to let Luis know that. The deep, masculine voice speaking to her of the rich Moorish past of his country was one pleasure she had no intention of denying herself.

'I can't wait to see inside the Royal Palace.' She opened up a map they'd been given at the ticket office and scanned it to find the best route.

'I'm afraid that you will have to. I pre-booked a time of two o'clock to visit there.'

Emma scowled at him. Luis knew that was where she wanted to visit most of all; she'd been chuntering about it ever since they'd reached Granada.

'The gardens of the *Generalife* first, I think,' he said, walking away.

Emma followed him. She might have known he'd take over and not take any notice of her. After a moment he looked back and then quickly away again. She noticed that his shoulders were shaking.

'What's so funny?' she demanded, grabbing his arm.

'You, *niña.*'

'Don't call me that.'

'Then stop acting like a child and I won't.'

'You know I want to see the Nasrid Palace,' she fumed.

Luis leaned casually against a pillar and smiled. 'Of course I do, which was why I chose two o'clock for our visit. At this time the tour groups will have dispersed to their lunch destinations, other visitors will be feeling peckish, and we should be able to view the apartments in relative peace.'

Emma stared at the ground, ashamed. 'You could have told me,' she muttered.

'That I could, and that I would if you hadn't immediately jumped to the conclusion that I was taking you to the opposite end of the complex out of sheer bloody mindedness.'

Emma's cheeks glowed warmly. Was she so predictable in her reaction to Luis? 'Sor – ' she said, but the word was like a boulder in her throat. She tried again and managed to dislodge it. 'Sorry.'

'You are forgiven.' With a broad grin, he kissed her on the brow, then offered her his arm. This time, she thought she'd better take it.

'We'll be walking broadly in a circle. After the gardens we'll enter the palace, and then when we come out of there you may choose between the

Alcazaba and Carlos V's palace. I doubt we shall have time for both.'

Emma was glad she'd taken Luis's arm. It was quite a climb to the *Generalife* and he did tend to stride along. Even with the flat sandals she'd worn especially she'd have been running behind to keep up with him.

'Oh, my gosh!' she exclaimed, as they made their way through avenues of wisteria and bougainvillaea and she glimpsed the gardens through a walkway of cypress trees.

'It's really beautiful.' She gazed in awe at the pools and fountains, at the geometrically perfect arches and pillars, and at the gardens crammed with shrubs and flowers. 'If you brought someone here when they were asleep they'd think when they woke up that they'd died and gone to heaven.'

'An Islamic version of heaven at any rate,' mused Luis. 'Paradise is described in the Koran as a shady garden refreshed by running water where the blessed may take their rest.'

Emma turned a corner and came across a hidden garden. 'I'm definitely going to be good while I'm on this earth, then. I want in.'

Time slipped by like a dream. It seemed only minutes later that Luis was pulling her gently away from the dramatic view over Granada from the gardens and telling her that they must leave if they were to reach the palace in time.

'It can't be nearly two o'clock!' She checked

her watch and found that it was. They bought some orange juice and some nuts from a kiosk, and then had to run the last part of the way.

'Thanks ever so much for bringing me here, Luis, I'll never forget today.' Emma hung on his arm and listened avidly to his commentary as they moved from the public to the state rooms and finally to the sultan's private apartments and harem.

Luis smiled at her indulgently. 'It's amazing to think that after they expelled the Moors my countrymen allowed this place to fall to ruin. It was used as a prison, a lunatic asylum, and Napoleon almost succeeded in blowing the whole lot to oblivion.'

'What a place to be banged up in, though.' She craned her neck to study the magnificent dome of the Hall of the Two Sisters. It looked like a giant sunburst frozen in space and was reputedly made up of five thousand separate cavities. 'I thought when I was looking at the pictures in the guide book that I might be a bit disappointed when I saw everything face to face, that it might be too ostentatious and slightly over the top, but it's not, is it?' She turned an excited face to Luis.

He shook his head. 'Everything is in harmony with everything else. Aesthetically it is perfect. Move one pillar or piece of stuccowork only a fraction and it would throw the whole completely out of balance.'

Finally, they wandered out into the Court of

the Lions at the heart of the harem. 'Now you have seen everything here.' He gestured to the fountain at the centre of the patio. 'Where to next – the *Alacazaba*, Carlos V's palace, or would you like to go somewhere to eat?'

Emma studied his expression. He'd seemed as delighted by the royal apartments as she'd been; she didn't think he was simply being polite. 'Would you mind very much if we went round here again?' she asked hesitantly.

He laughed, white teeth sparkling against bronzed skin. What had he said earlier about everything being aesthetically perfect round here? 'It would be an honour to escort you around the palace, my lady.' He gave a mock bow, then offered her his arm. Emma caught the envious glances of a group of young women nearby. It was strange how women seemed drawn to her companion; she'd noticed it all day. The surge of possessiveness that accompanied their notice was also incredibly strange.

Despite lingering in the Alhambra palace they managed to tour the fortress of the *Alcazaba*. Luis seemed game to visit Carlos V's palace in the three quarters of an hour before closing, but Emma felt that her beauty appreciation cells were completely saturated. 'Culture overload . . . culture overload,' she intoned like a demented robot before collapsing dramatically on the grass.

'The younger generation today, simply no

stamina.' Luis grinned and reached for his mobile phone.

'I'm really looking forward to seeing Carlos,' she said, as they waited for the Rolls to pick them up.

'You have missed him?' Luis looked bemused.

'I've missed what he's got in the boot. I hope he hasn't eaten it all.'

Luis burst out laughing. 'Don't ever change, *guapa*,' he said when he sobered up.

'You have enjoyed today a bit, Luis?' she asked anxiously. 'You haven't been bored out of your head the whole time, have you?'

Luis gave her a strange look. 'I have not been bored out of my head, as you put it, for any of the time, *guapa*. Thank you for suggesting here. I have enjoyed it enormously.'

'We could always come back tomorrow for Charlie's palace,' she grinned.

His answer was a playful swipe across the head.

CHAPTER 9

Friday arrived far too quickly. The week had passed in a blur of sightseeing, horse riding, and long conversations with Don Rafael. She felt so much part of the place now it seemed incredible that she would ever have to leave.

But here it was: her last day at the Villa Quevedo with Luis and Don Rafael was beginning. Tomorrow she would be leaving early for the airport, and while Luis and Ramón returned to London, she would be boarding a plane to Madrid. Her plan was to find temporary work in a restaurant or a hotel there and stay in Spain for the rest of the summer.

Following their disastrous beginning, Luis had behaved impeccably towards her. Apart from the obligatory public embraces he had never, since the incident under the lime trees, attempted to kiss her, but she was certain that, in his own way, he'd grown fond of her. The cuddles and hugs she'd received from him

144

hadn't all been for his grandfather's benefit, and here they were once more entwined together in sleep.

Luis's body, naked apart from the underpants she was sure he wore only for her benefit, was shaped around her back, one leg and one arm curled over her. His head nestled into her shoulder, and his deep, rhythmic breathing told her that for once she'd woken before him.

Every evening they lay in bed, keeping religiously to their own side. Emma yearned to drift off to sleep enfolded in his arms as she'd done that first fateful night, but Luis never touched her when he was awake. Somehow during the night their bodies came together, and were always snuggled close, as now, by morning. The touch of warm relaxed flesh against flesh aroused her enormously, but Luis usually made a joke of it because it was normally she who'd crept into his space.

A slight jerk of his head and a change in the pattern of his breathing alerted her to the fact that he too was now awake, but he remained unmoving for several minutes.

'Our last day together, *guapa*,' he reminded her unnecessarily as he stretched lazily against her.

'How did you know I was awake?'

'You snore when you are asleep.'

'Do I?' She twisted over and her stomach lurched as she met his laughing brown eyes.

145

'No, but your body and breathing feel completely different asleep from awake. Have you not noticed this with me? '

'Yes.' She looked up at him through eyelashes drenched with tears. 'I'm going to miss you, Luis.'

'Do not do this, Amanda!' His face hardened and he threw the covers back and climbed out of bed. 'You were brought here for only one purpose.'

Emma flinched as the bathroom door slammed behind him. How had she allowed her emotions to become so raw and entangled with regard to this man? She must have had a death wish, because any sane person could have predicted that a relationship between them was doomed from the outset. Like he said: she was here for only one purpose. That purpose was almost complete and she was rapidly approaching her sell-by date. He'd never lied to her. He'd never promised her more. That she'd allowed herself to become attached to him was sheer stupidity.

She traced her finger along the edge of the duvet, and frowned. He probably thought she coveted his luxurious lifestyle and that was what she'd miss about him, but he was wrong. The Villa Quevedo was certainly magnificent, but it was the people inside it who were important to her.

Her thoughts were interrupted as Luis strode

146

out of the bathroom and flung open his wardrobe door. It was as well it was solid wood and craftsman-constructed given the rough treatment it received from him.

'If you wish to come riding this morning you had better hurry up,' he snapped.

'I don't want to go riding with a grump.'

Luis paused as he was about to kick the door shut, and stared at her. The clouds lifted from his expression and he smiled. 'You're right,' he nodded. 'One should never go riding when one is out of spirits. The horses always sense such things. Perhaps I should begin again.'

He sat down on the bed, took her hand and kissed it with mock chivalry. 'Please come riding with me, *señorita*, you are the most adept pupil I have ever taught to gallop.'

Emma thought for a second. 'How many other women have you taught to ride?'

He raised his palms in a gesture of defeat. 'I believe you are the first.' They both laughed and thankfully the tension between them evaporated.

The ride was exhilarating. Emma had progressed to a three-year-old palomino that didn't have Estrella's character but was certainly a lot friskier. She was beginning to understand Luis's insistence on riding every day he was in Sevilla. She'd do exactly the same if she lived here. The miles of open space perfumed with the fragrance of wild herbs under a brilliant blue canopy would prove too much of a temptation.

As they cantered back to the yard, Emma lifted her head to the heavens. Oh, Lord, help me to forget all this, she asked silently. It was the first time she had prayed for years.

Don Rafael was not in his usual seat when they went to the terrace for breakfast. Luis went to him immediately, and looked grim when he returned. 'He has had a bad night and doesn't look at all well. I have called the doctor, which will not please him, but I think it is necessary. At least he has consented to remain in bed for the rest of the day, although he is adamant that he will get up for dinner this evening. Nothing will prevent him from missing the last evening of your visit here, he says.'

'Poor Don Rafael,' she whispered, her appetite gone despite the sumptuous buffet laid out on the terrace.

'He is an old man. He has had a good life. The doctors say it will be a gradual deterioration.' Luis sounded as though he were trying to convince himself rather than her, and when she looked up she thought she detected tears in his eyes. He turned away before she could be sure, and left abruptly.

Mechanically, she poured herself a cup of coffee and buttered a bread roll. The bread stuck in her throat like lumps of concrete and the coffee made her nauseous. She left them both and wandered aimlessly about the grounds. Luis

148

found her beside the ornamental pool an hour later.

'Forgive me. I promised to take you on a boat trip along the river today.'

Emma smiled at him. He still looked grim, but composed. 'Nothing to forgive,' she said.

'I have decided to extend my visit here. Perhaps I'm being foolish, it is probably only a false alarm, but . . .' His voice trailed away.

'I understand,' she said, squeezing his arm.

'I have been training my successor at the London office for the past few months. He is very capable. Perhaps it is time to relinquish the reins there and concentrate on the main business here.'

'Perhaps,' she agreed, wishing she could think of some sparkling words of wisdom that would make him feel better.

'I know it is a great deal to ask of you . . .' He hesitated, and Emma's heart juddered against her ribs. What was it he was going to say?

'Would it be extremely inconvenient for you to stay a little longer? Grandfather adores you. He may think it strange if I remain and you leave,' he continued, apparently unaware of the havoc his words had wreaked on her inner organs.

Emma's heart reverted to a more normal rhythm. What on earth was wrong with her? She must be suffering from heat stroke. For a second she thought he was going to ask her to make their arrangement more permanent for Don Rafael's sake.

She sat down on the edge of the pond and watched the golden carp darting below the surface. Oh Lord, she'd only just come to terms with leaving Sevilla. The longer she remained here the harder it would be when she eventually went. She trailed her finger in the water and watched the fish darting for cover. That was what she felt like doing, scurrying away and hiding. She was afraid. She didn't want to stay here and fall more in love with Luis, she didn't want to become more attached to Don Rafael, and she certainly didn't want to be here when Don Rafael . . . The word refused to form in her mind.

She was such a selfish cow! How could she think solely of her own feelings when Don Rafael might be dying and her presence might cheer him up.

She stood up, resolute. 'Of course I'll stay. I'll have to ring my mum and let her know.'

She strode back to the house before Luis could say anything. She had a feeling that he was going to discuss payment with her, and the way that she felt at the moment she'd probably hit him.

For once he seemed sensitive to her feelings, but when he rejoined her for lunch the dismal mood of the morning had vanished. He took her hand as he sat down beside her and squeezed it warmly. 'I have just seen Grandfather and he seems a lot better. The doctor gave him something to make him sleep and it has left him well rested. He would have got up but I dissuaded him.'

'I'm so pleased!'

'Yes, *chica*, so am I.'

Emma gritted her teeth. Luis was gripping her hand so hard that it hurt, but she didn't like to tell him.

'So what about tomorrow, then? Do I stay or do I go?' she asked, trying to lessen his hold on her.

'You must stay. Definitely you must stay. I have already told him so.'

This time she succeeded in pulling away. 'I can't stay forever, Luis,' she said. 'What will you tell him about our breaking up?'

'We shall not break up, not while Grandfather is alive.' He stood up, thrust his hands into his pockets, and strode over to the French windows. 'What was I thinking about bringing you here?' He leaned one arm on the window and stared outside. 'When I saw you in the hotel, it seemed that you had been sent by heaven to get Grandfather off my back.'

He turned round and stared at her accusingly. 'It never crossed my mind that he'd become so fond of you in such a short time. Girlfriends have visited here many times. He's never reacted like this before.'

Emma bristled. She felt guilty enough about the situation as it was. She wasn't going to accept

Luis's share of the blame as well.

'So what are you suggesting, Luis? That I sprinkled magic dust on his cornflakes and bewitched him?'

He pursed his lips in annoyance. 'This isn't a joking matter, Amanda.'

'Too right it's not! If you go around tampering with people's lives for your own convenience then don't whine when it doesn't turn out exactly as you expect.'

He clenched his fist, then gradually released it. 'You're right, of course,' he said, 'but we're in this together, *guapa*. You must visit here at Christmas. At Easter also, although I think that will be unlikely.'

'The odd phone call or letter to Don Rafael wouldn't come amiss either, I take it?'

He nodded.

'You've got a nerve, Luis.'

'I shall recompense you well for your trouble,' he said, then looked taken aback by the look of contempt she shot him.

'You will not do this?' he asked.

'Oh, I'll do it. I'll do it all right. But not for you, Luis, and not for any money you offer me. For Don Rafael. That's the only reason. Do you understand?'

'I believe so.' Luis looked unsure of himself. For the first time in their relationship she had the upper hand. It was very little comfort. She pushed her chicken salad to one side.

'I wish I'd never applied for a summer job in that hotel!' she said with vehemence.

Luis made work the excuse for staying out of her way for the rest of the afternoon. Emma took *Hard Times* with her to the inner courtyard, curled up on a wicker chair and finally finished it.

She stood up, stretched, and realized she felt a lot calmer. Maybe it was the book. It was a sad story, but therapeutic in its way: life could have been a whole lot worse, especially if she'd been born into poverty in Victorian times.

She left the book on the chair and wandered off to the kitchen to receive the latest news about Don Rafael.

'Sitting up in bed, reading *El País*, and calling for a glass of *fino*,' said María, giving Emma's arm a motherly pat. 'I tell you, Señorita Amanda, the old rascal will outlive us all.'

Thus reassured, Emma accepted a cup of coffee and stayed talking to María until it was almost dark. 'Better go and get ready,' she said, then on impulse bent over and gave the housekeeper a kiss on the cheek. She'd been so kind to her. Somebody else to miss, she supposed, hurrying away.

She'd wear the turquoise dress again tonight, she decided, as she looked in the wardrobe. May as well get some use out of it; it would look a little out of place at the student union disco. Her face creased into a grin as she imagined the expression on her friends' faces if she waltzed in wearing that.

Steam billowed out of the bathroom and she raced in to turn off the taps. Now, which bath oil hadn't she tried yet? She picked up a crystal decanter and sniffed. Mmm, that would do. She poured a small amount into the bath and swirled it around. Oh, to hell with it. She tipped the bottle up and the delicious fragrance of jasmine filled the air.

'Wonderful,' she sighed, slipping under the dense foam.

Three quarters of an hour later she was washed and moisturized, her face was made-up, and her hair was dry and shining. She wrapped herself in a bathrobe and walked back into the bedroom where her clothes were laid out on the bed.

Eight o'clock, she noted, glancing at her watch. Luis would be up soon. She stepped out of the bathrobe and put on white lace briefs, matching suspender belt and stockings. The dress had its own support for her breasts so a bra wasn't necessary.

'You are even more beautiful than I imagined, *guapa*.' The low, appreciative voice came from the balcony. It caused an instant burning over the top of her body.

'Luis!' She dived for her dress. 'You could have told me you were there.'

'I do not yet aspire to sainthood.' He came in from the shadows, grinning. 'Although I believe I have come quite close over the past week.' His eyes grazed over the soft ample curves of her breasts as he slowly made his way towards her.

Emma remained transfixed by the predatory gaze. The hand holding her dress slid to her side, and she knew by the ache spreading over her lower limbs that she was his if he desired her. There were times she hated him with a passion that shocked her, but it never came close to matching the intensity of the physical longing she also felt for him.

'Let me help you with your dress.' He was only inches away from her now, and the tang of his warm, male body was playing havoc with her senses. Her lips had become unbearably dry, and her tongue flicked out to moisten them.

'Your maiden blush against this amazing translucent skin of yours threatens to be my downfall,' he whispered, as he zipped her into the dress.

Emma gazed at him in confusion. She could only guess at the number of women he'd made love to. What was wrong with her that he showed no inclination to add her to the list?. 'Am I ugly or what?' she said, frowning.

He gave a low deep chuckle, then turned her gently towards the gilt mirror that hung above the dressing table. 'Look in the mirror, *guapa*.

The only male who could fail to be affected by your beauty would be a blind man.'

She saw herself: pale, blonde, petite, but her gaze locked on the arrogant-featured male behind her whose appearance contrasted so sharply with her own. They'd been in opposite queues when looks were being given out. The hands that gripped her shoulders were burnished mahogany, his hair was the deepest shade of black, and his height dwarfed her by a good eight inches.

She looked away. Was it really love that she felt for him, or was it a natural desire that most women would feel in his presence?

'You'd have thought that after a week in this climate, I'd have some trace of a tan,' she joked, in an attempt to hide her churned-up emotions.

'Difference is always desirable.' He stroked down her neck with exquisite gentleness.

She broke away from him angrily. 'Why are you doing this when you don't want it to go any further? I'm not a puppet you can play with until you get bored, then stash it away in its box. I do have feelings, you know.'

'Forgive me, *guapa*. I only thought that I was hurting myself. Why am I doing it? To prove to myself that I am capable of not making love to every beautiful woman that I desire.'

'So I'm not a puppet. I'm an experiment?'

'A very difficult one, yes, but you have no

justification for looking at me like that. It was your words that prompted my behaviour.'

'Congratulations, then, on remaining celibate for a week,' she said sarcastically, unwilling to acknowledge the truth of his statement. 'I'm sure you deserve a medal, but what about next week?'

'Next week? Who knows? One week was the target I set for myself.' His sardonic smile was so smug that she would dearly have loved to knock it off his face for him. Was there another man living who could infuriate her as much as this one? Had she really seen tears in his eyes this morning? It must have been a piece of grit.

'Don't look at me like that, *chica*. You can't believe the agony you have put me through these seven days. There were times I didn't think I would survive.'

'Well, pardon me for being such a bitch,' she said, reaching out for her jewellery case. At least the reason he'd never kissed her again was now clear.

'Don't let's argue. Not tonight.' He came behind her and fastened the pearl necklace deftly around her neck. His touch was feather-light, but she was so sensitive to him that it was almost as if he were branding her.

'It was meant to be a parting gift,' he said, handing her a matching pair of earrings.

'Mmm?' Emma gazed at him, uncomprehending, then she glanced again at the pearls in her hand. As realization dawned, she flicked open her jewellery case where a similar necklace and earrings lay.

'Oh, gosh! Real ones!' Her hands flew to her throat to touch the milky, opalescent beads that encircled it.

'I wished to buy you something more expensive, but nothing seemed as right for you as these.' He bent and kissed her cheek.

To her chagrin she began to cry.

'What a strange creature you are.' He shook his head in dismay. 'Certainly the first woman who has ever wept when I have handed her a present.'

'Why do you have to keep confusing me?' she sobbed. 'Why can't you just stay a swine, Luis? It's so much easier.'

Luis threw up his hands in surrender and stalked into the bathroom. She was fully recovered when he returned, and it amused her to see the wary glances he kept giving her while he dressed in a closely tailored white silk shirt and charcoal-grey trousers.

'Thanks for the pearls, Luis, they're lovely.' It was sweet of him to buy them for her. He was such a curious mixture; she didn't suppose she'd ever understand him.

He leaned over and smoothed her left earring between finger and thumb. 'Not as lovely as the lady wearing them,' he said silkily.

She pulled away from him. His freshly showered, freshly fragranced presence was altogether too much.

'There will only be the three of us for dinner tonight. I thought it best for Grandfather,' he said, taking her hand and leading her downstairs.

For once they were in agreement about something. They went straight into the dining room where Don Rafael was already seated, sipping a glass of sherry.

'How are you, *Abuelo*?' she enquired solicitously.

'Much better for seeing you, my dear,' he replied, taking her hand. Although his grip was firm and his eyes twinkled as brightly, Emma sensed an indefinable frailty about him which caught at her heart. 'I have learned to accept that some days are better than others,' he said, shrugging off further enquiry.

The meal was a pleasant one: *gazpacho*, the refreshing, chilled vegetable soup which they often had as a starter; *archoba*, a highly seasoned fish dish which was delicious; and *tocino de cielo*, a sort of sweet creme caramel which was a particular favourite of Don Rafael's, but which Emma found a little sickly.

'I promised to show you my old mare's foal today, Amanda. We can go now,' said Don Rafael pushing his dessert plate away and rising unsteadily to his feet.

'I don't think that's very wise, Grandfather. I can take Amanda and show her Negrito, or you could go tomorrow. There is no hurry now that Amanda is staying with us for longer.' Luis jumped up and tried to help Don Rafael back to his seat, but the old man became agitated and pushed him away.

'I'm not completely senile yet, boy. If I say I want to go to the stables then that is what I mean. Now take your hands off me and let me get up.'

Luis stepped back. 'At least let me accompany you, Abuelo,' he said.

Don Rafael shook his head in exasperation, glared at his grandson, and held himself bolt upright. Emma glimpsed the man he must once have been, and it was a shock; he seemed the image of Luis.

'Amanda is quite capable of running for help if I feel ill. Now sit down and let me be.' His tone was razor sharp and determined. Luis backed off, but Emma could see the effort it cost him. He looked about to explode with a thousand and one unsaid words battling to get out.

What happens when an unstoppable force meets an immovable object? In this case the older one wins, thought Emma, offering her arm to Don Rafael and helping him slowly out of the room.

A security guard who tried to accompany them across the floodlit courtyard was also given short shrift, but eventually they made it to the stables. Don Rafael sat down heavily on a bench outside. 'Forgive that scene, Amanda,' he said. 'I know Luis means well but I wished to speak to you alone. Time is running out for me and I haven't said everything to you that I wanted to.'

'I'm sure . . .' Emma was about to say that he had plenty of years left in which to say them, but she met his gaze and she felt it would be insulting his intelligence.

He seemed to understand and patted her hand. 'I'm not afraid of death, my dear. There are so many people I look forward to seeing again, and I have achieved what I set out to do in life. Luis was my greatest worry, but now that he has you I am content.'

Emma squirmed uneasily. Could it ever be right to deceive anyone like this? It had gone too far now to stop, but she would always have it on her conscience.

'When I see how he adores you and how you handled Carmelita the other evening I know that you possess the strength of character to achieve what I did not.' He stopped for a while to draw breath before continuing.

'I am to blame for Luis being the way he is. When he needed guidance and love at a crucial stage in his life I failed him. I was so devastated by my own grief and loss that I couldn't bear to have him beside me because he reminded me too much of my own son. My wickedness was repaid by raising a grandson whom I loved dearly but

161

didn't much like. Can you understand what I mean?'

Emma nodded. She could think of no words to say so put her arms around the old man and hugged him instead.

'You are a lovely girl, Amanda. For love of you Luis will renounce his old ways. He has always been a good boy underneath, just a little too eager to explore alternative paths.'

'I know that he loves you a great deal,' said Emma. This was awful. Her eyes misted with guilt and emotion.

'Enough of this for now. I don't want to upset you, but there is one more thing that I must say.' He gripped her by the upper arms and beamed. 'Welcome to the family, Amanda. You have my complete blessing.'

'Thank you.' Emma smiled back at him though she wanted to sob her heart out.

'Come on, let's go and have a look at this old mare of mine.' He opened the stable door and, chuckling, took down an old hurricane lamp and lit it. 'This annoys Luis. He says that we have electricity now. But the old ways are the best; this does not startle the animals as much when they are asleep.'

As they walked into the stables the pungent aroma of horses filled Emma's nostrils. All was quiet until they passed Hierro's stall, and he began to stamp and neigh loudly at the unaccustomed intrusion. His large black head and staring eyes suddenly thrust angrily over his door looked eerie in the gloom. Emma's heart began to pound uneasily.

'A fine beast and a fine temper,' muttered Don Rafael, motioning for her to give him a wide berth. 'Negrito is in the bottom stall with his mother, Cara. She was my favourite mount and her foal promises to have the same qualities which made her special. I will sit here and hold the light for you.'

'Are you all right, *Abuelo*?' The old man's face looked extremely drawn as he sat down heavily on a bale of straw.

'I must catch my breath and rest a moment. Nothing to worry about.' He waved his hand impatiently at her, indicating that she should go and see Negrito.

'Oh! What a gorgeous little thing!' A dark, gangly foal with wide, curious eyes rose enquiringly to its feet. She peered into the corner of the stall to try and distinguish its mother from the shadows, when what little light available was extinguished completely.

'*Abuelo*!' Emma swung round to witness the sight of the old man, head slumped on his chest, illuminated by a more sinister light below. She scanned the walls desperately for a fire extinguisher, but none was visible in the dim light. Racing over to Don Rafael, she tried to stamp on the flames, but they were already beginning to spread, feeding voraciously on the straw.

There must be an extinguisher near the door, she thought, beginning to panic as the old man's trousers caught fire. There was no time to look. She put out the flame with her hand. She'd have to get him out before she did anything.

It took every ounce of her strength to lift Don Rafael and pull him towards the door. His head lolled lifelessly forward, and Emma knew in her heart that her efforts were pointless, but she couldn't be certain. Finding hidden resources inside her, she struggled with his body until she could lay him safely outside and scream for help.

The clamour of the terrified horses was deafening and their plight pitiful, but she waited until she saw a guard running towards them before returning into the stables in an attempt to free as many as possible.

Poor Negrito and his mother! Tears streamed from her stinging eyes as she thought of them caught behind the now impenetrable barrier of flames. She had to blot out their painful image and concentrate on freeing what animals she could. At least the bolts were opening easily and the horses had the sense to flee the flames.

Emma turned to open Sombra's door. The mare seemed even more terrified than the rest, and was thundering on the wood with her hooves. She flicked the bolts and stood back to allow the horse passage, but she wasn't quick enough. Sombra had reared to pound the door again. Instead of meeting the wood when they descended, her hooves encountered Emma's head.

Everything went black . . .

CHAPTER 10

'Concussion . . . brain scan normal . . . the wound is healing well . . . superficial burns . . . smoke inhalation could be serious, possible pulmonary oedema . . . will know tomorrow.' The words floated in and out of her consciousness.

'Emma. Can you hear me, Emma?' The voice was familiar but unkind. It wanted to pull her out of the dark pit of oblivion and drag her back to the world of pain. Now this person was touching her, gripping her arms. Why couldn't he leave her alone? Didn't he understand that all she wanted to do was sleep?

'Emma. Listen to me. Open your eyes, *guapa.*' The voice was insistent. She tried to ignore it, blot it out, but it wouldn't go away.

'Wake up, Emma. Open your eyes.'

She felt herself surface, obedient to the voice's will. Her eyes flickered open, only to be blinded by a searing flash of light, while somebody took the opportunity of cleaving her skull open with an axe. Somewhere in the room someone was screaming. Why couldn't they be quiet? The noise reverberated in her ears. It was some time before she realized it was her.

'She's in pain! Do something, damn you!' There it went again. Shouting now. Angry. Didn't it realize it was the cause of everything? It was the one who'd dragged her back and made her head explode again.

Now someone was probing her arm. A sharp sensation there. Why couldn't they leave her be?

The voices became distant, distorted. A swirling blackness beckoned. Without hesitation she embraced it. This time she'd stay there. They wouldn't trick her again.

'Thank God you're going to be all right, Emma.'

Emma sat up in bed, drip and oxygen mask now removed, thankful that the nightmare of the last five days was now over. She smiled wanly and surveyed the haggard face and dark sunken eyes of the man, sombrely dressed in a black suit, who was slumped in a chair beside her.

'Don Rafael?' she whispered.

'It is his funeral tomorrow.'

Emma stared at the beautiful bouquet on a table at the bottom of her bed. The image in her brain wasn't flowers, but that of an elderly gentleman smiling kindly at her. She closed her eyes, but was unable to dam the tears that flowed relentlessly down her cheeks.

'You knew, Emma.' Luis grasped her arm as her hands were still bandaged. 'Surely to God you knew?'

'I did really.' She wiped her eyes on the starched white sheet. 'But until I heard someone else say it, I suppose I was hoping it wasn't true.'

'I know what you mean.' The pain in Luis's eyes mirrored her own. 'Even when one is expecting it, the shock is still great.' He lapsed into silence for several minutes, lost in his own thoughts. She longed to know whether he believed it was her fault for what had happened in the stables, but didn't feel strong enough to ask him outright. His hand, still resting on her arm, comforted her and allowed her to think that perhaps he didn't completely blame her.

Surfacing from his reverie, he attempted a smile. 'You are lucky that the horse only glanced your forehead with its hoof. There will be a scar, but it could have been so much worse. I'm so sorry.' He let go her arm and gripped hold of her blanket instead. 'You frightened me, Emma. There were times I thought you'd given up, that you wanted to accompany Grandfather into the next world.'

Emma shuddered as she recalled the experience of the previous few days. 'It was the pain. It was like someone ramming knitting needles into my skull. I could cope with it by letting myself drift away. It felt like it was happening to someone else then.'

'There is pain now?'

'No, not really.' She shook her head, then wished she hadn't as the unaccustomed movement jarred. 'I'll be a junkie when I get out of here I've popped so many pills,' she joked feebly.

Before he could say anything else a young, cheerful nurse bustled into the room. 'Time to change the dressings on your hands, *señorita*.' She turned to Luis. 'Won't take long if you want to stay.'

Luis stood up and plunged his hands deep into the pockets of his trousers. 'No. I shall go now. There are things to be arranged. I shan't see you tomorrow, Emma. You do understand?'

Emma nodded, and he made his way to the door. He turned briefly before leaving. 'Anything at all that you might want, don't hesitate to ask the staff. You will receive the best of care here, Emma. I guarantee it.'

'That is Luis Quevedo?' asked the nurse when he'd left.

Emma said that it was.

'Ay, *señorita*, what a man!' she giggled, blushing.

It was late afternoon of the next day. In the morning, a doctor had removed the stitches in her forehead, which had taken her mind off Don

Rafael's funeral somewhat. She gazed at the ugly line snaking across her brow and tried to console herself that at least she was alive. She wished Luis would come and see her. She wanted to see his reaction to her disfigurement.

She threw the hand mirror aside. Selfishness always disgusted her, especially when it was she who was guilty of it. The last thing that would be on Luis's mind today would be Emma Blackmore and her problems.

'Ah, *señorita*, a visitor for you.' The young nurse beamed as she put her head around the door.

Oh, gosh. Emma sat up and tried to compose herself. Poor Luis. Would she be able to comfort him? He must be in a terrible state after his grandfather's funeral. She wished she'd asked what time the service was being held. She directed a sympathetic smile at the door, but it froze on her face as the last person she expected to pay her a courtesy visit walked through it.

'Amanda.'

'My name is Emma.'

'Emma, Amanda, Luisa, Victoria, what difference does it make? I forget the names, he's had so many. I don't know why you should look so surprised to see me. Haven't you worked out yet that it's always yours truly who does Luis's dirty work for him?' Ramón's face twisted into a cruel smile as he threw her passport and an airline ticket on the bed.

'I'm not well enough to travel yet.' Invisible fingers clutched at her throat, making it difficult to speak.

'Yes, you are. Luis spoke to the doctors this morning. Once your stitches were out there was no reason why you couldn't be discharged.'

Emma shook her head in disbelief.

Ramón walked around the room, insolently picking up objects and opening doors. 'Private bathroom, hmm? Telephone, television.' He picked up the hand control and flicked it on. 'All satellite channels, I see. Very nice. I wonder how much these extras cost? Add them to all the treatment you've received, all those tests, I think we're talking of several thousand here. Pounds sterling, mind you. Not pesetas. Medical insurance up to date, I hope?'

Emma felt herself grow cold. The last thing she'd thought of doing when Luis had whisked her off to Spain was taking out medical insurance.

'He wouldn't make me pay for all of this,' she stated, but her voice lacked total conviction.

'Not if you do what he wants, he won't,' said Ramón. 'Sweetness himself if he gets his own way is Señor Quevedo. A total monster if you cross him. Haven't you noticed?'

Emma shook her head. 'I don't believe you.' Her voice was beginning to croak. 'The last thing he said yesterday was that I'd have the best of care here, and to ask for anything I wanted.'

Ramón started to laugh. 'Oh, but you're one thick lady. Of course he said that. He has a position to maintain in Sevilla. He can't be seen to throw anybody out of a hospital bed, even if they did kill his grandfather and his favourite horse. That's why muggins is here.'

Emma clenched the covers around her. This wasn't happening. It was a bad dream. Please God, let her wake up soon. Then she remembered.

'You're a liar!' she spat. 'Hierro didn't die in the fire!' Even through her panic that night she'd known that she had to save Luis's horse. He'd been one of the first she'd released.

'No, he didn't die in the fire, but he's dead all the same. He went berserk when he got out, leapt the wall leading down to the sunken garden and broke both his front legs. Luis shot him himself.'

'Oh, dear God.' Emma buried her face in the pillow and closed her eyes.

'Don't know why you're bothering with Him. He wasn't much help the other night, was He?'

'You're a despicable little toad!'

Ramón shrugged. 'Can't stand here all day making small talk. Are you going to get dressed or are you getting on the aeroplane in your nightie?' He heaved a suitcase on to the table beside her and opened it. Inside were all her belongings, neatly packed.

'He got one of the maids to pack it all up last night. Nice of him to let you keep all those

172

clothes, I thought. Would have burned them myself.'

Emma's head was spinning. Did Luis really want her out of the country so badly? Surely he wouldn't have sat at her bedside and appeared so concerned about her health if he had. It didn't make sense.

'I'm going to phone him,' she stated, reaching for the telephone and punching out the number with difficulty.

'You're an awkward bitch,' snarled Ramón. 'I could tell that the moment I laid eyes on you.'

'Villa Quevedo.' The phone was answered on the second ring by a female voice.

'Can I speak to Luis please. Luis Quevedo,' she added, remembering that one of the grooms shared the same name.

'May I enquire who's calling?'

'Emma.'

'Just a moment please.' A minute ticked by. It seemed like an hour. 'Would that be Señorita Emma Blackmore?'

'Yes.'

'I regret, *señorita*, that the *señor* does not wish to speak to you. He says that he has sent a message to you via señor Ramón.' The line went dead and so did Emma's heart. Defeated, she dressed meekly in the jeans and oversized T-shirt that Ramón handed her. It was true: Luis hated her. All his concern had simply been for appearance's sake.

She scooped up her belongings into a bag. 'What about this?' she asked, indicating the engagement ring that was lying in the drawer of her bedside cabinet.

Ramón snatched it up and flashed it under her nose. 'Yeah, take a good look at it. It'll be the last time you'll ever see jewellery as good as this unless you queue up to see the crown jewels.' He opened the patio doors in her room and pulled her towards them.

'Don't I need to sign something?' she asked vaguely.

'It's taken care of.'

'Why are we going this way?'

'Because it's quicker. The side entrance is over there, and that's where I've got a taxi waiting.' He slammed her case down in annoyance. 'But if you want to walk all the way through the hospital to the main entrance, Miss Awkward, that's what we'll do.' He stood with his hands on his hips and waited.

'This way's fine,' she whispered. She felt like a pillowcase emptied of all its stuffing. All the fight had left her body.

She must have looked a pathetic figure trailing after Ramón, but her last shred of self-respect restrained her tears until after he'd seen her safely through passport control.

Looking back, the only thing she could remember about the flight to England was the man sitting beside her making a fuss about her crying.

'It's too much for anyone to put up with,' he complained loudly to the flight attendant. 'I demand to be upgraded to first class.' She thought he got his way.

CHAPTER 11

'Letter for you. Another one,' said her mother pointedly when she returned from the library.

Emma sighed, flicked on the kettle, and waited for it to boil so she could steam the envelope open.

'It's harassment, you know. I've a good mind to go and see a solicitor. How he managed to get hold of our telephone number, I don't know, but I've told him if he ever tries to set foot in this house he'll get more than he bargained for.'

Emma stared out of the window in an attempt to blot out her mother's moans. She couldn't blame her for being annoyed, but she wished she wouldn't go on and on about it every minute of the day. She felt as if she were about to explode and her mother was stoking the flames. How much longer would Luis continue? Surely he would get fed up if she wouldn't speak to him and returned all his letters.

'I think maybe his grandfather's death unba-

176

lanced him mentally,' she said, watching the first threads of steam issuing from the kettle.

'Then he should be put away.' There was no grey in Mrs Blackmore's world, only black and white. 'He deserves to be put away for what he did to you in any case. To my dying day I'll never forget the state of you when you walked in here two weeks ago. If I'd had a gun I would have shot him.'

'Please, Mum, we've been through all of this. It's not doing any good.'

Mrs Blackmore glanced at her daughter's strained expression and nodded. 'All right, pet, I'll shut up about him. Have you finished with that kettle? I'll make us a pot of tea. Pity to waste all that hot water.'

Emma stepped to one side, slid the embossed notepaper out of the envelope and glanced at it. It was similar to the others:

Emma,
I understand why you hate me. I'm so sorry for what has happened, but I can't bear for us to part like this. At least tell me that you are well, whether I can pay for hospital treatment for you.
Oh, Emma, you're ripping me apart. Why won't you read my letters or answer the telephone? I can make amends if only you would allow it.
Luis

'Too late, Luis.' Emma folded the paper, returned it to the envelope and scrawled 'RETURN TO SENDER' over her address. Her head ached with trying to analyze Luis's motives. Why should he suddenly suffer this attack of guilt now after turfing her out of Spain like a criminal? The only explanation that fitted was the one she had told her mother: he was mentally unhinged. It wasn't that reassuring when she expected him to knock on her door any day.

He came on the Friday of the next week. Her plan of spending each day supposedly working in the reference library had paid off, and she wasn't at home when he arrived.

'The last you'll see of him. I gave him a right piece of my mind. Thought he was something special in his fancy car and his fancy clothes.' Mrs Blackmore's eyes were shining. She'd tackled the devil himself and emerged triumphant.

'What did he say?' Emma had to sit down; her legs seemed incapable of taking her weight.

'Didn't get the chance to say much at all, did he? I asked him whether he was stupid, whether he couldn't get it through his thick head that you didn't want anything else to do with him. I told him. I told him you were ill, that he'd made you worse and that you were staying with relations until you were better. I told him that we were making enquiries about getting a court order against him.'

'What did he say then?' she whispered.

Mrs Blackmore's mouth tightened into a narrow line. She picked up a scouring pad and scrubbed furiously at a ten-year-old stain on the bottom of her roasting dish.

'What did he say, Mum?'

Her mother slammed the dish down and threw the pad away in disgust. 'What did he say?' she spat. 'He only tried to give me money, that's what. Blokes like him should be lined up against a wall and shot. They ruin people's lives, but think it's all right if they offer them a few bob afterwards. I lost my temper, Emma. I'm sorry, but I did. Like I say, you won't be hearing from him again.'

Relief flooded through her. No more ridiculous letters, no more phone calls, no more hiding in the library and expecting to see his face around every corner. She could start rebuilding her life. It was a good life. One she'd been perfectly happy with until Luis García Quevedo had entered and shattered it into a thousand pieces.

The feeling lasted until the following morning. She awoke from a fitful sleep, dragged herself to the bathroom to wash the heaviness and lethargy from her limbs, and studied the haggard-looking woman in the mirror. It was as if she had been drained of all emotion. She felt nothing as she stared at the greasy hair, sallow complexion, and lustreless eyes of her mirror image. The thought came to her as though telepathically – she was nothing without Luis. Even that failed to trigger any reaction in the hollow features of the woman in the mirror.

'Hold on a minute, would you, Emma. You're not rushing off to another lecture or anything, are you?'

Emma shook her head, sat down again, and groaned inwardly. She'd been expecting this. Her tutor was patience personified, but even he wouldn't wait forever for her essay on Calderón and her last two comprehension assignments. She knew she had to get her act together. If only she could extricate herself from this fog of inertia that had settled over her.

'Fruit gum?' asked her tutor, offering her the packet.

'No, thanks, Mr Edmonds.'

He popped one in his mouth and sat down beside her. 'A fortnight ago I received an extremely generous donation towards our new language lab.' He stopped and looked meaningfully at her.

'That's good,' she said, feeling that she was expected to say something.

'Mmm. Naturally I wrote to the address on the letter to express my gratitude.' He tore some paper from the packet and inspected the next fruit gum.

'Naturally,' she agreed.

'I like the green ones best. What's your favourite?'

'The red.' Emma started to fidget. She was supposed to be meeting Kate in the coffee bar, but the way it was going they'd be here all day. 'Look, I'm sorry,' she said, taking the bull by the horns. 'I've had a few problems, but I promise I'll hand my essay in by the end of the week.'

'Good-oh.' Mr Edmonds smiled and slurped quietly.

'Could you wait a little longer for the comprehensions? The English department's on my back for my Hardy essay.'

'Come and see me when you're ready. We'll go through them together.'

'That's great. Thanks.' She placed her file in her bag, but he remained sitting.

'I was telling you about the donation,' he said.

'Right.' Kate would go spare when she finally made it to the coffee bar.

'Shortly afterwards I received a telephone call from the gentleman in question. Very courteous but rather persistent. He wanted to know about you. Had you returned to your course? How did you seem? Had the . . . ahem . . . scar on your forehead healed?'

Darkness opened in front of Emma and swallowed her up. When she came to, her tutor was dabbing at her face with damp paper towels.

'Sorry. I'm so stupid.' She sat up, fighting the nausea that threatened to engulf her. 'Really I'm all right. No it's not your fault at all. Low blood sugar probably,' she reassured the man, who was starting to flap. 'What did you tell him? What did you tell Luis Quevedo?'

'Yes, that was his name.' Her tutor looked embarrassed. 'I answered his questions briefly. I told him nothing he couldn't have discovered himself by pursuing other channels.'

Emma gave him a weak smile and stood up. She could always say she'd been swept off her feet by a man, she thought ruefully.

'Oh, dear. Now I don't know what to do, but I did promise.' Mr Edmonds stuck his hands in his pockets and walked agitatedly about the room.

'Promise what?' She might have known there'd be more.

'To personally hand you a letter which he sent me. It seemed an innocuous request, but now I don't know.'

Emma sighed. 'A promise is a promise,' she said, holding out her hand. He withdrew a bulky white envelope from his jacket pocket and her stomach contracted momentarily as she recognized Luis's bold scrawl.

'I'll be all right. Really,' she assured her tutor, as he hovered about waiting for her to open it.

'Then I'll leave you to it. I'm just across the corridor in my room if you feel the need.'

As soon as the door closed, Emma ripped open the envelope, her heart beating wildly. This was just like Luis. Why couldn't he send a letter through the post like any normal person?

Dear Emma,
I am pleased that you have returned to your
studies. Your tutor speaks very highly of
you and expects you to do well in your final
examinations.

'Get on with it!' she hissed through
clenched teeth.

Your mother left me in no doubt that you
did not wish to see me, and I have respected
your wishes, though it does not mean that I
have not thought of you often.
Don't worry, guapa, this will be the last
letter that you will receive from me unless
you desire otherwise. Enclosed with it is a
chequebook, which allows you to draw on my
account in London.
Before you rip this letter to shreds, Emma,
please read to the end, then think about it for a
while. If for no other reason, take the money
for the injury you received at my home. You
would have been granted as much in a court of
law. Use it for any purpose you like. Give it to
charity if you must, but I hope that at the very
least it will enable you to complete your course
free of any money worries.
My sincerest wishes for your happiness,
I shall not forget you,
Luis

Emma crumpled the paper and stared out of the window. Guilt was certainly biting deep into Luis's soul. Well, he deserved it, but if he thought for one moment that she'd touch a penny of his conscience money he was mistaken.

He wouldn't forget her, would he? Well, that was something, because she certainly wouldn't forget him. She had a permanent reminder of her short stay in Andalucia. Most of the time it was hidden by a thick fringe, but it was there to taunt her every time she cleaned her face.

Why couldn't Luis let go? Why was he trying to control her life? She could only guess at his reasons. Absentmindedly she traced her finger over the steamed-up window in the room while she puzzled over it.

What had he written? That she could have sued him or something for the accident? Maybe that was it. Maybe he'd taken legal advice and found he was liable. He might still blame her for killing Don Rafael and Hierro, but his Spanish sense of honour forced him to pay her off. Emma smiled to herself. She was a bad debt. Luis was a businessman; he abhorred bad debts. It was as simple as that.

Cheered by her discovery, Emma stuffed the letter in her bag and went off to see if Kate was still waiting for her. 'I'll definitely have that essay for you in the next couple of days,' she called to her tutor, who was sitting in his room with the door open.

He smiled and gave her the thumbs-up sign. She hurried past before he could call her back and ask how she was.

Outside, the October day was cold but bright. A hardy sun accentuated the ruddy bronze hues of the trees along the university's boundary. The sight made her pause on the steps of the Spanish department. It was so beautiful. A last glorious show of colour before the year ended.

As she walked across to the student union building, Emma felt like Mary Poppins; the weight that had been grinding her down since her return to England had lifted and she felt as if she could float over the building if she put her mind to it. By his letter, Luis had set her free. He'd cleared his debt and his conscience by giving her access to his bank account, but the main thing was he'd promised that she'd never hear from him again. He'd cut the final invisible thread that had held her prisoner – the anxiety that she'd never be free from him.

It was up to her now to get on with her life. She felt like a tender plant that had barely survived a harsh winter. Outwardly she might appear dead, but the sap was rising. It wouldn't be long before she was covered in green shoots again.

She took the student union steps two at a time. How ridiculous she'd been to convince herself that she was nothing without Luis García Quevedo! Her life had suffered a temporary setback, that was all. Now it was back on course, and there was a lot of catching up to do!

Emma walked into the coffee bar and over to the chair that Kate was saving for her by propping her boots on it. 'Hi, I didn't think you'd still be here.' She smiled and steeled herself for the mouthful of abuse that would shortly be winging her way.

Kate swung her legs off the chair and pointed to the table. 'I put the plate over your coffee to keep it warm. I was just about to eat your doughnut.'

Emma stared at her in disbelief. The girl with the vilest temper in the Northern hemisphere was actually smiling at her. She took the plate off her cup and downed the lukewarm coffee in one to fortify herself.

'What do you want, Kate?'

'Why should I want anything?'

'OK, I'll rephrase it, what have you done?'

Kate scowled darkly. 'You can be a right suspicious cow at times, Emma Blackmore.'

'The last time you bought me a doughnut you'd left my jacket on the bus.'

'We got it back.'

Emma tore pieces off the doughnut and waited. The path to a girl's heart was definitely ring-shaped, she decided.

'Brad's been evicted,' Kate announced eventually.

'That's what happens when you don't pay

your rent.' Emma licked the sugar from her fingers.

'Don't you feel sorry for him?'

'Nope.'

'You've turned really hard recently.'

Emma shook her head. 'Just realistic. If I'd spent all my grant on dope and booze I wouldn't expect sympathy. Why should he?'

'I didn't say he wanted sympathy, just somewhere to sleep for a bit.'

'For a bit of what?' asked Emma, then grimaced at her own joke.

'He could sleep on the settee. It wouldn't be that much different to the way it is now.'

'Yes, it would. If he was staying with us he'd expect to be waited on hand and foot. It's bad enough now – "Have you got the iron on? That's lucky. I've just come back from the launderette. Could you just run over these few things for me?" and "Mmm, that stew smells nice. Any going spare?"'

'He's very appreciative.'

'I've noticed. Our bedroom walls are like cardboard.'

Kate had the grace to blush. 'I didn't mean that. I meant the way he gets us free tickets for the gigs, and he's always first with his round in the pub.'

'What does Louisa say about it?'

'She doesn't mind. That's the thing about Brad: even when he's not sleeping with you any longer he manages to stay friends.'

'What a gentleman.'

'Lighten up, Emma. You've got to admit he's quite a stud. Might be just what you need. You should see the way he drools after you.'

'Two weeks. Just while he's looking round for somewhere else. I couldn't stand it any longer.'

Kate glanced at her watch and picked up her books. 'You can buy your own pigging doughnut next time,' she said as she left.

'Hiya, scarface, how did it go?'

Emma walked into the student union bar after the most gruelling hour she'd ever spent and gratefully accepted the cold beer Brad offered her.

'Terrible. I feel like a Wimbledon tennis ball.'

'Aw, poor Em, come here and have a cuddle.' He grabbed her and pulled her easily towards him.

Emma closed her eyes and allowed herself to be patted on the back like a child. Brad was idle, he was a pain in the neck, and he was a complete chauvinist, but after sharing her house with him for the last six months she loved him like a brother.

'Which interview was this one for then?' chipped in Kate.

'That sherry company, Herrero's, in Jerez de la Frontera. It's for a trainee public relations officer. I thought I might stand a good chance because of the information I'd picked up when I was in Sevilla, but I reckon that's another one down the drain. The blokes interviewing were reincarnated Gestapo.'

Brad released her and turned his attention back to his pint. She sat down but still felt the comforting warmth of his arms around her. It was he who had persuaded her to try for the job when she'd rejected it out of hand as being too close to Luis's operation. Well, at least she'd tried; it was out of her hands now.

'I told you they'd give you a hard time.' He put down his pint and wiped the froth from his lips. 'They're not going to employ somebody who buckles under the first bit of pressure, not in a job like PR.'

Kate nodded. 'They told us in business studies that all companies want staff who can stand up for themselves. They think there's more likelihood that they'll stand up for the company.'

'Oh, I stood up for myself all right, but I think I went too far the other way. They'll probably cross me off the list for being too aggressive.'

Brad started to laugh. 'Yeah, that's our Em. You think she's a bimbo until she lashes you sideways with her tongue. They probably didn't know what hit them. I bet you get the job, though. You certainly look the part.'

Emma smiled and picked up her beer again.

'Hey! Watch your drink on that suit! I need it for my interview on Thursday.' Kate threw her a beer mat and Emma dutifully wiped the drips from the bottom of her glass. She gazed wryly at the blue silk suit that she'd first worn to visit the Quevedos' villa. It was doing sterling service at the moment.

CHAPTER 12

Emma loosened her seat belt, smiled warmly at the flight attendant who was offering her a glass of wine, and counted her blessings. She'd been so busy with finals and the celebrations afterwards that the excitement of her new job hadn't quite sunk in. It was only yesterday that she'd heard she'd gained an upper second-class honours degree, and now her happiness was complete.

OK, she was broke. She was coming to Spain with a hefty overdraft. But her job was such a good one that she'd be able to pay it off relatively quickly. It was sad leaving her mum, but she'd keep in touch by letter and phone and send her a ticket to visit during the holidays. It probably wouldn't be that much different from her being away at university once they got used to it.

The air ticket was unlikely to be business class, as Herrero's had sent her, but who could tell what might happen in the future? Wouldn't it be something to fly her mum over first class and imagine her sitting on the plane sipping champagne with the best of them? Emma smiled, then shook her head. Her mum became tiddly on one glass. She'd have to rethink that one.

Emma sipped her own drink and saw out of the corner of her eye that the man across the aisle was still watching her. She'd have to stop grinning so inanely. He was either nervous about sharing the cabin with an escaped lunatic or he thought she was coming on to him.

She pursed her lips and tried to look serious. It was difficult. She felt like a child on her way to Disneyland. She was so lucky. Most of her friends were still job-hunting, except for Kate, who had landed a job at a chain store. How she'd managed to swing that had surprised her as much as anybody. Brad reckoned it was probably the suit. He was still waiting to hear from a record company, and was consoling himself in the meantime by pouring as much alcohol down his neck as he could.

'Would you like another glass?' The flight attendant reappeared, bearing a bottle, but Emma shook her head. She had no wish to repeat the performance of her last flight to Sevilla. The thought made her grin again. What on earth must Luis have thought of her throwing up in the toilet? It was a wonder he didn't change his mind and pack her straight back on the first flight home.

Her face grew serious. She hoped she didn't run in to him before she'd found her feet at Herrero's. The sherry houses were quite a close community. There was no doubt she'd have to face him eventually, and there was no doubt in her mind that she'd managed to get this job because of the knowledge she'd gleaned on her visit to the *bodega* and during her long conversations with Don Rafael.

What would Luis do when he discovered she was working for a rival company? It was one thing offering her money because his lawyers had told him he was liable and he thought he'd never see her again. It was quite another for the person he probably still blamed for his grandfather's death to turn up working in the same business as him.

Emma turned and gazed at the cushion of clouds outside. It was strange how her brain consistently refused to tackle this question. Would he let her be or would he use his influence and superior knowledge of the sherry industry to ensure that she was made to look a fool?

She sighed, picked up her fork, and toyed with the navarin of lamb in front of her. There was little point in agonizing over it. She'd chosen her path. All she could do now was be a model employee, work hard and learn everything she could about the industry. She'd probably never be a match for Luis – he'd grown up in the business – but she wouldn't go down without a fight if that was what he wanted.

By the time Emma had finished her lunch she'd managed to shake off any negative thoughts and her spirits were again high. The stewardess came round with the duty-frees, and she increased her overdraft with a bottle of Diorissimo. Who needed a man to buy her perfume? It certainly was a heady feeling sitting here courtesy of Herrero's, on her way to a new job that she'd achieved solely on her own merits. The years of study and her mother's scrimping and saving had been worthwhile. She vowed to do all she could to repay her by making her mum proud of her success and by trying to make her life easier.

The plane landed without incident. The airline hadn't managed to lose any of her luggage, and Emma piled it all on to a trolley and walked out once more into the main reception area of San Pablo airport.

It was strange being back. Her spirits nosedived for a few moments as she recalled the pathetic figure she must have appeared when she was here last. She refused to let the image gain hold, gritted her teeth, and pushed her trolley resolutely towards the exit.

Halfway there, a short, elderly man appeared from nowhere and stepped directly in front of her. Emma yanked the trolley back as quickly as she could, but it was too late. It dealt him a glancing blow and he fell to the ground.

'I'm ever so sorry. I didn't see you.' She helped him to his feet. He wasn't quite as old as she'd thought, which was a relief; elderly people and falls could be serious. He was probably only about fifty. It was his bald head that made him look older.

'Are you all right, *señor*? Can I get you anything?' He was rubbing his leg, but there didn't seem to be anything broken.

The man straightened up, then adjusted his suit, which she noticed was of good quality. Her eyes took in his expensive shoes, immaculate shirt and tie and neatly groomed appearance. He looked important. Not the type of bloke who was used to having trolleys bounced off him at airports. She glanced nervously around, wondering if anyone had noticed the accident; she was certain it wasn't completely her fault. But nobody was paying them any attention.

'Señorita Blackmore, perhaps?' asked the man, and she nearly hit the floor herself. As it was she stared at him in disbelief, her mouth hanging open. Good grief, Sevilla had already been alerted to her presence. A mad Englishwoman was on the loose, intent on maiming as many Spaniards as possible.

The man's eyes twinkled as he viewed her confusion. 'I see that I shall have to be quicker on my feet in future, Señorita Blackmore.' He extended his hand and she shook it automatically. His grip was warm and firm. 'Antonio

195

Jiménez at your service. I am the marketing director at Herrero's. On behalf of the company, allow me to welcome you to Spain.'

Emma's face glowed like a three-bar fire. She could safely say she'd never been so embarrassed in her life. Of all the people to flatten she had to pick one of her superiors at Herrero's. A niggling doubt wormed into her brain that perhaps luck wasn't smiling on her quite as much as she'd thought. What on earth was a director of the company doing meeting staff at the airport anyway?

Señor Jiménez seemed to find her consternation amusing. 'You'll be able to tell everyone that you bumped into me at the airport,' he chuckled.

'I'm ever so sorry,' she reiterated.

'I'm fine. Only bruised. I assumed that you'd seen me because you seemed to be looking directly at me. One thing I should have known after fifty-three years on this earth is that it is dangerous to assume anything. Now, shall we go outside? I have a car waiting.'

They walked out of the air-conditioned terminal and into the sweltering heat of a July midday in Sevilla. After a prolonged heatwave in Britain, Emma thought she'd be more prepared for it, but short of basting herself in an oven nothing could have prepared her for the ferocity of this Andalucían sun.

A white Mercedes was parked in the shade

nearby. The driver was reading a newspaper, but folded it quickly when he saw them approach. As he loaded her cases into the boot, Emma slipped gratefully into the cool interior of the car.

'I will be responsible for you during your probationary period,' Señor Jiménez began as soon as they drove away. 'I had a meeting in Sevilla today and thought it would be pleasant to get to know you a little before you start work with us officially.'

'That's very kind of you,' she murmured. The man was doing his best to put her at ease, but she couldn't quite shake off her initial embarrassment.

'We like to take care of our employees, *señorita*, especially those who have travelled so far to join us. Now I'm sure that you have plenty of things that you would like to ask me. I am at your convenience.'

The journey from Sevilla to Jerez whizzed past. Emma lost her nervousness as she realized that Señor Jiménez was as kind as he appeared. He really seemed to care that she should settle down well. He pointed out interesting places to visit and told her the best places to eat. Emma was still a little bemused by his meeting her the way he had, but counted her blessings that she'd found work in a family-run business that obviously treated its employees well. Catch any of Quevedo's directors meeting a new member of staff at the airport, she smiled to herself. Luis would probably sack them for wasting valuable time.

The Mercedes came to a halt before a modern three-storey building with tinted windows. 'Herrero's,' announced Señor Jiménez with a flourish.

Emma tried to conceal her disappointment. The man beside her exuded such an old-fashioned charm that she'd expected her workplace to be dignified and quaint as well. Trust her to make sweeping assumptions. She listened to Señor Jiménez's instructions about where she should report to on Monday, and her eyes travelled to the warehouse next door. This was more like it. The ancient *bodega* with its white stone walls and huge wooden doors looked exactly as it should. The modern building must have been added as an office when the company expanded.

'Your apartment is on the other side of that park.' He pointed across a busy road. 'It is within walking distance. A godsend in Jerez.'

Emma gazed across the road with delight. Any disappointment that she'd felt over the architecture of her workplace was immediately swept away. This was an unexpected bonus. She'd be able to walk to work through a green haven of trees and bushes. Her excitement mounted. She couldn't wait to see where she was going to live.

'It probably takes longer by car than it does on foot.' Antonio Jiménez gave a particularly Latin shrug. 'I shall drop you there now, then I really must get back to work.'

'I'm extremely grateful for – ' she began, but he waved away her thanks.

After a circuitous journey, they stopped in front of a modern four-storey apartment block. Like Herrero's, the architecture was functional, but she noticed with a thrill that each apartment had a tiny balcony overlooking the park. In her mind she was already outside, sipping coffee and admiring the view.

'Lovely,' she said, clasping her hands together.

Señor Jiménez took one look at her face and a huge beam lit up his own. 'It is the first time that you have the freedom of living alone?'

Emma nodded and grinned back. To be able to do exactly as she liked. No fighting for the bathroom or the phone. Nobody eating your food and leaving the dirty dishes for you to wash up. No squabbles over whose turn it was to buy coffee or clean the loo. Total bliss.

'I'm afraid that you are on the top floor,' said Señor Jiménez apologetically, as they waited for the driver to unload the car.

'Great. I'll have the best view.'

'And also the most stairs to climb. There is no lift.'

'It'll keep me fit.'

Señor Jiménez smiled. 'You have the key we sent you?'

Emma took it out of her purse.

'Then I shall bid you farewell and ask Juan to take your cases up for you. His legs are younger than mine.' He took a business card out of his wallet and gave it to her. 'My home address is there also. Please ring me if you have any problems whatsoever.'

'Thank you so much, Señor Jiménez.' She felt like kissing him, but restrained herself and shook his hand instead. 'I'm really looking forward to starting work on Monday.' Then she picked up a holdall and raced after Juan to open her front door.

As soon as he'd set her cases down in the living room and closed the door behind him, Emma opened the patio door, flung back the wooden shutters and walked out on to the balcony. Her view over the park was just as she'd hoped. She was close to the hustle and bustle of Jerez yet she could sit on her balcony sipping a drink and look out over trees, flowers, shrubs and even a pond where she could just make out children splashing about.

Emma was as pleased with the rest of the apartment. There was one bedroom, but the sofa in the living room folded down to a bed so she would be able to have friends to stay. The kitchen and bathroom were tiny, but as she wasn't the world's greatest cook, and she wouldn't have to queue in the morning for a shower, she thought they were ideal. Everything had been newly decorated, and it was all hers for a small monthly deduction from her salary. She was truly blessed!

The weekend passed quickly. Emma's mind was full of things she'd like to buy to make the apartment more personal: the walls were crying out for pictures, the sofa needed a colourful throw over it, a table lamp would be useful beside the armchair, and another shelf in the bathroom would be handy. In the end she settled for a pot of geraniums for the balcony. Her salary was a good one, but as her bank wouldn't see a peseta of it until the end of the month she didn't want to stretch their tolerance to the limit.

Excitement and nerves battled for supremacy as Emma set out early for work on Monday morning. Once again her blue suit was pressed into service. She'd bought some good working clothes but felt confident wearing this. And today she needed all the confidence she could muster. She felt as if she was eleven years old, was moving up to comprehensive school and had just been told that all her friends were going to a different one.

A leisurely walk through the park calmed her. She lingered by the pool, allowing the water and dappled shade of the trees to exert their soothing influence. By the time she crossed the busy road to Herrero's she was ready to face whatever the day had in store for her.

The receptionist phoned Señor Jiménez to tell him that she'd arrived. He emerged immediately from a room at the far end of the corridor and walked towards her.

'Bright and early. Well done.' He took her hand in both of his and smiled. 'Let me show you your room. It's right next door to mine, so there'll be no slacking,' he chuckled.

She followed him to a small office overlooking the car park. It was little bigger than a walk-in wardrobe, but it had a large window and good natural light. As soon as she'd put up a few posters and installed some houseplants it would be fine. He beckoned her to sit at her desk and he sat down opposite.

'As I told you at the airport I have been given the task of supervising you during your probationary period,' he began. 'You will remain with me in the marketing department for the first month. I shall give you a general overview of the company, answer any of your questions, allow you to sit in on meetings, and introduce you to people. This last is the most important and it's probably why you have been assigned to me. I've lived in Jerez all my life. I know everyone.'

'I'm looking forward to it.' If her boss knew everybody then he must know Luis. She'd have liked to ask him what he knew about him, but she kept quiet. The last thing she wanted was her former association with a rival producer to be common knowledge.

'Shortly, I'll take you around the departments to introduce you to everybody. It's pointless yet. Half of them won't have arrived.' For a moment his brows knitted together and he looked annoyed, but he was again smiling when he turned to her.

'In the meantime if you'd like to come into my office I've sorted out some information – old reports, press releases, that sort of thing – which you might find useful.'

She followed Señor Jiménez next door, but couldn't suppress a gasp of surprise as she saw the mountain of material piled on his desk. It would take her the rest of the month to read through it. She recalled the determination that she'd felt on the plane. Information was power. It was exactly what she needed. 'That lot should keep me out of mischief,' she joked.

'That is the general idea,' replied Señor Jiménez. He was smiling, but she detected an undercurrent to his words that disturbed her. It vanished as he took her on a tour of the building. Names and faces blurred into each other and her jaw ached with smiling so much, but everyone seemed remarkably friendly. The relaxed, laid-back atmosphere of other departments contrasted sharply with the bustling efficiency evident in Señor Jiménez's.

'What do you think so far?' he asked, showing her the staff canteen at lunchtime and sitting down next to her in a proprietorial fashion.

'I think this paella must be the best I've ever tasted.' She piled generous mounds of rice on to her fork, and grinned.

He watched her indulgently, a benevolent smile on his face as though he'd personally prepared the dish.

'We use outside caterers,' he murmured, sipping his wine thoughtfully. 'It is probably one of the few areas here that makes a healthy profit.'

Emma chewed her food more slowly. This must be the third hint Señor Jiménez had dropped that day that Herrero's wasn't quite the stable family-run operation it presented itself as being. She hoped that it was only a temporary slackening-off of trade, and that lack of any profit-sharing bonuses would be the only consequence.

'I'm certain your job is safe, my dear,' said Señor Jiménez, correctly reading her thoughts. 'Your contract is a good one, yes?'

Emma nodded, but her mind returned to Brad and the argument they'd had when the contract had arrived. He'd told her she was stupid for signing it, but she'd ignored his advice. She wanted this job and didn't want to run the risk of Herrero's changing their mind if she tried to renegotiate. After all, it was only one clause. The rest of the conditions were brilliant. 'Even if it's absolute hell I'll stick it for six months,' she'd assured him.

The cause of their disagreement was a penalty

clause in the contract, which stated that if she gave in her notice before her probationary period ended she had to repay six months' salary.

'They've got you over a barrel if you sign it,' Brad had said. 'What happens if your boss starts feeling you up on the first day or the place is an absolute hole? There's no way you can resign.'

'I'm sure that wouldn't happen.' Emma could see Brad's mocking expression and hear her own conciliatory tone as she tried to convince both him and herself. 'They're just protecting themselves. They need some kind of insurance that I'm not going to chuck it in on the first day. It's expensive bringing someone over from England and training them.' It was an occasion when neither of them had won. Eventually, for the sake of friendship, they'd agreed to drop the subject.

Thankfully, their argument had been academic. She was sure that she could work with Señor Jiménez or any of the people she'd met this morning. It hadn't entered her head until now that the company might be experiencing difficulties and that she might have to deal with the even greater problem of redundancy. Last in first out. Wasn't that how the system worked?

Emma put down her fork and stared at her empty plate. She'd eaten the rest of that wonderful paella without tasting any of it. What a waste! Perhaps if she spoke to other members of the PR team they might be able to put her mind at rest.

They'd have some idea how safe their jobs were.

'I don't recall meeting any other members of the PR team today,' she said in a light voice to Señor Jiménez.

'That's because there aren't any.' Her boss turned his face away and she realized it was to hide his amusement.

'What?'

'I'm certain you heard what I said. Until now Pascual Herrero has dealt with public relations himself. Suffice it to say, your appointment is long overdue.'

Emma swore to herself. It was an English word that popped out, and she hoped Señor Jiménez wouldn't understand it, but his expression told her otherwise.

This was one question she should have asked during her interview, but she'd been so occupied answering the Gestapo's questions that she'd had little chance to ask many herself. She'd assumed that a company as established and well-known as Herrero's would have a structured approach to public relations. Wasn't it Señor Jiménez who'd warned her only a few days ago that it was dangerous to assume anything?

Her boss seemed to find her discovery amusing. He sat back in his chair and regarded her with a smile. 'A challenge, my dear. Don't I recall reading on your application form that you thrived on them?'

Emma blushed. She'd hoped that the enthusiastic excesses of that document had been consigned to a filing cabinet in the personnel department and wouldn't see the light of day again. Most of their job applications in the house had been a team effort. It became a kind of hobby after a night out at the pub, when they'd spur each other on to more and more outlandish statements. One afternoon with a collection box outside a food store became 'a deep commitment to social work', and a Saturday job in a chain store became 'extensive retail experience'. Emma's various jobs had given them great scope, and her form was a masterpiece of ingenuity. She hadn't actually lied, but the truth had definitely been tampered with.

It seemed to be what employers wanted, however. The house ratio of applications to interviews was higher than anyone else's. Was it her fault that applicants were supposed to come across as the next Sir John Harvey-Jones just to get an interview? She glanced hesitantly at Señor Jiménez. To her relief his eyes were laughing. He was teasing her.

She smiled at him. 'I'm not afraid of a challenge,' she affirmed, but as she said the words they became fact. Had she really expected it all to be plain sailing? This was the real world. Things didn't happen like that. Nothing had changed: she still wanted desperately to do well in her job. A few obstacles along the way would make her appreciate the success more when it came.

She raised her glass to Señor Jiménez in mock salute. 'Here's to the best PR woman Herrero's has never had,' she grinned.

CHAPTER 13

'There is a management meeting at half past ten this morning, Emma.' Señor Jiménez placed an agenda on her desk, but didn't seem as inclined to stay and chat as he usually did.

'That should be interesting,' she said picking it up.

'I think you will find it so, yes,' said her boss, and he was gone.

Emma smiled after him. Over the last few weeks, she'd grown extremely fond of the man, but she would be pleased when her month with him was over. She immediately felt guilty at having such thoughts. Señor Jiménez was kindness itself, but his habit of accompanying her to the staff canteen at lunchtime and discussing marketing strategy during their meal, and also of keeping her late after work was a little wearing. He took his duties as her supervisor extremely seriously and it meant that she hadn't been able to make friends with any other members of staff.

One more week, though, and she'd be spending a couple of weeks in the finance department, then the same in other departments. It would be good to meet new people. She just hoped that they hadn't already dismissed her as aloof and a bit of a goody-goody because of the amount of time she spent with her boss. But how could she hurt his feelings when he so obviously expected to sit next to her each lunchtime? From what he'd told her she suspected that she reminded him of his daughter. She'd recently moved to Madrid with her husband and baby, and Emma could tell that he was missing her badly.

At twenty past ten she walked into Señor Jiménez's office. She was a little peeved that he hadn't advised her yesterday of the meeting. She would have worn a suit. Her white blouse and navy skirt were fine for general use, but they looked a little casual for a meeting attended by all the heads of department. Still, she supposed men didn't think of such things. A quick glance at her boss, however, altered her opinion. He always looked smart but he looked especially spruce and well laundered today. She was about to say something but changed her mind. It seemed petty.

'Will Pascual Herrero be chairing the meeting?' she asked instead.

'Not since the take-over, no.' Señor Jiménez seemed intent on searching through a pile of papers.

'Take-over! What take-over?'

'It was six months ago. Publicity was deliberately dampened down. The new owner wanted to maintain the brand image of a well-established family-run company.'

'Why on earth didn't you mention it, *señor*? I've been chuntering on about Pascual Herrero and you never said a word.'

Her boss gave one of his expressive shrugs. 'He is still part of the company, *señorita*, though without any executive powers.'

'So who runs the company now?'

'Mmm?' said Señor Jiménez, glancing at his watch. 'We really should head for the boardroom now.'

Puzzled, Emma followed him into the corridor, where a meeting with the finance director prevented her from repeating the question to her suddenly evasive boss.

'I see that you are prepared this time, Eduardo.' Señor Jiménez smiled and pointed to the large file the finance director was carrying under his arm.

'Yes,' replied the man vehemently. 'That man always seems to know what figures I've prepared and asks me about something else, but I'm ready for him today.'

'I'm sure you are,' he agreed, patting him on the shoulder.

Emma took her place beside Señor Jiménez at the huge mahogany table in the boardroom. The room was already full and there was a loud hum of conversation. Ever eager for information, Emma sharpened her hearing and listened. As she hoped, most people seemed to be talking about the new managing director, and none of it seemed very complimentary. The man sitting opposite, who she vaguely recalled being introduced as the export manager, seemed to share the opinion that the new owner was born out of wedlock. Whoever he was, he was certainly having an effect on the laid-back staff of Herrero's. More than one seemed to be finding the morning warmer than usual, and a young man at the far end of the table seemed to be actually praying.

'His last secretary didn't last long,' whispered the export manager to the man sitting beside him. 'This one looks as though she'll get her knickers off quicker.'

The man started to laugh and Emma shot them both a look of contempt. Maybe it was her fault for listening to other people's conversations, but she'd make sure neither of these two made it on to her Christmas card list.

The woman in question, a willowy blonde beauty, slid into her seat and smiled pleasantly around the table. Emma caught her eye and smiled back. Ignorance was bliss when it came to the things men said about you, she thought, then, despite her repugnance, prepared to tune in to the next snippet of conversation between the two men.

'Did you hear about him and that Scandinavian model?'

'Was she the woman who advertised bras or something?'

'I don't know about that but – '

'Have I shown you these pictures of my granddaughter, Emma? She looks just like her mother.'

Emma turned to Señor Jiménez with a smile. She'd never know about the Scandinavian model now, but she had to admit that Señor Jiménez's granddaughter was a little poppet.

'How old is she?' she asked, then realized that her voice was the only one in the room. She'd actually missed the entrance of the man himself, whose arrival had created a hushed air of expectancy in the room.

Her eyes immediately darted to the top of the table. They met a pair of piercing dark ones focused directly on her. The effect couldn't have been more dramatic if she'd encountered the devil himself. With his black hair, swarthy complexion, and dark suit, he might have been.

'No,' she gasped. All colour drained from her face, and her stomach levitated to her throat. She fought back the nausea, but couldn't drag her eyes away from the sardonic black orbs that held her own captive.

In her wildest imaginings she couldn't have thought up a joke as sick as this. She had to hand it to the man; his capacity for inflicting pain on her was supreme. His eyes flickered to the papers in front of him, releasing her, and she slumped back into her seat.

She supposed he had opened the meeting and was reading the minutes of the previous one. She could see his lips moving, but blood was pounding in her brain and she couldn't hear a word.

It had been a constant source of concern how she would react when she eventually met Luis. Nothing could have prepared her for the rage that swept through her body when the initial shock subsided. What God-given right did he have to tamper with her life? The interview, her job, it was just a sham. She thought she'd done so well, but she'd achieved nothing. He'd taken it all away from her. How he must have laughed at how easy it had been to manipulate her.

And what was his plan now? It must have really riled him that she'd ignored his letters and refused to speak to him to go to such lengths. Was he going to wait until she was happily settled in Jerez then fire her on a whim? She passed a hand over her aching head. Surely he wouldn't be so vindictive? Then she thought of the events after Don Rafael's death and realized that nothing was past him.

Until now she'd tried to make allowances for the way Luis had treated her. Temporarily consumed with grief at his grandfather's death, he'd wanted the cause of it as far away from him as possible. This was the theory she'd come to accept, but what if she was wrong? What if he was truly disturbed? What if it had given him such a thrill kicking her out of Spain when she was helpless that he'd determined to do the same thing again? Only this time he'd do it himself.

Her hands balled into fists and she glared at the dark figure at the head of the table. No way would she give him the satisfaction. Immediately this meeting was over he'd receive her notice. It wasn't too late to get another job; she'd apply for everything that was going, she wouldn't be fussy.

The throbbing in her head began to ease. She drank a glass of water and attempted to concentrate on the meeting. Señor Jiménez turned to her and patted her hand and she smiled weakly back. What on earth was his part in all this? It was blindingly obvious now that he'd been ordered to keep her apart from the other staff. Luis wouldn't have wanted her to learn the new owner's identity too soon. It would have spoiled his fun.

She jumped as Señor Jiménez suddenly leaned across, shook her arm and pointed to the top of the table. From the look of amusement on people's faces and the hint of annoyance on Luis's it seemed that he had been speaking to her and she had been ignoring him.

'What?' she snapped, shooting him a look of undiluted hate. She managed to inject the word with such pure venom that a deathly hush came over the meeting, and all eyes were raised expectantly.

Luis returned her stare, his eyes flashing a warning as he repeated his words pleasantly, 'I wished to welcome you officially to Herrero's, Señorita Blackmore. I hope that you will be happy with us.'

'Save your breath, I won't be staying that long.' If she hadn't been so angry, she would surely have balked at the look Luis gave her, but rage blazed within. She could have fallen into a den of lions and come out alive.

'I would like to have a word with you after the meeting, *señorita*,' he said quietly before returning to the agenda.

Whether this was a typical meeting or whether Luis had been fired by her anger, Emma had no way of knowing, but she watched in astonishment as senior members of his team squirmed in their seats under the force of his questions. He never lost his temper, was never openly discourteous, but the person was left in no doubt as to what their managing director thought of their weak answers and inconclusive projections.

This was his true character. A shell of hatred formed around Emma as she watched him in action. How had she ever deluded herself that she was in love with this man? She'd been out of her mind. He was a monster. He got off on controlling people and feeling superior to everyone else.

Now it was the turn of the finance director. Luis must have seen the huge file in front of the man. She could almost hear the click as his brain whirred into action then came up with a question that couldn't be answered by Eduardo delving into the papers in front of him.

The man turned crimson. The colour deepened as his managing director stared at him, waiting for an answer. Everybody including Luis knew that he had none to give, and relief was tangible as he turned away, the faint curl of his lip indicating exactly what he thought of Eduardo Valera.

Emma began to tremble, and she gripped her hands fiercely together. It was taking everything she possessed to control her temper. If Luis made the mistake of walking past her she'd rip him to shreds.

But it was good that she could see him like this. She could finally strip away the good memories of him that clung like dust to the deepest recesses of her mind. The memory of how vulnerable he looked when he was asleep, how desirable he was when he lay warm and naked beside her, the way her body yearned for him when he smiled at her, and the pure physical strength of him as he dominated his magnificent stallion.

That was what she hadn't been able to conquer: the overwhelming physical attraction he held for her. But that was all it was. Physical. Women were programmed to seek out the strongest male to provide for them. When she'd met Luis her cave-woman instincts must have been functioning on overdrive. He was the strongest male around all right. He'd trample on anybody who got in his path.

She wrenched her attention back to the meeting. Luis was questioning Señor Jiménez. Emma's fists clenched and she felt a fierce protectiveness for her boss. Maybe he had deceived her, but she didn't feel that this mild-mannered kindly man had done it with any malice. Señor Jiménez, however, didn't appear to be in any need of her protection. He seemed completely at his ease, speaking to Luis, as he did to everyone, with charm and humour.

Luis smiled at him, and it seemed that her boss was going to be one of the few that satisfied his exacting standards. Then he glanced at the paper in front of him and his brow wrinkled into a frown.

'It's unusual for you not to meet your monthly target, Señor Jiménez. Is there a problem I should be aware of?'

This was so unfair! Her boss had been ordered to stick to her like glue and now he was being taken to task for doing so. Before she could stop herself she'd opened her mouth.

'I think you'll find that the problem was me.

Señor Jiménez has spent the last three weeks baby-sitting.' As soon as it was out she regretted it. Why in heaven's name had she said baby-sitting? It had always irked her when Luis teased her by referring to her as a child, and now she'd set herself up for him.

A quirk of a smile fluttered across Luis's face before an inscrutable mask descended once more over his features. 'Thank you for your contribution, Señorita Blackmore. I believe, however, that Señor Jiménez is quite capable of giving me his own reasons.'

Nevertheless, he moved on to another subject, and the tone of the meeting lightened from that point. He moved swiftly to a close, ended the proceedings with a faint measure of encouragement, then chairs were being scraped back and she could feel the aura of relief in the air.

Señor Jiménez fielded small talk with his neighbours as he gathered his things together, then squeezed her shoulder encouragingly as he walked past. As soon as he'd gone Emma rose and stood by the window, watching the activity in the adjoining *bodega* where a tourist group waited to be taken on a sherry tour. By the time they came out again her career with Herrero's would be over.

'It is good to see you again, Emma.' Luis placed his hand on her shoulder when the last person had left the boardroom. The bolt of electricity that zapped through her from his fingers fortified her for the encounter that was to come.

'I hate you, Luis! I've never hated anyone so much in all my life as I hate you! I detested you from the beginning and nothing I've seen of you since has forced me to alter my opinion!'

Luis turned away, picked up a jug of water from the table and poured himself a glass. If she didn't know better she would have said that she'd hurt him. When he turned back she scanned his face for any trace of emotion. There was none. Why did she persist in searching for glimpses of humanity in him?

He sipped his drink and fixed her with a dark stare. 'I believe your feelings towards me were patently obvious to everyone today. That reminds me, before we exchange pleasantries, I must warn you that the little gems you contributed to the meeting this morning will not be tolerated in future. I made allowance for your obvious surprise at my presence, but I must insist that, at work, you adopt the normal attitude of an employee.'

'Which is what, Luis? Grovelling?'

The ghost of a smile fluttered across his face then disappeared without trace. 'I warn you, Emma, I have much more experience in confrontation than you. If you try it again, you will undoubtedly come off worse.'

'Oh, don't worry, I won't be doing it again. You won't have sleepless nights worrying about my attitude. You know why? As soon as I'm out of here I'm writing my resignation and you won't see me for dust.'

'Now why did I expect that to be your reaction?' Luis perched on the table and thrust his hands into his pockets. His fake air of sadness infuriated her.

'I don't know, Luis. You're just so brilliant, so wonderful, it must be difficult for you associating with us lesser beings.' Sarcasm dripped from her lips like butter.

His mouth tightened into a harsh line. 'I take it you're fully conversant with your contract?' He said no more but watched her closely until she caught his meaning.

The swine! That was why the penalty clause was included. He didn't want her resigning. That wasn't half as satisfying as firing her himself. Her not knowing when the axe was going to fall only increased his pleasure further.

She stared at her hands, unable to meet his cruel gaze. He knew as well as she did that she couldn't raise that kind of money. With her track record, the bank would laugh in her face if she tried, and her mother lived in rented accommodation and had nothing that her daughter could borrow.

Emma took a deep breath. She'd need it to hurl every insult she could think of at him. Then she stopped, but kept her head hunched as the idea hit her. It was brilliant! She'd use the money in Luis's London account to pay him back. She didn't have a clue how much it was, but if it wasn't sufficient she'd raise the rest somehow. She composed her face into a meek expression and looked at him.

'I'll have to resign when my probationary period is over, then.'

He stared at her for several seconds, his mouth twitching furiously, then to her astonishment he burst out laughing.

'I'm sorry. Forgive me.' He wiped across his eyes with the back of his hand and instantly became serious. 'You are delightful, Emma. I could live with you until I was a hundred and never be bored.'

He attempted a smile but when he met blank hostility he sighed. 'The account, which you have only just remembered, was closed the day you began work at Herrero's. It grieves me that you wouldn't take my money when you – '

He said no more. Only excellent reflexes saved him from the glass that whistled past and smashed into a hundred pieces on the wall behind him.

'It wasn't my fault your grandfather died!' she screamed. 'I couldn't have stopped him going to the stables that night. I did my best to save him, and I tried to save your horse.'

'Oh, Emma, *guapa*, please don't.' He leaped up and caught her rigid body to his. She struggled like a wildcat but he was too strong for her. Tears coursed down her cheeks and still he held her. Only when her body became still did he lessen his hold and draw her away from him.

Gently he parted her fringe and traced his finger along the silvery line of her scar. 'I'm so sorry, Emma,' he said. 'I would give everything I have to be able to replay that night, but it's not possible. What's done is done. But you, *guapa*, are still the most beautiful woman on God's earth.'

For a second she thought he was going to kiss her, and her deceitful lips parted in expectation. But he walked away, rested an elbow on the window ledge and gazed out.

'You wouldn't really take me to court for breach of contract, would you, Luis?' she asked, when it became clear that he wasn't going to say any more to her.

'Be assured of it. I wouldn't have asked for the clause to be included if I'd had no intention of implementing it,' he said, keeping his gaze fixed outside.

'Congratulations, then, Luis, you've won. You'd have laughed at how excited I was about landing this job.' She tried to keep her tone light, but failed. 'I spent a fortune in the student union bar that night,' she added bitterly, 'but I could have saved my money, couldn't I? Because I'd achieved absolutely nothing. You've taken it all away from me.'

'I've taken nothing away from you, Emma.' He turned round and looked at her with fake concern.

She sighed and flopped down into the nearest chair. 'You've taken any pride away that I had in getting this job on my own merits,' she explained wearily.

'Then I am sorry, for it because it was not my intention. You were the best candidate for the position.'

'Oh, spare me. I mightn't exactly be *Mastermind* material but I'm not completely thick, Luis. The only reason I'm sitting here now is because, like God, you decreed it.'

'Are you calling me a liar, Emma?' His dark eyes glittered dangerously.

Emma hesitated. Five minutes earlier she would have, and to hell with the consequences, but her rage had cooled and she was beginning to realize that antagonizing Luis unduly mightn't be her best course of action.

'You're telling me that my presence here is a sheer fluke?' she asked quietly.

'No, Emma, I won't insult your intelligence. I admit that I advertised the position at your university in the hope that you would apply. I had the interviews taped, as you know, and I also reserved the right to choose the successful applicant. In the event it wasn't necessary, I took Diego and Jaime's recommendation. I repeat: you were the best candidate for this position.'

'And what if I'd gone to pieces with nerves and made a total mess of the interview?'

'Then I'd have had you called for a second one. Knowing you as I do, I didn't think it would happen.'

'You know nothing about me, Luis,' she hissed, then immediately kicked herself as he scooped his papers off the table and made to leave. There were still questions she wanted answered.

'But why?' she shouted after him. 'Why go to all this trouble?'

He turned back to her and she saw the muscles of his jaw tighten. 'It should be obvious, Emma,' he ground out, before closing the door behind him.

Obvious to anyone with a crystal ball, a full pack of tarot cards, and an aptitude for tea-leaf reading, she fumed, but it wasn't obvious to her. He was such a complex personality, he gave off so many contradictory signals that it was impossible to guess what was really going on in his head. If he hated her then why had he appeared concerned and held her to him when she'd become upset? It was as if she was dealing with two different people. Was he schizophrenic? She had no idea. Her degree was in English and Spanish, not psychology.

She was about to leave when she caught sight of pieces of glass littering the carpet. Good grief. Thank goodness the glass hadn't hit him. She shook her head in disbelief at what she'd done. She abhorred violence. She was always the first in any fight dragging the opponents apart. What was happening to her? Perhaps Luis wasn't the only psychotic one in this relationship.

With a sigh, Emma retrieved an A4 envelope from the file she'd brought with her, then sank to her knees and began picking up pieces of glass and putting them in the envelope. The last thing she wanted was for anybody to discover the breakage and speculate on what had happened between the new employee and the managing director in the boardroom. She gritted her teeth. The new employee's behaviour in the meeting had given them quite enough scope for speculation.

Carefully, Emma wrapped the envelope around the glass. There was a discarded Jiffy bag in the wastepaper bin and she used this for added protection so that a cleaner emptying the bin wouldn't cut her hands.

Was the glass a symbol of her life? It was tempting to draw a comparison between it and her shattered hopes, but Emma refused to concede defeat. Luis had won the first victory, but he'd cheated: he hadn't told her battle had commenced. And he was still cheating by refusing to tell her the rules. She'd have to find them out as she went along.

So what exactly was her battle plan? She

deposited the bundle of glass in the bin and frowned. Thanks to Luis her options were limited. She had to stay here for six months. That was assuming he didn't sack her before then. If she was right about his motives he wouldn't do that immediately. He'd make her sweat a little, have her gain a false sense of security, and have a little fun by trying to intimidate her or make her look a fool at meetings.

She picked up her file and headed slowly back to her room. As far as she could see, Luis's need to keep her in the job for a reasonable period was his only weakness. She'd turn that weakness into her strength. Now that she'd had time to think about it she realized that her initial determination to resign would have been disastrous for her career prospects. The longer she could remain in this job, the more people she could meet, and the more she learned about the business, then the more attractive she became to a future employer.

That would be her course of action. She'd work as hard as she could, cover her back, and learn as much about the company as possible so that she didn't appear a total fool in any confrontation with Luis. Nothing much had changed, then: she'd already decided to do as well as she could in her job before Luis had come on to the scene.

Emma threw her file on to her desk and gave

an ironic laugh. Who exactly was she trying to kid? Nothing much had changed? Not much it hadn't. So much for her cushy job in the sun that her friends had told her she'd landed!

CHAPTER 14

'What did Luis tell you about me and him?'
Señor Jiménez was tucking into a beef stew as
she slipped into the seat next to him in the
canteen.

Her boss seemed unperturbed by her abrupt
manner. He looked up and smiled. 'Aren't you
eating, my dear? I can recommend the *caldereta*.'

Emma's stomach was still churning from the
confrontation with Luis; anything she tried to
shove down her throat would have come straight
back again. 'Please, *señor*,' she asked again.

He put down his fork and picked up his glass.
'Always so impatient, always so eager to know
everything. You will wear me out,' he chuckled,
drinking deeply.

'I'm sorry. I shouldn't have interrupted your
meal.'

Señor Jiménez shrugged and then smiled.
'You are a breath of fresh air, Emma. You
should go far in this company, and I don't

simply refer to your connections.'

'My connections.' Emma's body stiffened. 'Who else knows about them?'

'Nobody, as far as I am aware, although one or two people were curious about your behaviour at this morning's meeting.'

Emma raked her fingers through her hair. She didn't need Luis to make her look a fool, she was doing a good enough job all by herself.

'I told them you had received some bad news and were a little overwrought. I told them that I thought Señor Quevedo would overlook your rudeness when he was aware of the reason. The truth, I think.'

'Thank you.' Emma squeezed his arm.

'So, my dear, are you staying with us?'

'I can't afford not to,' she answered ungraciously. 'Oh, I'm sorry. I didn't mean anything about you. If it wasn't for . . . Oh, hell, it's such a mess.'

Señor Jiménez frowned and looked thoughtful. 'Is it? Is it really? You have a bright future with us if you want it, Emma. I presume that you and Señor Quevedo were once romantically attached. Is it so bad that he still retains feelings for you and wishes to help with your career?'

Emma laughed bitterly. 'If that really was his motive, *señor*.'

'And why shouldn't it be? More than one former girlfriend has found a place in his organisation.'

Emma raised her eyebrows in disbelief.

Señor Jiménez popped a piece of meat into his mouth and watched her thoughtfully. 'His present secretary is one of them,' he said, wiping his mouth on his napkin.

Emma fought and conquered an irrational stab of jealousy. 'Did he tell you that?'

The question appeared to amuse him. 'I think that's hardly likely, don't you?'

'I don't know,' she said, continuing to stare at him.

'It is like the Spanish Inquisition,' he muttered. 'You must meet my wife. You and she would get on extremely well, I am sure.'

'*Señor?*' It wasn't like her boss to be so constantly evasive.

Señor Jiménez sighed. 'My wife is an ardent fan of gossip magazines. I fail to see the attraction myself, but if it gives her pleasure . . .' He shrugged his shoulders in the Latin manner. 'Whenever anyone appears in them that I might have met she draws my attention to it. I recognize the secretary from a photograph – Consuela Javier. She used to be a model with some cosmetics company or other.'

'I see.' So Luis had a penchant for models. That horror Carmelita was one, there was the Scandinavian one they were talking about at the meeting, and now his secretary. Emma frowned. No wonder he'd had no difficulty resisting her charms when she was staying at the villa. 'You

231

are still the most beautiful woman on God's earth . . .' His recent words mocked her. Lying toad! He'd have said the same if she'd been Miss Piggy. He'd say anything to get his own way.

'Did you recognize me from one of those magazines?' she asked as the thought suddenly occurred. As far as she knew she'd never been photographed with Luis, but she couldn't be certain.

It seemed to be the best joke her boss had heard in a long time. 'No, *señorita*,' he said when he had recovered his self-possession. 'I can safely say I would have remembered if I had.'

'Why's that?'

'You aren't the type.'

Just what did he mean by that? What exactly did he know about her and Luis's relationship?

'Please tell me what Luis has told you about me, *señor*. It is important.'

Señor Jiménez smiled. 'This is the way my daughter wraps me around her little finger. She looks up at me with those wide innocent eyes and she knows I will do anything she wants.'

Emma's blush was instant. Had she really stooped to the equivalent of batting her eyelashes at a male to get her own way?

'Relax, my dear, I'm teasing you. Well, half-teasing at any rate. I have to admit your powers of persuasion are finely honed.'

Emma waited. She felt guilty as he pushed away the rest of his meal; she'd either ruined his appetite or the meat had grown cold and un-appetizing. She'd have to buy him lunch tomorrow to make amends. He refilled his glass, took a large mouthful and began.

'Some months ago Señor Quevedo told me of his intention to create a new post in the area of public relations. I agreed that it would be a good idea; my personal opinion was that it hadn't been handled very well in the past. He asked me how I felt about taking on responsibility for the new trainee. Naturally, I said I would be happy to oblige.'

'Naturally,' said Emma with some rancour. Nobody seemed able to deny Luis anything.

Her boss stared at her, uncomprehending, and she wished for the nth time that she had the ability to keep her mouth shut until she'd engaged her brain.

'He gave me a copy of your application form and a tape of your interview when he informed me of your impending arrival. "The lady in question is a former acquaintance of mine, Antonio," he said. "You would do me a great favour if you would take especial care of her. I particularly don't want her to know of my identity until she has chance to settle into her job here." You know the rest, Emma. I apologize if the way I interpreted Señor Quevedo's requests appeared a little odd to you.'

It was a fortnight before she saw Luis again. From her vantage point overlooking the car park she could see his Rolls-Royce come and go, and when he was at Herrero's she even avoided going out to the coffee machine in case she should bump into him. So far her tactics had worked, and he hadn't called her into any of his meetings, which was a relief.

It was the fifth day of her secondment to the finance department. Eduardo had spent the first day telling her how sexy she was and enquiring jokingly about her love life. The second day was a repeat of the first, and the third day she'd lost her temper and told him exactly what she thought of him. Workwise, it was probably a mistake, but she congratulated herself that she'd lasted almost three days. Her self-control was definitely improving.

Valera's attitude to her now was icy. He set her menial tasks and appeared to find withholding vital bits of information amusing. The contrast with Señor Jiménez couldn't have been more marked, but she wasn't going to let him beat her. She'd be ultra-professional. As long as he didn't harass her sexually she'd do everything he asked. If she did it with a smile it seemed to irritate him even more.

Crossing the car park to the main entrance of Herrero's on Friday morning, she saw Luis's car already parked there. Her first reaction was to quicken her pace, but she noticed his chauffeur examining a headlight. If Carlos was outside then Luis had already gone into the building.

She changed track and walked over to him. The man had been pleasant to her when she was staying at the villa and she didn't want to appear rude.

'Carlos!' She extended her hand in greeting. 'How are you? How's your wife?' Señora Machado had been heavily pregnant when she'd been introduced to her last year.

The chauffeur pumped her hand up and down. 'Twins, *señorita*,' he beamed sheepishly. 'Both girls.'

'How lovely. I bet . . .' Her voice trailed away as the rear door of the Rolls opened and Luis stepped out.

'I thought I recognized the voice. Hello, Emma.' He looked exceedingly pleased with himself as he raised his arms above his head and stretched languorously. It was his usual action when rising from bed in the morning, and it was impossible not to recall the sight and touch of his warm naked form as she watched his muscles flex and strain against the confines of his shirt.

Her heart began to thud, and as a slight flutter of wind carried his unique scent to her nostrils Emma felt an insistent ache spreading downwards from her stomach. It was all she could do not to reach out and touch him.

It was official: God had a sense of humour. Why else had he decreed that she should be hopelessly attracted to this man?

She turned away to hide her emotions at the same time as Luis reached into the car to retrieve his jacket. There was a faint whirr as a sun blind was lifted in the car, then his secretary stepped out.

'Shall I go ahead, Luis?' she enquired silkily, smoothing down her skirt and casting a cursory glance at Emma.

'Hmm? Yes. Be sure to photocopy those documents before the meeting, please.'

The blonde strode purposefully towards the building, leaving Emma glaring after her. She was so used to everyone referring to him as Señor Quevedo at work that the use of his Christian name by Consuela jolted her. Señor Jiménez's words about their relationship returned to taunt her. Was that why Luis had looked so smug when he stepped out of the car? Was he still going out with her? And was that why the blind was pulled? To hide their final embraces before beginning work?

Emma gnawed at her bottom lip. She didn't know why his behaviour should surprise or annoy her so much. This was Luis Quevedo here. The man who hired fiancées by the week, then threw them out like garbage afterwards.

'So how are you finding work, Emma?' Luis picked up his briefcase and smiled warmly at her.

'Very well thank you, Señor Quevedo.' Jealousy was an ugly emotion, and even though Emma winced inwardly at the pettiness of her tone, she couldn't help herself.

Luis's dark brows furrowed. 'What's the problem, Emma? You can tell me.'

'There's no problem, Señor Quevedo. I've said everything's fine.'

Luis swore and lifted his hand. For a second she thought he was going to hit her, but the hand continued upwards and raked through his hair. 'What the hell are you calling me Señor Quevedo for?' he demanded.

'I am an employee, *señor*. I distinctly recall you telling me to treat you with more respect.'

'You are the most infuriating woman,' he hissed. 'You knew exactly what I meant. I was referring to work.'

Emma looked around her insolently. 'Silly me. That's where I thought I was for the moment.' Before she could draw breath, he'd grabbed her hand, opened the car door, and pulled her inside.

'Get out and wait outside!' he barked at Carlos, who had settled in the front seat and was listening to the radio.

Luis sat beside her, his fists clenched and his eyes closed. Gradually his breathing returned to normal and he turned towards her. 'And now I shall have to apologize to Carlos,' he muttered. 'Eleven years and I have never shouted at him like that. Do you know that I never lose my temper?'

Emma gave a snort of derision. 'You could have fooled me.'

'It is true. Ask anyone.'

'I don't have to ask anybody, Luis. I lived with you for a week, remember.'

Slowly, Luis shook his head. 'Even then,' he murmured. 'Why should this be?'

'Because we're total opposites. I can't understand you and you sure as hell don't understand me. So let me go now before I upset you any more.'

He pressed his face close to hers. 'It's all a game to you, Emma, is it?' he hissed. 'Well, I'm sorry, *chica*, but this is one game you won't be winning. You will stay at Herrero's for six months unless you chance to meet your fairy godmother. And if you feel the need to insult me you'd better make sure you do it in private. I won't be made to look a fool in front of my staff. Do you understand?'

Emma was shocked by the vehemence of his response. She had meant that he should let her out of the car, but once again they were talking at cross purposes and he thought she was asking to be released from her contract. It took all of her acting ability to affect a bored tone of voice as she answered him. She managed it, though she was shaking inside. 'May I go now, *señor*?' she drawled, glancing at her watch. 'I really don't want to be late for Eduardo.'

A swear word with Eduardo's name attached

was her answer. It so echoed her own sentiments towards the man that her lips twitched involuntarily.

Luis reached across and gripped her chin between finger and thumb, forcing her face upwards. 'I don't understand you, Emma. It really isn't funny. It isn't a game, this thing between us.'

Emma wrenched herself away. 'No, it isn't funny,' she said bitterly. 'When I got back to England last year I certainly wasn't laughing.'

Luis leaned across her and opened the door. 'Go,' he said. 'You are impossible to talk to today.'

Emma raced into the building and up to the finance department, hoping that no one would notice that she was trembling. Damn the man! Why did he affect her more than anyone else she'd ever met? Why couldn't she shake off this ridiculous physical attraction whenever he was near? When he touched her it was as if she had swallowed a firework and it had ignited.

'Hey, hold on a minute.' A hand came out to halt her progress.

'Sorry, I'm a bit late.'

'He's not in yet, you're all right. And nobody hurries in this place. You'll get used to that. We save our energy for when they let us out at night.' José smiled widely at her.

Emma smiled back, amused. The young accountant positively lit up in the presence of women, and she'd already been warned about his ambition to bed the entire female workforce. They continued on to the finance department together.

'I was wondering if you were coming to the cinema tonight?' He opened the door for her and managed to brush his body seemingly innocently against her as she walked through.

Emma stepped away and affected not to notice. 'Yes, I'm going to the cinema,' she said.

The whiter than white smile almost blinded her again. 'Great! I could pick you up beforehand. We could visit some tapas bars; I know all the best ones.'

'Sorry. I'm meeting Carla.'

'Another time perhaps?'

Emma smiled noncommittally.

'Perhaps you could help me with my English some time. I'm thinking of taking lessons. Or do you think French lessons would suit me better?'

Emma laughed, then sat down at her desk. The man was handsome, funny, and had the body of a bullfighter, but physically he left her cold. It would be nice if she could remain friends with him when her lack of interest finally registered, but she was philosophical about it.

After her discovery of Luis's ownership of the company, Señor Jiménez had left her to her own devices at lunchtime. She was meeting staff from other departments and her circle of friends was gradually widening. It felt good. She was starting to be accepted. If only she knew what was in Luis's mind and whether she had any future at Herrero's.

CHAPTER 15

'Sorry. I'll come back another time.' Emma made to close the door when she recognized the lean, dark figure of Luis perched on the personnel manager's desk, reading some correspondence.

'Not on my account.' It was a command rather than a statement, and she had no option but to close the door and come into the room. She was aware of Luis's hawk-like eyes on her face and cursed the blush that immediately sprang to it. She'd successfully avoided him for the last week and had deluded herself into thinking that his effect on her had lessened.

'Would it be possible to book a few days' leave next week, Eugenia? I've checked with Señor Jiménez and he has no objection,' she asked.

'I'm sorry. Herrero's don't allow employees to take leave until they've been with us for three months.' Eugenia pulled a face to indicate that she was forced to trot out company policy in the

242

presence of their managing director.

'I see.' Emma nodded and turned away. So much for that. She'd have liked to take Brad round some of the local sights, but he hadn't given her much notice that he was coming to visit. He was a big boy; he'd have to find his own way around.

'Is that really what it says in the staff handbook?' The deep, resonant tones of the voice that was imprinted on her soul halted her.

'Page twenty-one, paragraph three,' said Eugenia, showing off.

'Really?' Emma noticed the corner of Luis's lips twitching. Why did he always try so hard to hide the fact that a sense of humour lurked beneath the stony exterior he presented to the world?

'It's rather an inflexible rule. I shall have to review it,' he said briskly. 'You may have your leave, Señorita Blackmore.'

'Thank you, *señor*.' She turned to Eugenia. 'Tuesday, Wednesday, and Thursday, please. I'll come back in on Friday for a rest.' She left the room with a smile and wondered vaguely why Luis was frowning.

The next management meeting passed without incident. There was a problem with their bottle supplier, and Luis devoted all his energy to this rather than to berating his management team's deficiencies.

Each time Emma was in the same room as

Luis she tensed up, waiting for him to turn nasty and try to intimidate her. Every time they met, however, he was unfailingly polite and pleasant. That unnerved her even more. He was either a grand master of the game he was playing with her life or she'd read his intentions completely wrongly. Either way she found she couldn't relax in his presence. It was always a relief when she could escape and her blood pressure and heart rate could return to normal.

The meeting broke up in a jovial mood and Emma guessed from the reactions of her colleagues that this was a rarity. She walked back to her office with Señor Jiménez. He'd just received another batch of photographs and was displaying them proudly to anyone who would look at them.

'She is the prettiest child I have ever seen, Antonio.' Luis caught up with them and reached for a photograph. 'I pity the youth of Madrid a few years from now when she is breaking all their hearts.'

Señor Jiménez chuckled and passed him the rest of the photographs. 'Just who or what is that?' he said, looking towards the reception area.

Emma followed his gaze and saw Brad, fetchingly attired in a shabby black T-shirt and ripped jeans, coming through the door. He tossed a battered rucksack to one side and swept a hand through his shoulder-length blond thatch. Immediately, two security guards swept down on him, and she saw Brad's hands curl into fists. His aversion to people in uniform ran deep, and she hurried forward before he received any provocation to hit them.

'It's probably a refugee from one of the guided tours next door. I'll handle it,' smiled Luis, getting to Brad before she did.

'Can I help you?' she heard him ask in English.

Brad ignored him when he spotted her.

'Hiya, scarface!' he shouted. 'It's damn hot, innit? I thought I was going to pass out when I got off the plane.' He grabbed her to him and kissed her soundly before she wriggled free.

'I thought you were going straight to the apartment,' she whispered, trying to push Brad back towards the door, but he loved being the centre of attention and refused to move.

'Lost the key. Sorry. I thought you might be a bit annoyed if I broke a window to get in.'

'You're right, I would have been.' She hunted in her bag for her own key, slapped it into his palm, and tried unsuccessfully once more to push him out of the door. He'd spent too many years trying to make himself heard in crowded bars and discos. His voice boomed around the building like a PA system and people stopped in their tracks to stare at him.

'Cross the road, go straight though the park, turn right and the apartment's opposite. You can't miss it,' she said briskly, picking up his rucksack and handing it to him. 'Help yourself to anything you need.'

'Ta. These letters came for you after you'd gone.' He opened the side pocket of the rucksack and pulled them out.

'Thanks.' She stuffed them in her bag.

'Oh, and the phone bill came. You owe me fifteen quid.'

'Fine. I'll settle up with you when I get back.'

'So, have I any other news to tell you? Louisa –'

'Go away, Brad, I'm supposed to be working,' she hissed, giving him another shove towards the door. This time, thankfully, he moved.

'Oh, do you want me to go, Emma?' he asked with exaggerated innocence. 'Why on earth didn't you say?' He tossed his bag over his shoulder, grinned, and sauntered towards the door.

'Oh, Em,' he said, pausing before pushing it open.

'Yes.'

His voice bellowed out, reaching parts of the building that other voices could only dream of reaching. 'Give us a ring before you leave and I'll warm the bed up.' He closed the door smartly before she could retaliate. She could hear him laughing as he ran down the steps.

Emma glanced warily at the faces looking after him. Most of them looked bemused but blank. Some of them spoke reasonable English, but

246

with any luck Brad's broad northern accent would be beyond them.

Her eyes found Luis's. They stared back at her, dark and unfathomable, giving nothing away. She noticed the tight line of his lips and the slight stiffening of his shoulders, and knew without a doubt that he'd had no difficulty in translating every word Brad had said.

'He's such a joker,' she said to no one in particular, before scurrying away to her office.

Three weeks later, Emma was running through the park and across the road to Herrero's. 'Any messages?' she gasped at the girl on Reception, who shook her head. It was the first time she had ever been late for work, and she didn't like it one bit. Luckily she had no arranged meetings for that morning, but she hated failing the high standards she'd set for herself.

It was typical of Brad to be still here two weeks after he said he was going. She didn't mind that, but she did mind that he expected her to accompany him to discos and stay up half the night talking about people that they'd met. It was different at university, it wasn't so important if she missed the odd lecture, but there was no way she was taking mornings off work here to recover from the night before. Brad never surfaced until the afternoon and couldn't understand why she was yawning and ready for bed when he was only just getting into his stride.

She raced through the corridor, glad that it was empty and that no one apart from the receptionist had witnessed her post-marathon beetroot face. Once in her office she'd be able to cool down a little before going in to see Señor Jiménez.

'I'm getting old. I can't stand the pace,' she muttered, pushing open the door and coming face to face with Luis, who was reclining in her chair with his long legs resting on top of her desk. He looked the epitome of cool, calm and collected, while she dragged air into her lungs and felt a trickle of perspiration snake down her spine.

'It's the first time. The first time I've been late,' she challenged, before he could say anything.

He swung his legs off the desk and started to laugh, then his face grew serious and he stared at her unnervingly.

'What?' she said.

He seemed to mentally shake himself and looked away. 'You wouldn't want to know,' he murmured.

'What?' she repeated.

'Antonio Jiménez advised me about your desire to know everything,' he said. 'Do you really want to know what I was thinking?'

She nodded. It would be a first.

He shrugged. 'It crossed my mind that with your dishevelled appearance and heated face you looked exactly like a woman who had been thoroughly made love to.'

He was right: she didn't want to know. The pink in her cheeks instantly darkened, and she walked over to the corner of the room and switched on a fan. 'What do you want, Luis?' she asked, standing with her back to the breeze.

One dark eyebrow lifted in enquiry, and she realized that her tone had been as cold as the air blasting her from behind.

'I mean, how can I help you, *señor*?' she said instead.

Again he started to laugh, and again he became serious. 'This is so difficult for you, Emma, isn't it? I'm sorry. I didn't mean it to be.'

Before she could wonder at his words or the sadness she detected in his tone, he turned to a report she'd been working on that was lying on her desk.

'I was reading this before you came in.' He indicated it with a derisory flick of his wrist. 'Interesting but quite inaccurate. You really must check your facts, *chica*.'

'It's a first draft.' Suddenly the fan seemed quite inadequate as Emma felt her temperature rise again. Luis could think all manner of things about her but she wasn't going to add incompetence to the list. 'I like to get my ideas down on paper first and then I know exactly what areas I have to research in depth.'

'I should have known we'd be different,' he

smiled. 'It's exciting, don't you think, to watch two people tackling a problem? They may arrive at the same answer but their manner of getting there will be diverse. We would work well together, I believe. I'd like to see your report when it's finished.'

Emma nodded, not entirely graciously.

Luis got up and walked to the window. 'You are happy with your boyfriend?' he asked suddenly, taking her by surprise.

'Brad's OK,' she answered carefully.

'A little fickle perhaps?'

Emma's head shot up. What a cheek he had! 'Maybe it's the breed of man I'm attracted to,' she answered caustically.

'He'll hurt you, Emma. Don't let him.'

'I don't intend to.' How, after what he'd done, he could stand there and feign concern was beyond her. 'And what basis do you have for this theory, by the way? Could you tell just by looking at him?'

Luis frowned then stared at the ground. 'I was in Sevilla on Wednesday and I saw Brad. He's difficult to miss, you must agree. He was kissing a woman in a doorway. It wasn't just kissing, Emma, he was practically making love to her.'

Emma flopped into her chair and covered her face with her hands. Her shoulders shook. Oh, this was too funny. She knew Brad had got lucky in Sevilla; he'd told her all the details when he came home, but why on earth was Luis telling her?

'Don't cry, *chica*, he's not worth it.' A hand rested on her shoulder and Emma stared up at him incredulously.

As he registered her mirth he looked as if she'd slapped him. 'I don't understand. Why should you think it is funny to know your boyfriend has been with another woman?'

'Oh for goodness' sake, Luis, there's nothing serious between me and Brad.'

His mouth tightened. 'Yet before you moved to Spain you were living with the man,' he said, then the door slammed behind him.

Emma stared after him. What was that all about? Surely Luis wasn't jealous? He didn't want her but he couldn't bear any other man to have her, was that it? It was a possibility. He was such a control freak it might make sense. And was that why he was angry when he saw she was laughing? Because his idea of splitting them up had failed?

She picked up her report, but when she had read the first paragraph three times without taking in any of it she tossed it aside. What exactly did motivate Luis García Quevedo? She'd bungee jump off La Giralda if someone would guarantee her the answer.

Another week passed and Brad moved on. None of the jobs he'd applied for had come to anything so he was going to London to pester a cousin who was a sound technician. His latest fancy was to be a roadie, and he thought that his cousin might have some contacts.

Emma watched his taxi leave for the airport and waved him goodbye with a mixture of regret and relief. She'd miss him and his irreverent outlook on life, but it would be good to have the apartment to herself again.

She whipped the sheets off the sofa bed and giggled. She sounded like a little old lady, but living with Brad would make anyone old before their time. His expectations of being fed and entertained by her every evening had become a strain. He couldn't speak Spanish so he wasn't interested in meeting any of her friends from work, and she realized that she'd neglected them a bit because of him. She'd have to apologize and be extra nice to them to compensate.

Before she left for work, Emma zoomed around the apartment picking up cigarette packets, mugs and empty bottles, and folding the bed back into a sofa. It was satisfying returning her home to its state of neat cosiness that she loved. Smiling, she closed the door behind her and set out for her morning stroll through the park.

She loved this part of the day, when the sun shone with a friendly warmth, compared to the savage heat it displayed later in the day. The plants and flowers looked refreshed after their evening rest, and she could look around at everything properly. At midday when the sun was at its height everything was affected by its blinding glare.

Walking through the park was the ideal transition from home to work. By the time she crossed the road to Herrero's her mind was full of the tasks awaiting her there. She loved her job. It would be good to be able to give it her best again. As she was becoming more familiar with the work and meeting people from other companies it was becoming more and more interesting. If it weren't for the ever-present dark shadow of Luis, her working life would be bliss.

But there was no getting away from Luis. He owned the company and the shadow cast by him was a long one. And there was no getting out of the management meetings which were held regularly and which were the bane of his employees' lives.

At twenty past ten, Emma picked up her file and joined her colleagues on the slow march to the boardroom. One and a half to two hours of non-stop Luis was a lot for anyone to swallow.

'Do us all a favour and unfasten a couple more buttons on your blouse this morning, darling,' said the export manager as he held the door open for her.

'Do us all a favour and fasten a cardboard box over your head,' she retorted icily.

'No need to be unpleasant. I wasn't being personal.'

'Didn't sound like it.'

'I just meant we needed all the weapons we could get on our side for this one.'

'You've lost me.' Emma threw her file on to the table. It gave her headaches trying to work out the hidden meaning in Luis's words. She wasn't even going to attempt it with this man.

'Haven't you seen the half-year figures, then?'

'Of course I have. They're atrocious.'

'Well, then. We need something to distract him and you're our best bet. Haven't you seen the way he looks at you? You could be in there, darling, if only you'd loosen up a bit.'

It was as well that Luis's arrival prevented her from saying the words that immediately sprang to her lips. She had to work with these people and, disgusting as she found some of the men, she couldn't afford to alienate too many.

At the first sight of their formidable managing director people's heads bowed, and they appeared to find a consuming interest in the documents before them or even in the grain of the table. Luis didn't waste time. He dispensed with the preliminaries at a stroke to discuss the more pressing matter of the company's losses.

Emma watched him with interest. His anger simmered like a pan on the stove. It entered into everything he said, and though he never allowed it to boil over there seemed the constant threat that it would. Staff panicked and made rash promises that he immediately cut to pieces.

With his dark suit, dark looks and dark, incisive remarks he reminded her of the Grim Reaper. Nobody present would have disagreed.

It was possible to make a success of the company, Luis concluded, and he intended to do just that, with or without the people present. He'd leave them to reflect on his words. He swept out of the room as briskly as he'd entered it, leaving in his wake a group of people who looked to Emma's imagination like the survivors in a disaster movie. Once again, she wondered why she hadn't featured in it.

Señor Jiménez checked his watch. 'Can I buy you lunch, Emma?' he asked in his normal cheerful fashion. He was one of the few, like her, who left the meeting unscathed.

Emma smiled. 'No, thank you, *señor*. If you don't mind I'd like to go for a walk in the park first. I need some fresh air.'

'To revitalize yourself with your natural element?' he chuckled, patting her arm and walking away.

Emma found a seat beside the pond and gazed out over the water. The bench was shaded all round by tall trees and even at this time of day was blissfully cool. It had become a favourite place for reflection and she usually stopped for a while whenever she walked through. Today, two young boys had been allowed by their mother to take off their shoes and roll up their trousers. Emma watched their visible delight as they probed the oozing mud of the water's edge.

A dark shadow fell across the water. 'It's a beautiful spot, isn't it? I imagined you sitting here when I negotiated the lease for your apartment.' Only one man had a tone so resonant, a voice so compelling that it had the ability to penetrate even her unconscious mind.

Emma stiffened at its sound. This was one place where she felt safe and free from Luis's influence. Now he'd invaded her sanctuary.

'Thank you, *señor*. Forgive me for not going down on my knees in gratitude.'

The seat shifted as Luis sat down beside her. 'What is it between us, Emma?' he said sadly. 'Why can't I say anything without you twisting its meaning?'

'I'm sorry. That sounded awful. It's a lovely apartment. I am grateful. I really am. It's just . . .' Words failed her. Where could she begin?

'Your friend has now left?' he asked, before she could attempt it.

She nodded.

'I came to apologize. I should have minded my own business. I hope his departure had nothing to do with me?'

'No.'

He thrust his hands into the pockets of his suit. 'I thought I was telling you for your own good, but I think now that my motives weren't completely altruistic.'

'I'd more or less worked that one out.'

'So how are you, *guapa*? How is work? Señor Jiménez has nothing but praise for you.'

'And the other heads of department? Finance, perhaps.'

A smile spread slowly across his features and her heart lurched. 'Now what did you do to upset Eduardo?' he enquired.

'You wouldn't want to know.'

He nodded. 'Suffice it to say I value certain people's opinion more than others.'

'I should go,' she said, rising to her feet. She had to go. She wasn't strong enough to resist his charm or the physical attraction he still exerted over her. When he was this close, being this nice to her, she found herself forgetting everything but the moment. But she couldn't let it happen. He'd hurt her too much before. Her only defence against him was a clear head, and to achieve that she had to keep her distance.

'Don't go yet. A few minutes more. I see so little of you.' He grabbed her hand and she made the mistake of looking into his eyes. They were dark and troubled and looked so unbelievably vulnerable that she allowed herself to be pulled back on to the seat.

'Thank you, Emma.' The warmth of his smile penetrated her soul. 'I miss the conversations we once had. Whenever I sit on the terrace I – ' He looked totally bemused as she scrambled to her feet again.

'I don't want to know about it, Luis.' Her

memory of the time she'd spent at the villa was still too painful. Whether his regret was genuine or feigned she couldn't bear to listen to it.

'I'm sorry, *chica*, I don't understand. What . . .?' He stood and gripped her hands as if they were the reins of a horse that might bolt at any moment.

Emma stared at the parched earth beneath her feet, refusing to meet his gaze. The moments ticked by and he didn't move. His fingers retained a constant pressure around her wrists, not hurting her but ensuring that she could not escape, and she could feel his eyes boring into her, willing her to look up and talk to him. The noises of the park receded. She fancied she could hear the deep, resonant thud of his heart, then realized it was her own. It was so loud that he must be aware of it. A faint breeze stirred the leaves on the trees above her. Normally this brought with it the wonderful scent of the rose bushes planted nearby, but today they were overshadowed by the subtler musky aroma of the male standing only inches away.

'Will you put that down! We're going to see Grandma.' The shrill voice of a mother calling to her child made Emma jump. She wondered how long she and Luis had been standing like this, and she began to feel faintly ridiculous.

'The past is the past,' she mumbled, pulling away from him. To her surprise, he released her immediately. 'I don't want to talk about it, it's too painful.'

'I understand.' He thrust his hands into the pockets of his suit as if he didn't trust himself not to grab her again. 'Sometimes though, *guapa*,' he said gently, 'it eases the pain to talk about things.'

'And sometimes it doesn't,' she replied. Not with the person who caused it at any rate, she added silently.

'All right, Emma.' He sighed and sat down on the bench. 'Nothing past, nothing personal, I promise, but I would still like to talk to you.'

She hesitated.

'A few minutes, Emma. Is it so much to ask? Do you hate me so much?'

'No.' She couldn't ignore the look of pain that flashed across his face. It vanished the moment she sat down beside him, and as she gazed at the relaxed open countenance smiling at her she wondered if it had ever been there.

'So what shall we discuss? I know. Tell me what you thought of the meeting today?'

Emma frowned. 'You're putting me in an awkward position here, Luis.'

He shook his head. 'It's not intentional. Speak to me as a friend, not as an employee.'

'You really want me to tell you?'

'Of course.'

'And what if you don't like what I say?'

He smiled. 'Then it is my fault for asking the question. Whatever you say, *chica*, I shall not take offence.'

'I thought the meeting was absolutely awful.'

'In what way?' His expression didn't change.

'You're a bully. You terrorize your staff and then wonder why they don't perform at their best for you.'

'You think I should congratulate them for losing a hundred million pesetas for me in six months, do you?'

'No, but shouting at them isn't going to make it better.'

'I don't shout.'

Emma conceded the point. 'I don't know, Luis. What you do seems worse somehow,' she said, and he started to laugh.

'Doesn't it worry you that people hate you?' she asked.

He stared at her a long time before answering. 'Not if it's purely business. Most people dislike change and I, as the agent of it, will be hated. It would worry me if it were justified – if I'd taken over the company and sacked half the workforce to make it more profitable. That would certainly have been the easiest option, but I view it as a last resort. Andalucía has always been one of the poorest regions in Spain and suffered from the highest unemployment. In recent years the situation has improved but the signs are not so good for the future. As a rich man and an employer I am in a privileged position. I have no wish to add to the hardships of my people.'

Emma snorted. 'You're such a saint, Luis.

What was that – your acceptance speech for your Nobel prize? Or are you rehearsing what you're going to say to God when he kicks Gabriel out and gives you his job?'

The bench shook with his laughter. 'You are such a cynic, Emma Blackmore. Don't you believe it is possible to be a good businessman and a good Christian?'

Emma shrugged. 'Anything's possible, I suppose. What's probable is more to the point.'

'I could take offence at your words, Emma,' he said darkly.

'No, you can't.'

He lifted an eyebrow in enquiry.

' "Whatever you say, I shan't take offence,"' she reminded him.

'I didn't realize I'd given you licence to insult me,' he murmured.

'Oh, come off it, Luis, you're a businessman. Making money must be your objective.'

'Of course. I don't dispute that, but how I make that money is important.'

She gazed at him, unconvinced.

'How can I explain this?' He ran a hand through his hair and studied the cloth of his trousers. 'Right. I shall try.' He looked up again and fixed her with intense brown eyes. 'As you say, I am a businessman, and I am good at what I do. This is fact, not conceit,' he added as she smiled. 'I have been raised in this industry. It would be stranger if I did not know everything about it.'

'OK. Go on.'

'As soon as I acquired Herrero's I made it my business to know all its strengths and weaknesses. I soon realized that if I rationalized the workforce and pared down the company's operations it would be possible to drag it out of the red in the short term. That would probably be enough to attract another buyer. The brand name is still respected. Any problems that the company has faced have not been reflected in the public's image of it. The way was clear for me to make a quick profit if I chose. Do you accept this?'

Emma shrugged. 'I suppose.'

'If I followed that route, however, it would leave in my mouth a taste similar to that left by the rubbish sold in your country as sherry.'

Emma bristled. She might agree with him, but she never let a slur on her country go unchallenged. 'Students might disagree. You can get drunk a lot cheaper on the supermarket sherry than you can on your stuff.' It sounded a feeble retaliation even to her own ears. What was it about Luis that she had to try and provoke him even when he was trying to be serious?

He raised his eyes momentarily to the heavens, but continued, 'I am fortunate that I have never been in that position, and it is fortunate for Herrero's that I can afford to view matters in the longer term. People are always a company's greatest asset. This perhaps isn't as true as it ought to be in Herrero's case, but much of the blame must lie with the previous owner's incompetence. I hope that I am a fair man. I don't expect people to change overnight, but most will adapt to my requirements eventually. Those that do not will be removed from the positions they abuse. As you point out, *chica*, I am a businessman. The angel Gabriel is assured of his job for some time yet.'

He paused and wrinkled his brow. 'Now have I just refuted my own argument? I don't think so. What I am trying to make you understand, Emma, is that if one makes a company profitable by investing in people, enabling them to share the fruits of success, then that is a good feeling. It leaves a taste in the mouth similar to the finest sherry.'

Emma smiled. 'You sound exactly like Don Rafael sometimes,' she said.

'I truly hope so, *chica*,' he said grimly.

The thought of Don Rafael saddened her too much to end the conversation there. 'Didn't you know the mess Herrero's was in before you bought the company?' she asked.

His expression cleared and his eyes glittered. 'Of course I did. That was its attraction. Herrero's has been sinking steadily for years. There's not another company in Sevilla that could offer a greater challenge. I have no doubt that I can turn the company around, though not perhaps as quickly as I had hoped. Certain key employees are proving rather intransigent, wouldn't you agree?'

'I'm not a spy,' she said, and he nodded thoughtfully.

'Your position is a strange one.' His brows knitted together in a frown. 'I would have preferred you working for Quevedo's, but I didn't think there was the remotest possibility of you applying for a post there. If you had, you would have found the set-up completely different. Most of the staff are loyal and there is no need for this unpleasantness. I gain no satisfaction from it, Emma, believe me.'

Emma gazed into the dark, persuasive eyes directed at her and wished with all her heart that she could believe him. At times like this he seemed so open and genuine that it was difficult to remember how he'd hurt her, but she couldn't allow herself ever to forget. Maybe it was true what he said about the responsibility he felt towards his employees. If you were rich you could afford such sentiments, though to be fair he'd already acknowledged that. But hadn't she in a sense been his employee last year in Sevilla? His treatment of her then hadn't been that responsible or Christian.

She looked away. Her heart wanted to embrace everything he told her but, like some key personnel at Herrero's, her head was proving more intransigent. Deep inside, she could never trust him.

Luis continued, unaware of her thoughts, 'Perhaps it would be useful for your training if you spent a couple of weeks at Quevedo's, learning how another company is run?'

Emma kicked at a clump of daisies. 'I don't think I could work in the same building as Ramón.'

At the mention of his name Luis started. 'You wouldn't have to. Ramón is no longer in my employ.' He glanced at his watch. 'I must go now, Emma. Thank you for talking to me. It has meant a great deal.' He rose and walked briskly away.

She watched him retrace his steps until his lean pinstriped figure was hidden by a clump of bushes. Why did it always feel as if he were taking a small part of her away with him whenever he left her?

She sat back on the seat and stared at the water. Had she been wrong about Luis? Surely he couldn't still hate her and talk to her the way he had just now? Perhaps he'd brought her to Spain as a way of saying sorry for his actions after his grandfather's death. That seemed to make more sense now. His abrupt departure at the mention of Ramón's name certainly suggested he still felt guilty.

She could never trust him, but perhaps she should try harder to forgive him. If she kept in mind that he'd been temporarily out of his mind with grief after the fire, and that his meddling in her life had been prompted by guilt, then perhaps she could.

A rumbling in her stomach reminded her that she hadn't eaten since breakfast. She picked up her bag and walked back to Herrero's. Whether the canteen had sold out of hot meals was probably a more pressing problem at the moment.

God was good. One slice of tortilla remained in its terracotta dish waiting for her. Her hunger satisfied, Emma could think more clearly. She was undecided whether or not to have a piece of peach flan afterwards, but she did come to a decision about Luis. She didn't want to turn into a bitter, twisted person because of the hurt he'd inflicted on her. If he wished to make amends then she'd go halfway to meet him. If he was pleasant to her then she'd be pleasant back; she wouldn't continually search his words for hidden meanings, and she wouldn't duck behind coffee machines and turn back if she saw him at the other end of the corridor.

They could never be true friends, but perhaps they could share a good working relationship. Proceed with caution was the key.

CHAPTER 16

'See you at half past eight!' Emma shouted
across the car park to a group admiring the
production manager's new BMW. They waved
and whistled, and Emma grinned back. She'd
already paid suitable homage to the car at
lunchtime, when Diego had demonstrated its
features as proudly as if he were displaying his
first-born son for adoration.

José detached himself from the group and ran
across the car park. 'We're meeting at El
Cuchillo first,' he said, slipping an arm around
her waist.

'Yes, I know.' She smiled but continued
walking.

'I'll pick you up. Quarter past eight all right
with you?'

'Thanks, but I want to walk. I need the
exercise.'

'Oh, well, if it's exercise you need, Emma . . .'
His hand slid suggestively over the curve of her

bottom. 'Look no further, I'm your man.'

'That's great, José.' She pulled away. 'I might just take you up on your offer. I've been looking for a tennis partner for ages.' There was a break in the traffic and she took the opportunity to dart across the road. Poor José. If he wasn't afflicted with testosterone overload he'd be quite a nice bloke.

She soon forgot him as she walked through the park. This must be the best place on earth to live. Mid-October and it was as warm as midsummer in England. For the first time ever she had a suntan. The pale milkiness of her skin had been replaced by a light golden glow that pleased her inordinately by its novelty.

She reached her apartment and hurried up the steps. There was still time to take a coffee on to her tiny balcony, prop her legs on the railings, and enjoy the last of the sunshine before getting ready for a hard Friday night's partying. What a life! It was getting better and better.

Her decision to take Luis at face value had been the right one. She was certain now that he hadn't brought her back to Spain through malice. Whenever they met he was courteous and charming, and she no longer felt the need to hide when she saw him at the other end of the corridor.

If truth be told she might even have been guilty of lingering in the places where she was most likely to bump into him, but she convinced herself that this wasn't the case. The times when they'd met accidentally she'd always had a good reason for being there; she'd had to return that file to accounts on Tuesday, and when she'd seen Juanita in Reception it would have been rude not to have stopped and asked her about her holiday . . .

The weekend whizzed past and Emma walked into work on Monday slightly fuzzy around the edges. Not for the first time she marvelled at the Spanish capacity for enjoying themselves. When did they sleep? It always seemed to be her that sloped off to bed first, and this was at three o'clock in the morning! She'd have to go into serious training a few weeks before *Semana Santa* or Holy Week, which was the biggest event of the year in Sevilla.

'Emma, Emma, you will help me, no?' She'd barely sat down at her desk when the sales manager appeared with a sheaf of papers. 'That girl has rung in sick again – in bed with influenza, she says. Hah! In bed with someone but his name is not influenza. These must be given out at the meeting.' He slapped the papers contemptuously with the back of his hand. 'So what am I to do?'

'Just this once, Rodrigo. I've my own work to do, you know.' She took the papers. It was beyond her why he hadn't told his secretary to prepare them on Friday. She couldn't leave things to the last minute like other people seemed to do.

'You are an angel, Emma, I think I shall marry you.'

'I thought you were already married?'

'Ah, my wife, she does not understand me.' He shrugged his shoulders in the continental fashion and turned to go. 'I'll see you at the meeting.'

'Hang on.' Emma grabbed the sleeve of his jacket before he could escape. 'Where are you going?'

'I have important things to do, *señorita*.'

'I'm sure. Like having a coffee and a quick cigarette beforehand?'

The man snorted. 'When do I have time for such luxuries?'

Emma dropped the papers on the table and folded her arms. 'If I'm photocopying, you can jolly well sort and staple.'

'And now you sound exactly like my wife,' he said, but he was grinning.

What kind of mood would Luis be in this morning? she wondered, taking her place at the table which must have taken an hour to polish to such perfection. The company was still losing money and, according to rumours, Luis had personally interviewed the heads of departments to issue an ultimatum. Señor Jiménez, however, had refused to be drawn on the matter when she'd asked him.

The mood around the table was grim. It was strange to see these normally ebullient men

270

looking as if they were attending their brother's funeral. And it was mostly men present. When she got the chance, Emma would have to take Luis to task about his policy or lack of it for promoting women to the higher posts.

'*Buenos días, señores.* Señor Quevedo asks me to apologize for his absence – a last-minute problem with one of our British buyers. I hope I shall not disappoint as his replacement.'

Hushed sniggers and broad smiles followed this announcement by the silver-haired distinguished looking gentleman who took his place at the head of the table. They were acting like a bunch of children given an unexpected holiday from school, thought Emma, acutely aware of the dull, empty ache in her stomach. She was probably the only one present who was at all disappointed by their managing director's absence.

'I am Alfonso Bécquer, deputy managing director of Quevedo's . . .' The man continued his address while Emma studied his features carefully. The name sounded familiar. Had she been introduced to him and his wife that first night at the villa? She couldn't be sure. It seemed a lifetime ago.

His brief must simply have been to go through the motions. He galloped through the items on the agenda, and though he paused for questions nobody asked any. People's attention drifted, and even Señor Jiménez doodled on the corner of his pad.

271

'And I'm certain that you'll all continue . . . Gracious me! Amanda, isn't it?' As he beamed around the table their eyes had met, and although Emma had immediately transferred her own to studying the pattern on her skirt she'd seen the frown furrowing his brow.

'Emma. Emma Blackmore, *señor*,' she said miserably.

'Emma? Pardon me. I'm so terrible with names. How are you, my dear? I had no idea Luis's fiancée was working here. You really must come and visit us soon. My wife would love to see you again. We were deeply shocked by Rafael's death, but I know how happy he was that you were going to marry his grandson.'

Emma was beyond words. The room spun and she hoped that she was going to pass out, but her body was strong and refused to allow her the easy option. She endured Señor Bécquer's apology for embarrassing her, then managed to control herself until the meeting ended, when she was out of the door before anyone else and didn't stop until she'd reached her peaceful sanctuary in the park.

It wasn't like her to run away from anything, but there were limits. What could she possibly have said to the man? Luis would have to sort it out; he was the one who'd got her into the mess in the first place. It had been wrong to deceive Don Rafael, Emma was still ashamed of herself, but she thought she'd already paid the price.

Surely Luis hadn't set her up? Her head ached and she dismissed the thought; she had to stop these suspicions. But she couldn't prevent herself wondering why he hadn't warned Alfonso Bécquer of her existence before the meeting.

She rested her elbows on her knees, cupped her head in her hands and gazed out over the pond. 'It's a lot easier being a duck,' she sighed, getting up and going back to face whatever was waiting for her at Herrero's.

It was probably her imagination, but people seemed to interrupt their conversations to stare at her when she entered the canteen. It was her being over-sensitive; she'd been accused of that before.

'Thanks for keeping my seat.' She slipped into her usual place next to Eugenia.

'That one's taken.' Eugenia barely glanced at her.

'That's OK. I'll get another one.'

'Don't bother. We mightn't have any choice over who we work with, but he doesn't control our social lives. Not yet anyway.'

'News travels fast.'

The girl glared at her, and Emma flinched inwardly as she registered the hate in her eyes. 'That's the conclusion we've all come to, Señora Quevedo. How does it work? Do you tell him all about us before or after sex?'

'Before,' muttered someone else. 'It'd probably turn him on imagining all the different ways he can sack us.'

'I've never spoken to him about anyone here,' protested Emma.

The jeers around the table suggested she wasn't believed.

'If you'd been up-front with us we might have listened to you now. We're not stupid. We knew something was funny, the way he hangs around you, but we decided he just fancied you. He's got the reputation after all.'

'I didn't say anything because we're not engaged any longer. I didn't even know he'd taken over the company until I got here.'

There was more laughter.

'Public relations officer,' sniggered someone. 'More like private relations officer. Nobody could figure out why he had to go all the way to the UK to appoint someone when there were plenty of people around here that could have filled the post. But you seemed nice enough so we were nice back. We're one big happy family here. Least we were when Señor Herrero ran the business.'

Emma bit her lip to stop herself retaliating.

'Yeah, and we know why she was so nice and friendly to all of us now, don't we?' added someone. 'Quevedo knew we didn't trust him so he sent in his girlfriend to have a snoop around instead. I don't know how you've got the nerve to look any of us in the face or how you can sleep at night.'

'It's not true. I've told you the truth; I'm not a spy.'

Eugenia snorted with derision. 'And you're not his wife either. I thought you were smart but you're as thick as a brick. Do you really think he's going to marry you when he's got what he wanted? He's stringing you along, you stupid bitch. He's using you. If I didn't despise you for what you've done I might even feel sorry for you.'

Emma shook her head. 'You've got it all wrong,' she said, making one last appeal to them, but the eyes that met hers were shuttered and hostile.

She picked up her plate and sat down at a nearby table. Her tortilla tasted like cardboard but she forced herself to finish it. The only thing she could do now was to act normally and hope that their hostility would diminish. She could understand their anger. Everyone was a little jumpy about the threat of redundancy at the moment and she conveniently presented herself as a scapegoat.

She finished her meal and walked out of the canteen, making a conscious effort to slow her pace and appear relaxed. It was going to be unpleasant working with such antipathy but she wasn't going to allow it to affect her work. She loved this job. As the weeks passed and she became more confident she loved it all the more. Her probationary period would be over just after

275

Christmas and she'd already decided to stay on. She wasn't going to let this change her mind.

'Thanks, Mum. I love you too. Bye.' Emma replaced the phone, and for the first time since she'd arrived in Spain a wave of homesickness swept over her. It was kind of her mother to ring her up to wish her a happy birthday but somehow it made it worse. Birthdays were special. Her mother had always made a fuss about them, and when she'd gone to university it was a good excuse for a party. Nobody here knew that she was twenty-two today, and they wouldn't have cared if they did.

For a few minutes she allowed herself to wallow in self-pity; it was her birthday, she was allowed to indulge herself a little bit. She hadn't felt like this since she was twelve and the whole class had stopped speaking to her because Jennifer Roberts had told them she'd stolen a pound from her purse. At the time it was as if the world had ended, and she'd begged her mum to let her change schools. Her mum had refused and said that they'd soon realize who was telling the truth. It had seemed the longest week of her life but at the end of it people were talking to her again as though nothing had happened.

Emma recalled the incident as she walked to work. She wasn't so stupid as to think that people here were going to forget what they'd heard about her, but she had to hope that eventually they'd realize it wasn't true or it would cease to matter quite so much to them. She couldn't let them see how much their remarks hurt her, and though her determination to stay and succeed despite everyone's hostility hadn't altered it was much more difficult than she thought it was going to be.

Emma's mood lightened as she pushed open the heavy glass doors of Herrero's and she shifted into work mode. She was working on a leaflet to give to tourists visiting the *bodega* next door, and it had been interesting delving into the archives and picking the older workers' brains for anecdotes.

Luis's Rolls-Royce was already in the car park, she noticed, but there was no sign of him. She also noticed the quiver of disappointment in her stomach as she made this discovery, and her forehead puckered into a frown. With the benefit of hindsight she realized, with regard to her colleagues, that it had been a mistake being friendlier towards Luis. He'd seemed aware of her change of heart almost telepathically and had taken every opportunity to talk to or be close to her.

He seemed hell-bent on proving that he wasn't the ogre the staff at work thought him. Invitations arrived for outside functions that she knew he'd be attending. She went because it was necessary to meet as many people as possible. In her job she was finding that who she knew was equally as important as what she knew. And Luis, it seemed, knew everyone.

She watched him closely as he interacted with people. Surely if he were putting on an act for her benefit then someone would remark how different he was. But nobody said a word. Apparently this charming, good-humoured Luis was the norm for such occasions.

Yesterday, she'd attended a wine-producers' conference. Luis had been a speaker and had been in fine form. As she watched his seemingly effortless performance Emma had felt proud of him. That was ridiculous. How could she feel proud of a man who had kicked her out of his life as unceremoniously as he had? Not for the first time she wondered if she needed her head examined. But if the psychiatrist came she probably wouldn't let him anywhere near her. Luis was becoming like a drug; if she didn't get her daily fix life lacked colour and it was more difficult to cope with the attitude of her colleagues.

The morning ticked past and she had almost finished the final draft of her leaflet when there was a loud rap on the door. Her pen shot upwards, crossing out what she'd just written. She swore softly.

'Did I hear you say, "Come in"?' Luis entered and closed the door behind him. 'Happy birthday, *guapa*!' Smiling, he held out his hands and before she realized what she was doing she'd thrown herself into them. The hardness of his body against her soft curves forced her back to reality.

'Thank you,' she mumbled, pulling away, her body sensitized and tingling along the entire length that had pressed against him. It was a friendly hug she'd sought, not a reminder that the sexual attraction she felt for Luis was as potent as ever.

Luis rested his elbow on her window sill and gazed at her, his mouth curving sensually. It crossed her mind that he knew exactly the havoc his presence caused to all her senses, and she felt her cheeks grow warm.

'So, *chica*, how does it feel to be the grand old age of twenty-two?' he laughed softly.

She shrugged. 'Just a normal day.' She'd meant the remark to be light-hearted, but she couldn't quite keep the disappointment out of her voice.

'Then we shall have to rectify that. You will come with me to lunch. We shall celebrate.'

'Oh, no, I don't think . . .' she said, and watched his face harden.

'Can we not be friends, Emma? I was beginning to think we could. Is it such a daunting prospect spending an hour or so with me?'

'No, but . . .'

'It is all arranged. It was the only present I could think of giving you that I thought you would accept.' He looked at her with such hurt in his eyes that she crumbled.

'I won't be a minute.' She grabbed her bag and raced to the bathroom, where she ran a comb through her hair and gazed at her slightly flushed appearance in the mirror. 'What the hell,' she murmured, slinging her bag over her shoulder and walking back to her room. A lunch with Luis couldn't hurt. It was nice of him to think of her, and she didn't want to cut him out of her life entirely just to please the gossips.

'Where are we going?' she asked as they climbed into the back of the Rolls.

'A surprise,' he answered, his face lighting up with almost boyish enthusiasm.

'Not the villa. I couldn't, Luis-'

'Relax, *guapa*.' He grabbed her arm as she grappled with the door handle. She didn't know where the thought had come from, but it was accompanied by an irrational blind panic.

'I swear to you I am not taking you there. Do you really think I would be so insensitive?'

'I'm sorry.' She cooled her face against the window and attempted to control her errant breathing. 'I still have nightmares sometimes. Fire and horses and your grandfather. It always seems so real. It's stupid after all this time.'

'It's not stupid.' He took her hand and rubbed gently across her wrist with his thumb. It was the most soothing sensation. 'It was a terrible experience,' he whispered, and she closed her eyes and began to relax.

'Poor Emma.' He continued the smooth hypnotic strokes, and she felt her body grow heavy and warm. She could have drifted off to sleep in a few minutes, but she dragged herself back to reality.

'I feel OK now,' she said, gently pulling away from his touch.

'I told María that you would find it difficult coming back to the villa. Since she heard that you'd returned to Spain she has given me no peace about inviting you. She knows that you were never my fiancée, by the way. I confessed everything to her afterwards.'

'And she still wants to see me?'

Luis smiled. 'Of course she does. It was me she was angry with when I told her, not you. Why should knowing you are called Emma and not Amanda make any difference to her?'

Emma stared at him. It made all the difference in the world. She wouldn't have been surprised if María had wanted nothing more to do with her, and she was touched by the housekeeper's generous nature.

'Tell her I'd love to see her again. Perhaps she'd be able to visit me?'

Luis nodded. 'She'd like that. Carlos can bring her. I'll tell her to ring you and arrange it.'

The car slowed and Emma glanced out of the window. A wry smile formed on her lips. Where had Luis chosen to take her for lunch? Where else but Jerez's premier hotel.

Although she was growing more accustomed to visiting hotels like these in a work capacity, Emma always found the splendour and magnificence of such places slightly intimidating. She accepted Luis's arm without hesitation as they walked up the marble steps to the entrance. At least, as Brad would say, she looked the part; she'd decided to wear her new lavender-coloured suit this morning to cheer herself up.

'Señor Quevedo. It is always a pleasure to see you.' The manager, a beaming, corpulent man, dressed in a severe black suit walked forward to greet them. 'If you would kindly follow me, I shall take you to your table, *señores*.'

He led them to a lift, and Emma was puzzled when it jolted to a halt to find herself stepping out into the open air. She stared around in astonishment at her surroundings, aware that Luis and the manager were watching her closely.

'This is amazing! I've never been anywhere like this!' she said finally, her face radiant with pleasure. They were standing in the middle of a beautiful rooftop garden where the heady aroma of roses, bougainvillaea, and herbs assailed her senses. Underneath the shade of a vine, commanding a spectacular view over Jerez, a table for two was laid.

'Your table is ready, *señorita*,' said the manager, clearly gratified with her reaction.

'Lovely.'

Luis walked over to the table, took a bottle of

champagne out of an ice bucket and poured her a glass. 'Happy birthday, Emma,' he said, handing it to her.

The bubbles fizzed and exploded on her tongue, then travelled through her blood stream, lifting her mood and making her feel more light-hearted than she'd been for a long time.

'This is perfect.' She waved her hand, encompassing the garden, the view, and the plate of exotic fruit that a waiter had placed before her.

Luis opened his napkin with a deft flick of his wrist and smiled.

'Is this where you wine and dine all your women?' she joked, then instantly regretted it. The open countenance snapped shut, leaving a thunderous mask in its place.

'I'm sorry. Don't answer that. It's none of my business.'

He speared a slice of melon, lifted it to his mouth, and chewed it slowly, all the while staring deep into her eyes. It was as if he had hypnotized her. She stared back, incapable of touching her own food.

'This is the chef's private garden,' he said eventually. His tone was soft and even, masking the anger that she knew simmered below the surface. 'He comes up here to unwind, and guards his privacy jealously. It took a great deal of persuasion before he would agree for us to use it today. No one, as far as I am aware, has ever been granted that privilege. It was meant to be special: for a special lady on her special day.'

'And now I've spoiled it all. I'm good at that.' She grabbed her glass and finished her drink, hoping to recapture her previous gaiety that had spluttered out like a damp firework.

'It is not spoiled.' Luis reached over and kissed her hand, then replaced it gently on the tablecloth. 'You simply take me aback some-times with your statements and your perception of me.'

'I'm sorry.'

Luis shrugged. 'Not knowing what you are going to say next is part of your fascination.'

As he refilled her glass, Emma tried to decide if he was being sarcastic, then gave up. The champagne was having its desired effect. Her mood was again turning mellow and for now she'd treat the remark as flattery. She could analyze it tomorrow.

'Are you trying to fatten me up?' she asked, as chicken breasts in a thick creamy sauce and several tureens of vegetables were placed on the table.

'I'm afraid Felipe never did get the hang of *nouvelle cuisine*,' laughed Luis. 'To be fair to him he did ask if you were one of those ladies who were constantly dieting. I said no.'

'So chomp along with Miss Blobby,' she grinned, scooping an artichoke on to her plate and trying to remember which part of it was edible. Just the heart, she decided, probing it with her knife.

'You are delightful.' He took off his jacket and draped it across the back of his chair. His tie was next and this was thrown unceremoniously to one side. Thankfully he stopped at that.

'For a moment there I thought I was getting the Chippendales for my birthday,' she giggled to mask her confusion. A doctor feeling her wildly racing pulse and sounding her erratically beating heart would probably have prescribed bed rest.

'What is the Chippendales?'

'Who, and you can find out the answer to that one yourself.' She cut another slice of chicken and placed it in her mouth. 'Oh!' She closed her eyes in appreciation. 'This is food to die for.'

'It's good to see you happy, *guapa*. I feel so responsible for taking that away from you.'

The hand holding her fork began to shake and Emma let it drop to her plate with a clatter. 'Please, Luis, not today. We have to talk about it some time, I suppose, but not on my birthday. I don't want to spoil it. Tell me how you got on at the London office. Did you solve that problem with your buyers?'

A frown clouded Luis's expression, but it was momentary. He began telling her about the mix-up over orders and how they'd eventually tracked the shipment to Hull. As she listened she relaxed again. His was a voice that could recite the telephone directory and make it sound interesting.

'That's enough about me.' He pushed his plate away and refilled her glass. 'What about you, Emma? Are you happy at Herrero's?'

'I love the work.' She traced her finger slowly around the rim of her glass.

'But?'

'Why does there have to be a but?'

'The tone of your voice, your manner, the sadness in your eyes. What is it, *guapa*?'

'The people. I don't think they'll ever accept me. Oh, forget I said that, I sound such a wimp. They will in the end, I'm sure.'

'I'm certain that they will also. My impressions were that they had already. Haven't I seen them laughing and sharing jokes with you?'

'Señor Jiménez hasn't said anything, then?'

'About what, *guapa*? He speaks to me about work. I don't pay him to report on your movements.'

'Señor Bécquer?'

Luis shrugged. 'I pay him to run Quevedo's. At the moment most of my energy is taken up with Herrero's which, as you know, is going through a difficult period.'

Emma chased a breadcrumb around the table with her fingertip.

'What is it? This is not like you, Emma. Normally if you have something to say you hit me with it between the eyes.'

'Do I?'

'You most certainly do.'

'Well, here goes, then. The staff at Herrero's weren't too chuffed to find out that I'd been planted there as a spy to report on their movements and to tell you which of them wasted the most time and should be sacked.'

'You're not making any sense, Emma.'

'That's what they think. At least that's what they've thought since Señor Bécquer announced to everybody that I was your fiancée.'

Luis's reaction was gratifying; she was left in no doubt that he'd known nothing about the situation until now. When he stopped looking as if she had actually smacked him between the eyes he mimicked the action himself and slapped his palm harshly against his forehead.

'What an idiot I am! It never occurred to me that Alfonso and you had met before. Of course. At the villa. Idiot! Idiot! Idiot!' He emphasized the last words with successive blows to his head, and then he stared at his empty plate as though it would give him the answer he was looking for.

'I don't regret deceiving Grandfather, but it seems that the fates have decreed that I should be continually reminded of it.' He looked up. 'You must come and work at Quevedo's. You'll be happy there, Emma. The people are content and work hard. You can sense the different atmosphere the moment you enter the building.'

Emma shook her head. 'It's my problem, Luis. I'll get there in the end.'

'I feel responsible. It is impossible working under such conditions.'

'Difficult, not impossible.'

'You are the one who is difficult. Yes, and impossible.' His dark eyes flashed angrily. 'Why won't you ever accept my help, Emma?'

'Why did you buy a company that was doing as badly as Herrero's?'

'Don't change the subject!'

'I'm not. Answer the question.'

'I've already told you – for the challenge.'

'And how will you feel when it stops losing money and starts showing a profit?'

'You know how I'll feel.'

'Exactly. And if you were granted three wishes, would one of them be to have Herrero's as the top sherry producer tomorrow without you having to lift a finger?'

He stared at her, not answering.

'You wouldn't, would you, Luis? You'd feel cheated. People would congratulate you on your success and it would mean zilch.'

He sighed. 'I begin to follow, but it doesn't alter the fact that the position you are in is my fault. My lack of foresight has made your working life unbearable, therefore it is my duty to do something about it.'

Emma shook her head. 'You've done enough. I'm still not convinced that I would have got a job as good as this one on my own. That rankles, but there's nothing I can do about it. I think I know now that you were doing it to make amends and not just to meddle in my life. But that's what it is, Luis – it's my life – and if you take away all the obstacles in my path then what have I to feel proud of when I make a success of it? Don't get me wrong, I'm not a masochist. I don't go around looking for trouble. I'd much rather this hadn't happened, but it has. I can't change it but I'm damn well not going to let it beat me.'

'Quite a speech.' His eyes glowed warmly with amusement.

'If you laugh at me I'll hit you,' she hissed.

'I'm not laughing at you, *guapa*. I'm laughing at myself, at my preconceptions, and how you shatter them with the force of a sledgehammer.'

'Such as?'

'Such as I always assumed our attraction was due to us being total opposites. Now I see we are not so different after all.'

'I think I'd argue with that.'

'I'm sure you would, *guapa*, but if you'll excuse me for a moment I must signal the waiter. The poor man has been waiting in the full sun for the past five minutes.'

'You are ready for dessert, *señores*?' The waiter approached with alacrity.

'Oh, gosh, I don't think I could eat another thing. Tell the chef everything was wonderful.

There aren't many people who can beat me, but he has.'

'Coffee?'

Emma shook her head.

'A brandy each to finish, then,' said Luis. Emma was about to shake her head, but the waiter had taken it as a command and had walked away.

'If I drink this I'll be in no fit state to do anything this afternoon,' said Emma when her drink arrived.

'Then I shall give you the afternoon off. Nobody should have to work more than half a day on their birthday.'

'You're doing it again, Luis. Why should I be any different from anybody else?'

'Because you are, *guapa*. You're totally different from anyone I have ever met.' He caught her frown and raised his hands in mock surrender. 'All right. If it pleases you I shall decree it. I'll have them write it in that rule book of theirs. That should make me more popular, don't you think?'

Emma watched as he hooked his feet on to a wall and reclined in his chair. She couldn't tell if he was joking or not.

'Good food, good company, and good brandy to finish. What more could a man ask of life?' he said, raising his glass to her.

'You're in a good mood.'

'A remarkably good mood. You are stimulating company, *guapa*. I haven't enjoyed a lunch so much for a long time.'

'Nor me,' she said, and she wasn't entirely referring to the food. The sight of his fit, lean physique barely a metre away was also appetizing, and deeply disturbing. The thoughts running through her brain would definitely not qualify for a PG certificate. She took a sip of her drink in an effort to dispel them, and absent-mindedly ran the fingers of her free hand across a rosemary bush. The pungent aroma that wafted upwards succeeded in distracting her.

'I could grow some herbs on my balcony. I hadn't thought of it before.' She rubbed a leaf between finger and thumb to release its volatile oil. 'Mmm, rosemary would be nice. The chef won't miss a bit, will he?' she said, snapping a piece off and putting it in her pocket. 'It might root.'

Luis started to laugh. 'As I said – like no one else. When María comes to visit you I'll tell her to bring some cuttings.'

'That'd be great,' she said, and he laughed louder.

'What's so funny?

'You, Emma. Don't ever change.'

Not sure if she cared to be laughed at by Luis, she scowled at him, but she couldn't take offence with the dark eyes glowing at her so warmly, so she changed it to a smile.

'I suppose we should go.' Luis rose to his feet

and she felt the regret in his voice.

'Can I take a quick look round first? I won't be a minute.'

'Take your time, *guapa*. There's no rush.' He sat down again under the dappled shade of the vine, but she felt his eyes follow her as she walked around sniffing lavender and roses and admiring the way the chef had crammed so many different plants together in such a small place.

'Right. I'm ready.' She leaned against a clematis-covered pillar and breathed in the scents of the garden, closing her eyes in an attempt to fix the fragrance in her mind.

When she opened them again Luis was standing only inches away from her. She knew he was there. His own subtle fragrance had mingled with the others and she was aware of the heat emanating from him. It wasn't possible, but she felt that if she touched him she'd scorch her fingers.

'Beautiful,' he murmured, his eyes dilated to dark fathomless pools, drawing her deeper and deeper into their dangerous currents. She took a step back, but escape was blocked by the clematis.

'Luis, I – ' She got no further before his warm, sensual lips descended, forcing her own open with one skilful kiss. A tremor of anticipation vibrated through her body, followed by a warm, pulsating ache deep within her. Of all the men she'd ever met why was it only Luis who could trigger such a reaction? The scents of the garden diminished; all she was aware of was warm, virile male.

She lifted her arms, twined them round his neck and gave herself up to the magic of his kiss. It was as if her body had been in limbo since his last embrace and he was leading her back to the light.

Too soon it ended. He tore his lips from hers with a groan, but held her body in a vice-like grip against his. 'Emma, Emma,' he whispered into the golden strands of her hair. 'Do you have any idea of what you do to me, *guapa*?'

Emma could feel an urgent hardness pressed against her stomach. She thought she had a fair idea of the effect she was having on him. So why had he stopped?

'Come.' There was a haunted, faraway look in his eyes as he took her hand and pulled her after him. The aftermath of the kiss had left her too languid and dreamy to protest, and she followed him meekly to the entrance of the roof garden. They went down one flight of steps and then another that brought them to a small patio dotted with tubs of flowers.

By this time her brain was starting to function again. She was pleased they were taking the stairs rather than the lift. It gave her time to unscramble her thoughts. When they reached the foyer she wouldn't look quite so spaced-out.

What was the purpose of that kiss? Was it

another one of Luis's experiments? Was he trying to prove that he could turn her to jelly in less than thirty seconds? Whatever his purpose had been it was probably as well that he'd stopped when he had. No man should be able to wield such power over a woman.

They came to a halt before a low wall. Emma had thought Luis knew the way, but it seemed he was as lost as she was. 'It's a dead end,' she smiled, making to turn back, but he restrained her. To their left were large French windows which overlooked the patio. She stared blankly at him as he took a key out of his pocket and opened them.

'It's all right, Emma,' he soothed as the penny dropped, and she remained standing stiffly outside, her blue eyes wide with apprehension. She moved imperceptibly backwards, but not quickly enough. Before she could gather her senses, Luis lifted her off her feet and carried her through an opulently furnished suite into an equally sumptuous bedroom, where he gently put her down.

'No.' She shook her head vigorously. 'What do you think I am?'

'I think you are the most wonderful woman I have ever met,' he said, folding his arms around her. 'Relax, *chica*, I promise not to do anything unless you want me to. I want to kiss you again, but this time in private without a waiter's prying eyes on us.'

She should have laughed and asked him if he thought she'd been born yesterday. If it had been Brad or José or any other male standing there she would have. But it was Luis gazing at her with his dark hypnotic eyes, tempting her with his irresistible mouth hovering above her own.

Afterwards, she couldn't recall who made the first move, whether he came to her or she strained to him, but seconds later they were kissing as if the three-minute warning had sounded and the end of the world was imminent. Her defences lay in ruins; her mouth opened for his plundering tongue which shamelessly ransacked any lingering shred of resistance.

'If anyone could bottle the taste of you, *guapa*, they'd become a billionaire overnight,' he gasped as he broke for air.

Ditto, thought Emma, closing her eyes as his lips kissed a painfully sweet trail down her neck. They lingered in the hollow of her neck and there they caused havoc. The sensations ricocheting through her body were both excruciating and erotic. It was too much and she begged him to stop. She gazed up at him sheepishly, every nerve-end on fire and her face glowing as if she'd completed a five-mile jog.

'Ticklish?' he murmured, and she nodded, but she saw from the curve of his lips that he suspected the true reason. So that was a Gspot? She wondered vaguely from the fuddled depths of her brain if she had any more, and whether they became less sensitive with use.

She didn't have to wonder for long. He kissed her again, more gently, but this time proving that his fingers were equally as dexterous as his tongue. They stroked her face, her hair, her neck, and moved slowly downwards to open the two buttons of her jacket.

She offered no resistance as he slipped the jacket from her shoulders and even lifted her arms so he could divest her of the lace camisole underneath more easily.

'Exquisite.' He cupped her breasts and began a painfully sweet massage of their delicate buds. His kiss became more demanding and she answered by scraping her fingers down the taut muscles of his back and pressing herself urgently against the hard contours of his body. Her flesh ached to be pressed against this potent male body, and she tore at his shirt in an effort to remove that barrier.

'At last,' she sighed when they were naked above the waist and he clasped her to him. She exulted in their differences: the dark skin next to golden; her soft curves moulded around the hard musculature of his chest; his masculinity so urgently aroused, and her femininity, hidden but equally as demanding.

'You are perfect. Totally perfect,' he said, stepping away slightly and gazing at her with midnight-black eyes. Emma glanced up shyly and made to cover her breasts, but when she saw the way he was looking at her, with total adoration, she dropped them to her sides and smiled. For the first time in her life she felt perfect. Her breasts, slightly too large for her own liking, were firm and voluptuous, and her pale skin, which branded her instantly as a foreigner in this southern land, was delicate and feminine.

Luis stepped towards her and scooped up her breasts, weighing them with the palm of his hands. Then he kissed each in turn before taking one bud into his mouth and suckling it hungrily.

'Luis.' She threaded her fingers through the lustrous strands of his hair and held fast in case the sensation became too much and she should fall. Just when she thought she could take no more he transferred his attention to the other breast. The feeling of relief lasted only seconds before his suckling took her to an exquisite peak of wanting and she dragged his head away.

'Emma – beautiful girl, beautiful woman,' he murmured cryptically as he hooked an arm underneath her and carried her to the bed. Her skirt and underwear were removed in an instant and he tore off the last of his clothes, holding her in his gaze while he did so.

'Oh, gosh,' she muttered as she viewed his magnificent maleness. Experienced through the confines of his clothes it had excited her, but now she turned her eyes away. Having only a vague idea of her inner proportions, its size seemed daunting. A tiny splinter of fear pricked the euphoria that had surrounded her like a bubble up to this point.

'It's huge,' she said as he lay down beside her.

'Thank you,' he laughed softly, 'but there is no need to flatter me, Emma.'

'No, really,' she said, and he lifted himself on one elbow and studied her face.

'It is not so big,' he said gently. 'And even if it were, Nature is a wonderful thing; she has built woman to accommodate all shapes and sizes of man.'

That was more or less what Emma had read; she hoped it was the truth. She had no more time for wondering as he pulled her to him and his mouth and hands smoothed away her fears. Her body seemed so responsive to his touch now that he only had to rub his thumb roughly over her nipple for it to recall all former sensations that he'd caused her and replay them in glorious colour.

She didn't think it was possible to want him more than she already did until his fingers brushed over the blonde strands between her legs then tentatively delved deeper. A fierce surge of longing radiated through every nerve in her body, and she heard the gurgle of triumph in his throat as he encountered the hidden evidence of her arousal. His fingers began an intimate journey of discovery, caressing and probing, smoothing and stretching, until she thought she would explode with the ecstasy of it. But each time she began to lose control Luis subtly changed technique, and the delicious torture began all over again.

'Please,' she moaned, drawing him to her. Her body was screaming for release and she knew that he was the only one who could give it.

He crouched above her on all fours. 'What is it that you want, *guapa*?' he enquired, teasing.

'You. Oh, I want you,' she said, clawing him to her.

'I believe you,' he said, resisting her efforts to move him. 'Do you want me to use protection, Emma?'

'Protection?' She stared at him, as uncomprehending as if he'd asked whether she'd care to dance the can-can.

'Oh, yes. Of course I do,' she said as she saw the packet he withdrew from the bedside table. Did she have a brain? She slumped back on the bed to consider. After everything she'd read about AIDS, after the years of brainwashing she'd endured from her mother, how could something so important have completely slipped her mind?

There was no time for further thought as Luis loomed over her, his weight supported by his elbows. She gasped slightly as he eased her legs apart, but there was no time for nerves as he pushed himself inside her. There was a sharp pain and she cried out. It was masked slightly by the deep groan he emitted.

'I know, Emma. I've never felt anything like this before either.' His eyes were tightly closed, his muscles were rigid, and he appeared to be concentrating deeply. 'Please don't move. I shall gain control in a second.'

Emma lay still and marvelled at the moment. She was no longer a virgin, there was no longer any pain, and the man she wanted more than anyone else in the whole world was part of her. He was joined to her and the sensation had overpowered him.

A surge of power flooded through her. Her body was capable of this. She stirred slowly beneath him and the movement caused ripples of delight to course through her.

He opened his eyes and smiled, a warm, glowing smile like sunshine after weeks of rain. 'Have I told you before how beautiful you are?' he whispered, before bending to kiss her again. His tongue mimicked another part of him as it moved at first slowly and luxuriously then embarked on a more thorough, urgent exploration.

From the first, Emma's eyes snapped shut. Nothing had prepared her for the intensity of this experience. All previous caresses paled into insignificance as she hurtled headlong to oblivion. At the brink, she hesitated. She hovered there for a full minute in an agony of expectation and frustration. Her body demanded release, and though she felt she might die when that happened she surrendered willingly to its command. Whatever happened she couldn't stay in her present state any longer.

Above her, she sensed Luis losing control; he pounded into her, his breathing hot and rapid, his body glowing with perspiration. It was his excitement that finally pushed her over the edge, his release that triggered her own.

She dug her nails into his back and shouted his name as she soared into space and her body exploded into thousands of glorious glittering atoms.

'Emma,' he groaned, slumping on top of her. 'I love you. I love you so much, *guapa*.'

Pinioned to the bed by his dead-weight, she traced her fingertips lightly down his spine and smiled. What a thing this making love was. At last she knew what all the fuss was about; no drug on earth could guarantee such a high and create such a relaxed euphoric aftermath.

'I'm sorry, I'm squashing you.' Luis stirred, then rolled carefully off her. She experienced a moment's dreadful abandonment before he drew her to him with one hand while he flicked the duvet over them both with the other. She snuggled into him, aware of their combined scent, headier and more potent than any perfume.

'Never have I felt anything like that,' he said, kissing her brow, her cheeks, her hair, anywhere his lips could reach. 'Your boyfriend is a good teacher.'

'Mmm,' she murmured, drifting away on a cloud of happiness, 'he certainly is.' She thought he was joking, referring to himself, then it struck her that he meant Brad.

'Who are you talking about?' she asked, but there was no answer. Deep rhythmic breathing and a face that resembled a child's in its vulnerability confirmed that he'd fallen asleep.

Emma gazed at him for a long time before sighing and resting her head once again on his chest. If she'd been in any doubt before she was in none now: she loved him. In capturing her body he'd captured her soul. Wrapped in that certainty, she listened to the slow, regular thudding of his heart, and drifted off to sleep.

Why she should wake later and feel like Cinderella on the stroke of midnight was a mystery.

CHAPTER 17

It was several seconds before Emma recalled where she was. Her mouth was parched and her head felt fuzzy – champagne, birthday, lunch, Luis. Luis! Had it been a dream? No, the all too real presence of her sleeping companion confirmed that her active imagination couldn't be blamed for the erotic images springing into her mind.

She fumbled for her watch. Twenty past four. Good grief, what was she doing here? She recalled a meeting arranged for three o'clock, and groaned. What would they say at reception? 'I'm sorry, Señor Márquez, Señorita Blackmore went to lunch with Señor Quevedo and she hasn't come back yet.' Then 'No, *señor*, I'm afraid she still hasn't returned. I'll get her to ring you the second she comes in.'

But she wouldn't be coming in this afternoon. And the reason? She was lying in a hotel bed with the managing director of the company.

She turned on her side and gazed at the sleeping form of her lover. Physically, he was gorgeous, and it took all her self-control not to reach out and run her fingers over the relaxed muscles of his back. They would tense at her touch, she knew, thrilling her with their hardness and strength.

But she didn't want him to wake up. Not yet. She needed time to think. Time to come to terms with the situation she found herself in.

And what exactly was that? Could it be that after an excellent lunch with one of his employees Luis Quevedo had skipped dessert, deciding there might be something tastier on the menu? He'd fancied her and taken her afterwards as easily as unwrapping an after-dinner mint. Her cheeks burned as she realized how simple it had been for him.

Hadn't he once said that the more difficult a challenge was the more satisfaction he felt? She gritted her teeth. She must have represented a difficulty factor of minus one. And the love-making? Her mouth relaxed and her body tingled as she thought of it. Like Luis it had been physically perfect and, for her at least, spiritually so.

But what did it mean to him? There was no doubt he'd enjoyed it. Again her body tingled as she recalled his ardour and enthusiasm. But was it special for him? He'd told her so. He'd even told her he loved her at one point, but wasn't that what all men did? According to her mother, her father had declared his undying love to her the night before he'd left for good.

She had to face it: she was another in a long line of Quevedo conquests, something she'd sworn never to be. Perhaps she meant more to him than the others? Even as she thought it she realized she was fooling herself. Hadn't he brutally kicked her out of his life once already?

Carefully, she slipped out of bed and gathered up her scattered clothes. If she stayed here Luis would wake up and they'd make love again. Of course it would be wonderful; she could arouse herself instantly just by thinking about it. And then what? 'Thank you, Emma, that was most pleasant. I'll take you home'? It was a possibility, but she dismissed it; the physical attraction that sizzled between them was deeper than that.

So how long would their relationship last? A week? A month? A year? His new secretary had already been given the boot after only six weeks in the job. Was that what he would do to her? Kick her out of her job when she became a personal embarrassment?

With a sigh, she retrieved her camisole from under the bed and crept to the *ensuite* bathroom. All manner of thoughts were bombarding her brain. She needed to get away from Luis so that she could sort them out and think more clearly. It was a pity she hadn't given any of them a thought a few hours ago.

'Where are you going? Come back to bed, *guapa*. I'm sorry, I must have dropped to sleep.' The deep caressing tones of her lover froze her in her tracks, but glancing at the bed she saw that he was only half awake.

'I'm just going to the bathroom,' she whispered.

'Don't be long. We've only just begun.'

Emma shivered at the promise in his voice. What in heaven's name did he do for an encore? Whatever it was she wasn't strong enough to face it. He'd made a coward of her, and she had to get out before she fell any deeper in love with him.

She studied herself in the mirror above the washbasin. One glance at her face and the whole of Jerez would know what she'd been doing. She splashed it continually with cold water until the flushed vacant expression changed into something more presentable.

Luckily her suit was of crease-resistant fabric and didn't look as though she'd spent the night in it. She dressed quickly and drew her fingers through her hair as a final touch. She'd pass. If she ever managed to get out of here, that was.

From the doorway, Luis looked as if he'd fallen asleep again. She tiptoed past the bed and breathed a sigh of relief. Confrontation, in her highly emotional state, was something she wanted to avoid.

'At last,' he murmured. He sat up, but the

smile on his face quickly turned to a frown as he took in her appearance and the look of horror that sprang to her face.

'Emma,' he growled. He threw back the covers and leaped out of bed, but she was too quick for him. She took off for the door as though the devil himself was at her heels, and succeeded in opening and slamming it just as his arm came out to grab her.

Luis was capable of many things, but she gambled that running naked through hotel corridors wasn't one of them. It wouldn't take him long to dress, though, and she looked around frantically for the lift. It was directly opposite, and she gave thanks to the Almighty as it purred open seconds after she punched the button.

'Ground floor, please,' she gasped, and when the boy looked bemused by her agitation she pushed past him and thumped the button herself.

'I'm in a bit of a hurry,' she apologized as soon as the doors had safely closed again. Less than a minute later they opened on the ground floor.

'Thanks,' she said and darted out, belatedly wondering if she should have tipped the boy. But she'd done all the work, she thought, suppressing the urge to giggle as the farcical element of the situation hit her.

It seemed that everyone was staring at her as she walked through the foyer. She told herself they weren't, and forced herself not to take to her heels and run; it would be all too easy to allow hysteria to take over.

At last she was standing on the steps of the hotel. She'd made it. The glare of the sunlight blinded her for several moments as she peered around in vain for a taxi. The doorman signalled to her that he would call one, but she ignored him. It would take too long; Luis would be down at any moment. Already she was beginning to feel totally stupid for running away. She couldn't face Luis now.

Across the road, about a hundred yards away, Emma could see the Rolls-Royce parked in the shade. There was no alternative. She raced over and rapped on the window. Carlos was stretched across both front seats, fast asleep.

'Take me home, please, Carlos,' she said, as he sat up and rubbed his eyes.

'Of course, *señorita*. I'm sorry. I didn't expect you. Señor Luis usually phones me and I pick him up at the entrance to the hotel.'

Emma clenched her fist as she wondered just how regular an occurrence that was.

'Oh, I didn't want to wake him, Carlos. He'd fallen asleep,' she answered, amazing herself at how light her tone sounded.

Carlos didn't seem to think anything was amiss. He started the car and pulled out into the traffic while she sighed with relief. She rested her cheek thankfully against the cool leather upholstery and tried to relax. She'd almost succeeded when the ringing of the car phone jangled the silence and made her jump.

'Will you answer it or shall I stop the car?' Carlos turned to her, puzzled. He was probably wondering why she was staring at the phone as if it were an unexploded bomb.

'It's Luis,' she said, still not attempting to pick up the receiver.

'Then I think one of us should answer it,' the man said deliberately. 'He will be angry if we don't.'

The car slowed and Emma grabbed the receiver. 'Hello,' she said, annoyed at how her voice wavered.

'What are you doing, Emma?' His voice had the tone of a kindly uncle patiently dealing with a recalcitrant child.

'Carlos is driving me home. I couldn't find a taxi.'

'Come back, Emma. I need to talk to you.'

'No.' It might have been what he needed but it was the last thing she did. 'Please, Luis, I can't.' She replaced the receiver and thankfully it remained silent during the short drive to her apartment.

'Thank you, Carlos, the *señor* is waiting for you at the hotel.' She climbed out of the car and hurried up the four flights of steps to her home. With a sigh of relief she closed the door behind her and breathed in the familiar safe scent of her living room. This was one birthday she'd certainly never forget. What was needed now was a warm shower, then peace and quiet to put the events of the day into perspective.

The hammering on her door began while she was shampooing her hair. It was still thudding insistently when she walked, dripping, into her living room. 'Go away! Leave me alone!' she shouted, and it stopped.

'I need to talk to you, Emma.'

She scrubbed furiously at her hair with a towel. Need. Need. Always Luis's need. Did he ever consider hers?

'I don't want to talk to you.'

'Come on, *guapa*, this is ridiculous. Let me in. Don't be so childish.'

The accusation stung, probably because it was the truth. But how could she tell him that she was afraid of letting him in because she knew if she did she wouldn't be able to resist him? She needed time to build up her defences, to create a shell around her that he couldn't penetrate.

'We need to talk about us. About our future,' he insisted.

'There is no us! It was a mistake! I was drunk!' she yelled.

'I can't believe you're saying this. Open the door so I can look in your eyes while you repeat it.'

'Go to hell!'

'Open the door, Emma. What are you afraid of? All I want to do is talk to you.'

'Oh, yeah? And all you wanted to do when you took me into your hotel room was to kiss me. Remember?'

There was silence, then what sounded like a deep sigh. 'I'm sorry, you have reason to be annoyed, *guapa*, but I did keep my promise to you. Whatever happened afterwards was because you desired it.'

Emma snorted with derision. 'Oh, don't worry, Luis, I'm not crying rape. You needn't live in fear of the police hammering on your door and carting you away.'

'That's the last thing I would have worried about,' he answered crisply.

'Sorry. Silly me. I forgot you were Mister Big around here. You'd simply have paid them to hush it all up wouldn't you?'

His fist crashed down on the door and he swore loudly. Emma regretted her words the instant she said them, but she didn't regret the fact that there was a solid wooden door between them.

'Does it amuse you to make me lose my temper, Emma?' His voice sounded sad, and she could imagine the hurt look he was able to project into his eyes for her benefit. 'I'm sure you knew what I meant. I wasn't worried about the police coming to the villa because I knew you weren't the type of woman to call them.'

An apology sprang to her lips, but she clamped her hand tightly over her mouth to stop it slipping out. 'Just go, Luis,' she said when she'd gained control. 'I'm not going to open the door. You can stay there all night and I'll not change my mind.'

'Very well,' he replied, and relief flooded through her until she heard what came next. 'I shall contact Carlos to bring me a sleeping bag and some refreshment. I shall remain in your doorway until you come out. I will discuss my feelings with you, Emma, but only to your face. I'm damned if I'm going to shout them through this door!'

Emma ran into her bedroom and threw herself on to the bed. 'Stupid! Stupid! Stupid!' she yelled as she pummelled her pillow. What had she done? She'd only issued a challenge to a man who thrived on them. There was no doubt in her mind that he was capable of staying outside all night. So who was being childish now?

She picked up her clothes and got dressed. If that was what he wanted to do, then let him. She wouldn't say another word to him. She'd ignore him. Maybe that would irritate him enough to go away.

She walked back into the living room and began a letter to her mother, but she couldn't concentrate and pushed it to one side. She picked up a book, but it might have been an advanced guide to nuclear physics for all the sense it made to her fuddled brain. The room was too quiet. She imagined she heard the sound of Luis's breathing; it made the tiny hairs at the back of her neck prickle. She switched on the television for distraction, but even through the bubbly chatter of a game show she was aware of Luis's lurking presence. It was intolerable. It was harassment. She clasped her arms tightly around her body and stalked backwards and forwards across her living room. She had to get rid of him.

'What more do you want, Luis?' she shouted, checking through the peephole on her door that he was still there. He was. He was leaning against the wall with his hands in his pockets, staring at the ground.

'We've had sex. It was an experiment.' Yeah, that was good, it had just come to her. He'd told her once that she was an experiment, and it had hurt. See what he felt like when the shoe was on the other foot.

'I wanted to see if you were better than Brad.' That had hurt as well, the way he'd assumed they were sleeping together. Had he thought she was fair game now she was soiled goods?

She dug her fingernails into her palms to steel herself for the final insult. It was as well there was a door between them; she'd never have had the nerve to say it to his face.

'And guess what? You weren't. Why do you think I couldn't get out of there fast enough? Stop making a fool of yourself, Luis. Go away. I don't want you.'

She turned and ran into her bedroom and curled up on the duvet. The bed shook to her sobs. Now he'd hate her and leave her alone. Wasn't that what she wanted? Somehow it didn't seem so clear any more. What had happened to her that she was capable of lying and hurting another human being like that? He'd pushed her into it, but it was no excuse.

Wiping a hand across her eyes to dry her tears, she rolled off the bed. She'd apologize, but ask him firmly to go and leave her alone. One thing was certain: with her eyes puffed up like Yorkshire puddings, he wouldn't want to go to bed with her again tonight.

'I'm sorry, Luis . . .' She opened the door but spoke to herself. Her plan had worked. He'd gone.

CHAPTER 18

It was fair to say that Emma was a nervous wreck the morning of the next management meeting. It would have been better if she could have seen Luis beforehand, but he hadn't been in Herrero's since her birthday. According to Señor Jiménez there was an urgent problem at Quevedo's that needed his attention.

Perhaps he wouldn't come this morning if things were so bad at Quevedo's. She offered up a prayer as she kept vigil at her window overlooking the car park. At a quarter past ten the Rolls purred to a stop and Luis stepped out. God was obviously in need of a hearing aid.

She rushed to the loo, then raced back to her room to retrieve her folder. Her palms were damp and she wiped them on the inside of her jacket. Her folder shook as she picked it up and she took several deep breaths before stepping out into the corridor once more. Well done, Luis, he'd made her the same as all his other employees – totally terrified of him.

What had possessed her to insult him the way she had? It would have been bad enough doing it to any man, but to insult a red-blooded Latin male in such a way was tantamount to a death wish. Listening to the Spanish, you'd think they'd invented sex. Many of them would rather suffer the loss of a limb than a slur on their manhood.

She sat down next to Señor Jiménez. Her mouth was dry and she would have liked a drink of water, but she didn't dare pick up the glass for fear of spilling it.

At half past ten precisely, Luis walked into the boardroom. There were dark circles under his eyes and he looked tired. Whatever the problem was at Quevedo's it must be serious.

Not having the courage to meet his eyes, Emma stared at the table as he extended a general greeting to those assembled. As was his wont he ploughed straight into the meeting, but without the usual autocratic style that made so many of his staff quake. People visibly relaxed, but Emma wasn't one of them. She felt sure that Luis would exact some kind of revenge for her humiliating him. She was only surprised he hadn't done it already.

He waited until the end of the meeting. Most people had packed up and gone, but those who hadn't seemed in no hurry to leave when Luis held out an arm to halt her own escape from the room. 'A word if you please, *señorita*,' he said, halting her as effectively with the dark sombre glint of his eyes.

'Perhaps you could explain this?' He threw her a letter. It was a complaint from Vicente Márquez about her missing an appointment with him. It had caused him a great deal of inconvenience, it said, and she hadn't even had the courtesy to ring and cancel. This was the first time he'd ever had occasion to complain about any employee of Herrero's; they were usually so reliable etc etc . . .

Emma gritted her teeth. She'd phoned Márquez first thing the next morning and followed it up with a letter of apology, but the man was a friend of Eduardo Valera's. She'd bet what was left of her credit card limit that Valera had a hand in this. He was staring at her now, a triumphant grin on his face.

But why should Luis make an issue out of it? The reason she'd missed the meeting was because he'd taken her to bed. He wouldn't exactly appear a super-hero if she announced the fact. Of course! Her mouth curved as she scanned the letter again. The swine had deliberately omitted the date of the meeting, Luis had taken the bait, and Vicente Márquez had earned himself a golden spoon for stirring.

'I fail to see any cause for amusement.' Luis's voice was quiet, calm, and deadly. She glanced at him but it was like looking at a statue. His eyes

317

seemed dead and his features expressionless. 'It is not a good idea to antagonize the press, Señorita Blackmore, especially with the position you hold in this company. I shall overlook it this time, but in future please ensure that having friends to stay does not interfere with your work.'

Emma stared at him in disbelief. So that was what he thought. He'd immediately jumped to the conclusion that she'd skipped a meeting to be with Brad. 'The meeting was scheduled for last Wednesday,' she said, as calmly as she was able.

Luis frowned. 'I see, so what is your reason for missing it?'

A rush of anger tornadoed through her. Last Wednesday! she wanted to scream. When you showed me how making love was the most beautiful experience in this world. In her mind she leapt across the table and smacked him in the mouth. The bastard had forgotten! She'd been filled with remorse about hurting him, when all the time he'd simply shrugged his shoulders and filed her in his dossier of sexual experiences best forgotten.

'I'd be grateful for an answer, *señorita*.' His tone was well modulated, with only the faintest hint of impatience. It must have taken years to perfect.

'Last Wednesday,' she repeated. 'Ring any bells?' Her tone was sharp and brittle. It took no time at all to perfect.

This time, his reaction was gratifying: his head jerked back as though she had indeed punched him, and two red weals appeared along the line of his cheekbones. Seconds later they had vanished. He reached out to take back the letter and scanned it, as she had, for a date.

'I understand,' he said. 'The phrase "some time ago" misled me. Intentionally, it seems.' He turned his attention to Eduardo Valera, who was still seated, watching the drama unfold. Luis said nothing, simply stared at the man, but Eduardo grabbed his file, muttered something about an urgent phone call, and dashed out of the room.

Luis sighed, folded the letter and placed it in his pocket. 'Please accept my apology, Señorita Blackmore, I shall write to Señor Márquez personally.'

'And that'll be the second letter he's had on the subject,' she said bluntly.

He nodded, picked up his things and left.

So that was it. She'd had her first professional tussle with Luis and lived to fight another day. It had been stupid working herself into such a state before the meeting. It was pure conceit thinking that she was anything special to the man. He'd even forgotten the date of their encounter, for goodness' sake!

Her eyes misted over as she acknowledged to herself how much that hurt, and she picked up her folder and hurried out of the room before she gave the stragglers any more free entertainment.

Luis was climbing into his car when she reached her office. She stood at her window and watched him leave, half expecting that he would look up, but he didn't. She tossed her file on to the desk and berated herself for her weakness. Would she never learn?

It seemed not. Seconds later she was back at the window, watching as the Rolls was gobbled up by the traffic and disappeared from sight. Where was he going now? Perhaps he was taking his new secretary out to lunch. Perhaps she would take his fancy afterwards, as Emma had. She closed her eyes in pain. Why was she doing this to herself? Why couldn't she just let him go?

She paced around the tiny room, needing to calm her mind before she did anything else.

It was twenty minutes before she saw things more clearly. The reason she'd become so agitated after the meeting was because she'd worked herself into such a frenzy before it. All that anxiety and adrenaline pumping through her system was bound to have an after-effect.

And it had been for nothing. Whatever else she thought about Luis she had to admire the way he refused to allow his personal life to interfere with business matters. She must have hurt his pride when she'd mocked his sexual prowess, but he wasn't going to retaliate. He'd had the perfect opportunity when he thought she'd skipped her appointment with Vicente Márquez because she'd been with Brad, but he'd been prepared to overlook it.

Emma sighed. No matter how hard she tried she couldn't cast Luis in the role of villain every time. If their positions were reversed she wondered if she'd be capable of such restraint.

Life went on. It never became easy meeting Luis unexpectedly at meetings or functions, but she managed it. Sometimes she felt his eyes on her, but when she looked up they seemed so blank and emotionless that she imagined it must be wishful thinking on her part.

People at Herrero's remained convinced that she and Luis were an item, but it had become so much part of her working life that it ceased to worry her unduly. She met so many other people through her job that she received more social invitations than she could cope with.

Christmas came and her mother arrived from England. It was wonderful taking her everywhere; Emma never needed an excuse to visit Sevilla's many attractions. It would have been a good time to visit the Alhambra again, but even though she knew of a bus company that arranged trips there, somehow Emma couldn't pluck up the courage to go again. Like the Villa Quevedo, it held too many memories.

Señor Jiménez and his wife invited them to dinner and she accepted on condition that Luis's name was taboo. What he thought about this she couldn't fathom. 'Cut out my tongue if I utter his name,' he declared dramatically, making her laugh and dispelling any awkwardness in his own inimitable fashion.

Mrs Blackmore returned home with a stash of photographs and memories, ready to bore anyone who would listen with the details of her holiday and the marvellous job her daughter had.

The middle of January marked the end of Emma's probationary period. It seemed incredible that six months had passed since she'd started work at Herrero's, but they had. Señor Jiménez called her into his office to tell her officially that her work was more than satisfactory and she was now part of the permanent staff.

It struck Emma that she was now free to leave. Six months ago she'd never thought she'd make it to this date, and now it was here she wanted to stay. She was bursting with enthusiasm about a new project that had occurred to her the previous day when she'd met the mayor of Jerez at a charity lunch. He'd told her about the cycle race that was held every year in the run-up to *Semana Santa*.

'Why doesn't Herrero's sponsor it?' she asked Señor Jiménez. 'It would be an ideal opportunity. There'd be so much publicity. Supposedly everywhere around here's bursting at the seams then.'

Her boss nodded. 'That's true.'

'So can I go ahead and work out some details? I can't think why no one has thought of the idea before.'

'It will do no harm gathering more information, but you will have to obtain final approval from Señor Quevedo. He likes to vet all such matters personally.'

'Is there time to include it on Friday's agenda?'

'There's no point, he's away on business. I suggest you leave a message asking for a meeting on his return.'

Emma frowned. So far she'd managed to avoid all personal meetings with Luis. That was how she liked it.

'It's entirely up to you, my dear, but if you don't act quickly you won't see your project developed this year. There's not that much time before the race.'

'I received a communication that you wished to speak to me as soon as possible.' The tone was cool, his manner composed, and his dark presence dominated her small office.

As she started to stammer out her proposal, the tired expression on Luis's face intensified and he raised his hand to silence her. 'We shall discuss it over lunch.'

'No.' The memory of their last lunch together was too raw.

He shrugged. 'As you wish. I have not the patience to argue with you. I have just spent a hellish week in your country. Is it the constant rain which makes your people so bloody-minded?'

He seemed to be waiting for an answer, and now didn't appear to be the time to be patriotic. 'Maybe,' she muttered.

'On my return I check my messages and find there is one from you. This is intriguing. Since . . . since your birthday you've made it abundantly clear that if I was to emigrate to Mars it wouldn't be far enough away from you. So what is it you wish to say to me? Do you want to hand me your notice in person perhaps? Or do you finally want to discuss this relationship between us that you've done your damnedest to destroy?'

He stopped and waited for some reaction, but when she said nothing, he continued.

'Whatever it was I felt it must be important, and I wanted to know. I asked Carlos to turn the car around and came here straight from the airport. What do I find?' A bitter smile twisted his mouth. 'That madam wishes to discuss a cycle race!'

'It is my job.'

'So it is.' He laughed sardonically and walked over to the window, where he rested his elbows on the sill and slumped over. Her heart gave a lurch. He looked totally exhausted. She wanted to hug him and give him some comfort. But she stayed where she was. Eventually he straightened up and seemed to mentally shake off his tiredness.

'Now I'm here I intend to stay for lunch. I didn't eat on the plane, and hunger isn't improving my temper. Once again I invite you to accompany me and discuss your project. Either that or you can ring Ana and schedule an appointment. I believe my diary is rather full at the moment, so I warn you that you may have quite a wait if you pursue this through the normal channels.'

'I'll get my jacket,' she said, slipping it off its hook on the back of her door.

He strode ahead, then waited for her on the steps of Herrero's. She automatically made for his car, parked in its usual spot, but his caustic tone stopped her.

'We'll walk. I haven't quite lost the use of my legs yet.'

Once again he strode ahead, but good manners forced him to stop and take her elbow as they negotiated the busy road. Emma suppressed a smile; this habit of the Spanish male never failed to amuse her. How on earth did they think their womenfolk managed the precarious business when they weren't there to help them?

As soon as they reached the other side he dropped her arm and he was off again; she had to practically run to keep up with him, and with high heels this wasn't easy. They snaked down narrow streets that she wouldn't have dreamed of venturing into by herself, the characters in them looked so shady.

Just as she was beginning to think that he was taking her on a wild goose chase they stopped outside a small hotel. By the look of it it had been built when Columbus was alive.

'You come here when you want to be incognito, I take it?' she said, taking in the crumbling walls and flaking paint of the building. What was he trying to tell her? If she slept with him she got the best. If she didn't he took her to the worst flea-ridden joint he could find.

To her astonishment he began to laugh.

'I thought you were in a bad mood,' she snarled.

'How could I possibly be with such delightful company?' he said enigmatically, leaning back against the wall and thrusting his hands into the pockets of his linen suit. 'On the way here it crossed my mind to wonder what your reaction to this establishment would be. It's cheered me up considerably to discover I'm not totally deficient in understanding the workings of your mind.'

'I'm not that hungry, but don't let me stop you. I'm afraid cockroaches running around in the kitchen always seems to have that effect on me.'

'You've turned into a snob, Emma. Where are your cockroaches? I defy you to find any. You look at the outside of a building or a person and immediately jump to conclusions. Be careful, *guapa*, it will land you into trouble.'

'Deny that you've brought me here because it's the total opposite of the last hotel we were at.'

'I deny it. It never entered my head until we were halfway here. I came because it serves the best *archoba* in the province, but don't tell María I said that.' He pushed open the carved wooden door and stood back to let her enter. 'And if we don't go in soon they'll have none left.'

The aroma of roast meat, fish, garlic and other herbs combined to assault her senses as they walked into the small dining room that was already crammed to capacity.

'Five minutes, *señores*.' A harassed-looking waiter ushered them to the corner of the bar and presented them unceremoniously with a glass of *fino* each.

Luis sipped the sherry and seemed preoccupied with his thoughts while Emma glanced nervously around the room. Did Luis realize that every person in this restaurant was male and that their conversation had suddenly become hushed while they examined her as minutely as if she were dish of the day?

Her hand fluttered to her forehead. Had they hurried here so quickly that the breeze had blown back her fringe and made her scar visible? Was that what they were looking at?

'When this happened when I was with Brad he'd stare at people so they'd leave sooner,' she blurted out.

Luis's mouth tightened and antagonism practically sparked from him. 'Really? How noble of him,' he ground out.

Emma groaned inwardly. Why on earth had she come out with a stupid remark like that? It was because she was feeling self-conscious, but it was totally inappropriate. She'd tried to lighten the situation for herself, but had succeeded in infuriating Luis again.

'I never slept with him,' she hissed, turning her back to the room and staring at a frayed beer mat on the counter.

'What did you say?'

'Brad. I never slept with Brad.' It wasn't the moment. It certainly wasn't the place, but it felt good laying the lie to rest. She should have known she was no good at deception after the agonies she'd suffered over deceiving Don Rafael, yet she'd made the same mistake with Luis. Never again. It would be the whole truth and nothing but the truth from now on.

She was so intent on this resolve that she failed to notice Luis hadn't answered. She glanced up now and a smile tugged at her lips. He looked like a cartoon character who'd just had a frying pan slammed in his face.

'This isn't funny!' His stunned expression flashed instantly to anger. 'Why do you provoke

328

me in this way? Does it amuse you so much to hurt me?'

'Why should the fact I never slept with Brad hurt you?' she asked, deliberately misunderstanding.

Thankfully the waiter showed them to a table at this point. Luis's fists were clenched. If he was ever going to break his rule about not hitting women, now seemed an appropriate time.

'You were living with the man.' Luis waited until the waiter had spread a clean paper cloth over the table, taken their orders and walked away, before speaking to her slowly and precisely in English.

'Yeah, me, Kate, Louisa, and Sharon when she wasn't with her boyfriend. That's why he stayed so long; he used her room because she was never there.'

Luis adopted the flattened by a frying pan look again.

'His comments about warming your bed when he came for your key?' he asked eventually.

Emma reached for her glass of wine. She hadn't intended to drink at all, but she had a feeling she might need it. 'You've met him, Luis. You even warned me about his character. You work it out.'

'And your comments after we'd made love?' he said gently.

'Lies. At least as regards Brad they were.'

He reached over and grasped her hand. She

snatched it away as a familiar electric sensation shot up her arm. 'But why, Emma?' he asked sadly.

'I needed time on my own, but all you cared about was your own need. I told you I didn't want to talk to you, but you wouldn't leave me alone. You went on and on. You forced me into a corner and I retaliated. I hit you with the one thing that would make you go. I'm sorry. It was a horrible thing to say, but it worked.'

'I'm sorry too, *guapa*. I felt that if only you would open the door we'd be able to work things out. I – '

'Enjoy!' The waiter plonked two huge bowls of fish stew before them and bustled off. Seconds later he was back with a basket of bread which he practically threw at them.

'Spain's answer to Basil Fawlty.' She smiled and reached out for a piece of bread.

'Ah, but just taste it.'

She broke off a piece of bread and put it in her mouth. 'Tastes much like the stuff I get round the corner from the apartment,' she said, and he grimaced.

'It does smell rather wonderful, though.' She spooned up a succulent piece of white fish with its sauce, sniffed it, and plopped it in her mouth. 'Oh, my goodness, that's good.' For the next ten minutes there was no sound from her but tiny murmurs of appreciation as she ate.

She swirled a piece of bread around the bowl

to capture the last drops of sauce, then picked up the menu again.

'Do you wish to change your order for dessert?' Luis asked. She looked across. He still had half of his *archoba* left. She was such a pig.

'No. I'm checking how much it cost. Whether I could afford to eat here every day.'

He started to laugh. 'You are delightful, Emma. Watching you eat is a sensual experience.'

'Mmm,' she said, not so sure about that. The usual remark when people saw how much she could consume was that they'd rather keep her for a week than a fortnight.

Luis picked up his glass and twirled it slowly by the stem. 'This Brad,' he said, speaking to her once again in English, 'you and he seemed close. I could tell that he appreciated you as a woman. He didn't appear the type of man that would easily take no for an answer. Weren't you ever tempted, being together so much?'

A broad smile spread over Emma's face as she recalled the subtle and not so subtle manoeuvres Brad had employed to get her into bed when he'd first moved into their house. He'd seemed to take her virginity as a personal affront, and had never really given up on her. During his stay in Jerez he'd tried it on twice, but to her mind his seduction had lacked conviction. It was probably his way of being polite, to show her he still thought her attractive.

'Nope,' she said, as Luis continued to stare at her.

'May I ask why?'

Emma frowned. She certainly wasn't going to admit it was because she could think of no man but Luis in that way. But there was another reason.

'I hated the way he flitted from one girl to another. He'd had so many he couldn't always remember their names. I didn't want to be number two hundred and sixty-four, or whatever total he was up to.'

Luis gazed at her thoughtfully. 'He's young, Emma, he's searching for his perfect mate. Perhaps you might have been the one.'

Emma choked on her drink and spent the next minute coughing, then she swore at Luis. 'Only a man could have come out with something as stupid as that, but there were plenty of girls who believed it. They'd come round to the house, crying because he'd finished with them. We'd sit them on the settee and make them a cup of tea while Brad was upstairs in bed with somebody else.'

Luis winced with distaste, but Emma continued.

'One girl slit her wrists because of him. That shook him up. He visited her in hospital every night. It put him off sex for . . . oh, let me think . . . almost three weeks. A record.'

'Everything all right, *señores*?' enquired the waiter briskly as he whisked their empty plates away and deposited gargantuan portions of chocolate sponge in front of them.

'Excellent,' they answered in unison.

'I suppose you can't defy nature,' mused Emma, for once ignoring the tantalizing temptation of chocolate. 'A woman will go with a man because she sees him as the one to father her children, whereas men are programmed to scatter their seed over as large an area as possible to ensure a good harvest.'

'You have a certain way with words, *guapa*.' Luis toyed with his dessert but ate none of it. She realized that he hadn't really wanted it; he'd ordered it so that she wouldn't feel guilty eating hers.

'You can't deny it's true, though.'

'There may be an element of truth in what you say, but in my experience all women are not as you describe and certainly not all men.'

Emma fixed him with a clear blue gaze. 'But some are, aren't they?' It was clear that she was referring to him, and he had the grace to look embarrassed.

'Reports of my philandering have been greatly exaggerated.' He dropped his spoon into his dish and gave up any pretence of eating it.

'The names Carmelita and Consuela spring to mind.'

'I understand the first but not the second. What is her surname?'

'I can't remember. Your secretary. The one

you got bored with after a few weeks.'

Luis propped one elbow on the table and rested his head in his hand. He laughed softly. 'You'll have to do better than that, *chica*. Consuela is a family friend. She might have been willing; I was not.'

'You got rid of her because of that?'

He clicked his tongue in exasperation. 'No, Emma, I did not. Consuela was doing me a favour, helping out until I found a replacement for my previous secretary. And before you accuse me of anything with her I shall tell you that I fired her because she was passing information to a competitor.'

Emma took a mouthful of sponge and considered. Luis's explanation fitted with the familiar attitude the woman had had with him. It also fitted with *her* habit of jumping to conclusions, she realized. 'OK, I believe that one,' she conceded.

'That is so reassuring,' he said sarcastically, and she laughed.

'More questions?' he invited. 'May I prove to you that recently my life has been exemplary?'

'You don't have to prove anything to me, Luis.' He was clever. He could probably prove to her that black was white, but nothing altered the fact that she couldn't trust him.

'I have changed, Emma. I want you to know that.'

'Right. I know it now,' she answered flippantly, refusing to acknowledge the hurt expression in his eyes that he could conjure at will.

She tackled the rest of her sponge while he chased a crumb around the tablecloth with his fingertip and appeared deep in thought.

'Am I right in assuming,' he said finally, 'that when we made love you were a – '

'Gosh, that was filling.' She pushed her plate away. 'I'd love a coffee if you don't mind.'

The restaurant was emptying, and when Luis raised a finger the waiter rushed across and took his order.

'Aren't we supposed to be here to talk about the cycle race?' she hissed when he'd gone, though to be honest it had slipped to the back of her mind until now. 'We're not going to have time.'

Luis smiled. 'I shall make time. I can always ring Alfonso and ask him to take my next appointment. As to the other, you do not have to reply. I now know the answer.'

'But you didn't, did you? I thought blokes were supposed to know things like that. How does that make you feel?'

'Knowing that I introduced you to love makes me feel privileged, wonderful, special . . . I can't think of enough superlatives.' His smile widened and he gazed at her with such blatant acknowledgement of their union that she had to look away.

'Well, don't get too carried away, because it

won't be happening again,' she muttered.

'I can always dream.' His eyes were wide with longing and the look that blazed from them was pure sex. She felt her insides contract.

'The first I knew of the cycle race was when I was speaking to the mayor,' she began. Luis heaved a sigh that was so deep it must have originated at his feet. He spooned sugar into his coffee, stirred it, and then gave her his full attention.

'. . . and Herrero's has got something of an old fogey image, you have to admit. Bicycle racing mightn't exactly be formula one, but at least it's a youth sport. By sponsoring it we become associated with that and drag the company to the notice of a new generation, to potential new customers. I've checked and it's already covered by the media, but a bit low-profile. I'll have to come up with some ideas to persuade them to heighten that. It shouldn't be a problem. I really can't understand why nobody's pounced on the idea before.' She stopped, her face flushed and eyes glowing with excitement. Luis had said nothing, but he'd listened intently and nodded encouragement.

'I'm impressed,' he said, rising to his feet. 'Now I really must phone Alfonso. Would you like another coffee?'

She glanced around the restaurant. It was practically empty but they weren't the only ones lingering over their meal. She nodded.

'Does that mean I can go ahead?' she asked, the instant he joined her again.

He started to laugh. 'And if you were God you would say – Seven days to create the world? Pooh, I could do it in three.'

'There isn't much time,' she reminded him.

'Exactly. Perhaps it would be as well to set the wheels in motion for next year.'

'Oh, Luis!' Disappointment flooded her features and she gazed at him bleakly through long golden lashes.

He swore, then turned away. 'Don't look at me in that way, *guapa*. It isn't fair to manipulate me like this.'

'Like what?' she demanded, stunned by his reaction.

He frowned, but didn't elaborate.

'Your outline is good, more than good, but that's all it is, Emma, an outline. There is so much to do before it could come to fruition.'

'So? I'm not afraid of hard work.'

He smiled. 'I'm sure you're not, and with any other employee that came to me with such a project I'd be tempted to tell them to go ahead. I'm a great believer in letting people learn by their mistakes. Unfortunately, Emma, I can't afford you that luxury.'

'Why should I be any different?'

'Because you are, *guapa*. You've already pointed out that the sherry community here is, in the main, a group of conservative, traditionally minded men. Your arrival in Jerez, a young, beautiful foreigner, created quite a stir among them; several questioned my wisdom in appointing you. It has amused me watching them change their opinion as you've talked to them and charmed them with that engaging manner you adopt with everyone, it seems, but me.'

Emma stared into the empty dregs of her coffee. She wished she was able to behave with Luis as she did with other men, but it seemed impossible. 'I don't quite see how this is relevant,' she said.

'You will. We move now to Herrero's. A quiet little backwater where the staff had such a cosy stress-free life until the nasty new owner hurled them protesting into the twentieth century.'

Emma smiled at his description.

'They haven't forgiven me for it. I doubt some of them ever will. I stand in front of them and I can feel the emanations of hatred directed at me from certain quarters. It's not pleasant, Emma, despite what you seem to think of me. Sometimes I leave the building completely drained. But it's working. Slowly, very slowly, things are starting to change.'

'And generating wider publicity for the product can only help,' she protested.

'I'm not questioning the wisdom of your idea. I think it is brilliant, but don't you see the delicate situation you're in, Emma? It's my fault. I take all the blame for placing you there.'

'Because people associate me with you?'

'Precisely. There are some at Herrero's who would love to see you fall flat on your face. They could then trawl their theory around the community that of course it was only to be expected when a woman is appointed because of her skills in the bedroom rather than in the boardroom.'

Emma flushed scarlet.

'I'm sorry for being so blunt,' he said gently. I assure you it is not my opinion, and it's probably not even theirs, but they'd milk it for all it was worth.'

'Why are you so certain that I'm going to fail?'

'The time factor, purely. Without it you would probably still make some mistakes, but you would have time to correct them yourself and nobody would be aware of it.'

Emma sighed. 'So it's a no, then.' At least he'd had the courtesy of telling her why.

'It should be. I can think of only one solution to the problem, but it is up to you whether you decide to accept it or not.'

'Go on.'

'You must accept my help on this one. It will be your project. You will do all the work, but you must liaise with me. Antonio Jiménez is busy at the moment. I can't justify adding to his workload, not after the favour I owe him for looking after you when you first joined the company.'

Emma pondered his suggestion while Luis flicked open his personal organizer. 'I can meet you for lunch here next Tuesday, and I give you permission to leave messages on my personal line. I would prefer it if nobody else knew we were working together.'

'And it would still be my project?' The last thing she wanted was Luis to stamp his dictatorial style all over it and give lip service to the fact it was hers.

'Completely. I shall act as devil's advocate, pointing out the pitfalls and possible solutions. Naturally I reserve the right to hold the casting vote, but I shall only use it if I see you heading for total disaster.'

'And any further projects?'

'You are on your own, unless of course you ask my advice as a friend. Once you have had one success you will have won credibility. They can't take that away from you even if you do make a mistake in the future.'

'Next Tuesday, then. Thanks, Luis, I appreciate it.' She reached across the table and offered him her hand. He looked surprised but took it and shook it firmly.

'To a successful working relationship,' she said.

'To more than that, I hope,' he countered.

Emma frowned. 'If I meet you, Luis, it's only to discuss work, nothing more.'

'Absolutely. I never mix business and pleasure.' He signalled to the waiter and paid him. 'Well, hardly ever,' he added, getting to his feet.

'Luis, I – ' She got no further before he pressed a finger against her lips.

'Joke,' he grinned. 'Now come along, woman, am I paying you good money for sitting on your backside enjoying yourself in restaurants?'

'Careful, Luis, if you develop a sense of humour you'll confuse everybody.'

'Now that could be a useful tactic. I'll have to remember that one.' He smiled, refusing to take the bait.

They walked back to Herrero's with Luis in top form, making her laugh. Anyone seeing them together could have been forgiven for thinking that she was with a totally different man from the one who had accompanied her to the restaurant.

When he was like this she forgot all his faults, but she couldn't allow herself to do so. Only by keeping his unreliability to the forefront of her brain could she save herself pain. He was so easy to love, and the physical attraction she felt for him was almost overpowering.

CHAPTER 19

'Oh, María, you can't go! I'll miss you too much.' Emma stared in horror at the well-padded woman on her sofa and felt tears prick her eyes. She hadn't realized how attached she'd become to María in such a short time and how much she looked forward to her regular visits.

'I'm sorry. I'm being selfish. Of course you must go and live with your sister and her family if that's what you want.'

'It isn't really a case of wanting, Señorita Emma. My sister has cancer. Her husband is a good man but he will not be able to cope.'

'Oh, how awful.' Emma wrapped her arms around the older woman and hugged her tightly. María was a demonstrative woman who gave and accepted love in equal measure. She rested her head on Emma's shoulder and wept freely.

'It hurts me to leave Señor Luis,' she said, lifting her head and dabbing at her eyes.

'What does he say?'

'Ay, *señorita*, he is so upset. He tries not to show it, but I know him too well.'

'Poor Luis.' He would take it hard; María must have been like a mother to him.

'It would be a heavy burden lifted from me if I could see you and him together again before I left.'

'Don't, María, please. You know that we only pretended to be engaged because Don Rafael was dying.'

'Ay, poor Don Rafael. He adored you, *señorita*. He died happy, you know.'

'I'll put the coffee on, María.' Emma stood up and hurried into the kitchen. María followed her.

'You can't run away from the past, Señorita Emma. It has happened. You can't change it. It was no one's fault. If it was anyone's it was Don Rafael's for being so stubborn.'

'I know, but it still hurts to think about it. Can we change the subject?'

María nodded. 'But you do know now it was no one's fault?'

'Yes.'

'I shall tell Señor Luis what you said.' She smiled and walked out of the kitchen.

Emma gave sigh of relief. What on earth was that about? María didn't usually come on so heavy. Having to leave the villa must be really shaking her up.

She returned to the living room with a pot of

coffee and a large plate of cakes. María immediately picked one up and began to eat it. Emma smiled. She'd miss María; she was probably the only person she knew who ate more than she did.

'Señor Luis insists that I have a party at the villa to say farewell to all my friends.'

'That's nice of him,' said Emma guardedly. María's one fault was that she was convinced the sun rose and shone from her employer's nether regions.

'Ay, *señorita*, he is such a good man. If once you touch his heart he cannot do enough for you.'

'Hmm.'

María finished her cake, took out a handkerchief and wiped her fingers. 'Of course you must come to my party,' she stated.

'No, María, I'm sorry. Too many bad memories. Perhaps I could take you to the theatre or something before you go. We could say our goodbyes then. Barcelona isn't the end of the world, you know; we will see each other again.'

'I so hoped you would come to my special night, Señorita Emma.' Emma looked on, appalled, as two large tears rolled down her friend's cheeks and landed with a plop on her black skirt.

'Oh, María, I – '

'It won't be the same without you there.'

Emma felt ashamed of herself. She didn't know why her presence should make such a difference to María, but obviously it did. Surely she could steel herself to enter the villa again for her friend's sake?

She shifted uneasily on her seat. 'If I came, María, I might only be able to stay for a short while.'

María's face brightened; she rubbed roughly over her face with the back of her hand, and reached for another cake. 'I knew you would come, *señorita*. You are a good girl.'

Emma stared at her as she munched happily on a chocolate doughnut. She had the distinct impression she'd been conned.

'Ramón's not likely to be there, is he, María?'

María's face curdled as if she'd bit into a lemon, and she pretended to spit on the floor. 'He certainly will not.'

'Luis mentioned he wasn't working for him any more. He was a bit funny about it.'

María raised her eyebrows. 'Terrible man. Thought he was above the rest of us because his family had worked for the Quevedos for generations. Even had some idea of his sister marrying Señor Luis. Can you imagine? That strumpet!'

Emma smiled at the thought of Carmelita as Señora Quevedo, lording it over the household. María, for one, would have left her job sooner.

'So what happened?' she asked.

'Well, the *señor* met you, didn't he? How could he have eyes for anyone else after he'd found you?'

Emma winced. 'No. I mean why did Luis get rid of Ramón?'

María folded her arms and looked indignant. 'It was after Don Rafael's death. After the fire and after you'd gone back to England Señor Luis was ill. I've never seen him like that.' María pointed to her head and mouthed the word 'depressed'.

Emma listened to her, shocked. So she had been right: his grandfather's death had unbalanced Luis.

'It wasn't like the *señor*. He even gave up riding, and you know what he's like for that. All of us were so pleased when he came home one day and announced he'd bought this company that was heading for bankruptcy. Quevedo's was no challenge, he said. It was too efficient. A five-year-old could run it.'

'It seemed to take up quite a bit of his time when I was at the villa,' mused Emma.

María nodded. 'Perhaps he was fooling himself a little, but there was no doubt that he started to get better, became more like his old self after he bought this company.'

'How does Ramón come into this?'

'Well, he seized the opportunity, didn't he? The evil little man. With Señor Luis out of the way, and with him as finance director, he moved Quevedo money into bank accounts all over the world. I think his plan was to disappear, but the *señor* got to him before he could.'

'Good gracious. So he's in prison now?'

Again María pretended to spit on the carpet. 'He should be. Señor Luis should have handed him over to the police and be done with it. He's too soft-hearted, *señorita*. Ramón's betrayal cut him to the quick, but he couldn't bear to be the one to send him to jail. I'd have done it.'

'And me,' murmured Emma, and wondered what that said about her, then wondered who did Luis's dirty work for him now.

'Wonder why he's in a good mood? He must have had a good night last night.' The export manager glanced lewdly across at Emma as he spoke in a loud whisper to the man sitting next to him. She stared back at him as though he were something unpleasant she'd found on her shoe, and was pleased when he was the first to look away.

Luis did seem in a good mood, though. He'd mentioned to her that he hoped to break even by the end of the financial year. Perhaps that was it.

They covered all the items on the agenda in record time, then he sat back and looked at his watch. 'We still have some time to run, *señores*,' he said, scanning the table until his eyes alighted on Emma, seemingly at random. 'Ah, Señorita Blackmore, perhaps you would tell the meeting something about your idea for the company to sponsor the forthcoming Jerez cycle race.'

'Oh!' she said, hoping her face didn't reveal

the sudden terror that gripped her insides. 'The file is in my office, Señor Quevedo. Shall I fetch it?' He could have warned her he was thinking of doing this. She wouldn't have looked so stupid for being unprepared.

He shook his head. 'That will not be necessary. I simply want to know how matters are progressing, what stage you have reached. But please begin at the beginning for the benefit of others.'

Emma made a shaky start. She was totally unprepared for a speech, but her nerves settled down after a few minutes. She'd already sold the idea once to Luis in the restaurant, and she found it easier second time around. When she'd finished, Luis asked her a few questions, ones he'd already asked privately, and she started to congratulate herself on how simple it was.

Then he turned her over to the wolves.

'Would anyone care to comment or ask Señorita Blackmore any questions?' he asked mildly, and it began.

The savagery of the attack almost overwhelmed her as one after another tried to pick holes in her arguments and cast aspersions on her judgement. She glanced over at Luis. Had he set her up? Was he enjoying this? His face was a mask – expressionless – but there was something about his eyes that seemed to glint encouragement.

She was being paranoid. Of course he hadn't

set her up. All the questions she was being asked were ones he'd already grilled her on. He was giving her a chance to prove herself.

As she adapted to the new situation, Emma felt her hackles rise and her temper grow. What did they think? That it was open season on the boss's bimbo? Well, they wouldn't do her down without a fight.

All decisions that had been reached on the project had been arrived at for a purpose. Luis had explained everything and she had listened carefully, not wanting to concede any of her ideas without a good reason. She now turned his arguments into her own, and cut to shreds those who voiced opinions that had once been hers.

When Luis announced that the meeting had overrun she felt bitterly disappointed. The adrenaline was surging through her veins and she wanted it to continue. She sank back into her chair, only half listening to Señor Jiménez's chatter as the room cleared.

'Well done, Emma,' he said, when there were only the three of them left. 'You have received far better tuition than I could have given you.'

Emma glanced at Luis. His face had been the picture of impartiality throughout the proceedings, and even now wore an inscrutable expression.

'They really do hate me,' she said when they were alone.

Luis shook his head. The mask lifted, and he smiled warmly at her. 'No, they don't. I've told you, it's me they hate, and they thought they could get at me through you. They thought you were an easy target. I doubt there's one among them who still holds that opinion. Congratulations, *chica*, you were wonderful.' He took her hand and held it to his lips.

'I went a bit too far, though, don't you think? They made me so angry.'

'A couple of times I thought you were going to overstep the mark. You might have noticed me holding my breath as I wondered whether it had been a wise move throwing you in the deep end like that. I needn't have worried, *guapa*, you were totally professional. Your attacks always stopped short of being personal, but the victim was left in no doubt that there was more you could add if you were so inclined.'

Emma grinned. 'That's a relief. I do tend to get carried away.'

Luis started to laugh. 'Oh, Emma. I believe it's the hardest thing I have ever done in my life – to sit there and not burst out laughing. Such passion! Such shamelessness! Using my arguments like that. Why didn't I have the foresight to video-tape the meeting; it would have seen me through to my old age.'

Emma smiled at him. 'Thanks, Luis. I wouldn't have stood a chance without you.'

'Yes, you would. Given the time, you would

have found everything out for yourself. I simply speeded up the process. You're a natural, *guapa*. You research everything thoroughly, you're not afraid to ask for advice, and you perform well under pressure.'

'Oh, gosh, I don't know about the last one. I was shaking like a leaf when I started, didn't you notice?'

Luis shrugged. 'It soon passed, and it convinced everyone that your performance wasn't rehearsed. And what a performance it was! Without a script as well. Brilliant! It is rare to find someone who not only lives up to one's expectations, but actually surpasses them. You and I make a good team, Emma.'

Emma smiled into the smouldering dark eyes regarding her so warmly. The physical attraction between them seemed stronger than ever. When she went to sleep at night his face hovered in her dreams, and simply by closing her eyes she could conjure up every detail of his charismatic presence.

For the past few weeks she'd worked harder than she'd ever done; Luis's good opinion was like sustenance to her. She'd realized straight away that it had to be earned. He wasn't one to praise lightly, not in business.

Her major coup had been to get one of the national weeklies to cover the race. Luis had given her his contact on the newspaper, but hadn't held out much hope of them accepting.

It had taken endless phone calls and a meeting where she'd been forced to use her trump card of Herrero's using the paper for future advertising before they agreed. Luis told her she was more persistent than a timeshare salesman. Although it was spoken half in jest, the remark meant more to her than any compliment he'd ever given about her appearance.

'May I buy you lunch to celebrate?'

Emma started. She'd been in a reverie, and had the suspicion that she'd been staring into the hypnotic depths of Luis's eyes for far too long.

'That's kind of you, but if you don't mind I want to buy some rolls and eat them in the park. Suddenly I feel exhausted – definitely in need of a little nature.'

It was more than that; her stomach was churning with longing. She felt so close to Luis at the moment. It was too dangerous. Every cell of her body wanted him to make love to her, and the way he was looking at her suggested he'd be only too willing to oblige.

'I understand,' he said, as she scraped her chair back. He looked so sad as she picked up her bag that, on impulse, she bent down and kissed his cheek.

'Thanks again for everything.' She hurried to the door, but paused as she opened it to look back. He was staring at the window, but his fingertip probed his cheek as if she'd burnt it.

The park was almost empty and this was the

way Emma liked it best. The natives of Jerez were dressed in coats and scarves at this time of the year and probably thought it was too cool for sitting outside. For Emma, brought up on the chilly North coast of England, seventeen degrees centigrade was summer. She took every advantage of it.

Sitting on her favourite bench beside the pond, Emma relaxed. What a morning it had been. Thank goodness Luis hadn't warned her about what he had planned; she wouldn't have slept last night.

She'd have said the chances of her actually enjoying such an experience would have been zilch, and she would have been wrong. It had left her with a buzz. She could make it in this profession. With or without the co-operation of her colleagues, she was going to carve out a successful career for herself. She hoped that their attitude would eventually change towards her, but if some of them remained hostile . . . well, she could live with it. She'd just have to make sure she always covered her back and didn't leave herself open to criticism.

Emma picked up a stone and skimmed it across the pond. It landed with a disappointing plop. One of these days she'd discover how to make it bounce. Luis would be able to do it, she thought, and then she groaned. Would she never get him out of her head?

It was probably because she'd spent so much

time with him recently. And he'd been so nice. Although he'd grown up in a sherry-producing family, and his knowledge of the industry was vast, he hadn't talked down to her as she'd expected. He'd treated her as an equal and carefully considered all the ideas she brought him.

She wondered if he guessed how much she desired him? It was a miracle she'd managed to retain any information at all with the seething mass of emotions that churned inside her whenever he was present.

If he had guessed, he hadn't taken advantage of it. He'd teased her about not mixing business and pleasure, but while they were working on the sponsorship deal he'd taken it as his watchword and been completely professional.

Emma sighed. She was so contrary. Part of her – her heart – wished that Luis would sweep her off her feet and make love to her again. The other part – her head – couldn't allow it to happen. It wouldn't allow him to hurt her again. It knew that she loved him. It knew that the experience would be wonderful. But it also knew that ultimately he'd let her down again. It was in his nature.

She reflected on the changes of the last month. Despite all the odds, she and Luis had developed a good working relationship. They respected each other and she'd even go so far as to say that they were friends. She didn't want to lose all that.

One thing she knew for certain: she'd need to be hard-headed and hard-hearted this coming Saturday when she returned to the villa for María's leaving party.

CHAPTER 20

Luis's Rolls-Royce arrived outside her apartment at one minute to seven. Emma was watching from the balcony. She grabbed her bag and hurried down the steps to prevent Carlos having to walk all the way up to fetch her.

'Lovely evening, Carlos. Definitely getting warmer the last couple of days,' she chattered inanely as Carlos held the door open for her. Her heart was thudding wildly and she felt sick with nerves. The Villa Quevedo was the last place she'd ever thought she'd visit again.

As they drove away, Emma leaned back on the soft leather upholstery and closed her eyes in an effort to calm herself. Images of terrified horses enclosed in a ring of fire immediately filled her mind. Her eyes flew open in a panic, and she gagged on the acrid stench of smoke which seemed to fill the car.

The back of the Rolls was vast, but she felt as if she were in a coffin. Blindly she searched for the button that operated the window, and heaved a sigh of relief as a blast of air hit her in the face. It buffeted her and tangled her hair, but at least she could breathe again.

She saw Carlos watching her in the driver's mirror, a strange expression on his face. He must think she was a complete idiot. The last time he'd seen her was during her mad flight from Luis, and now she was behaving oddly again, sticking her head out of the window while he was hurtling down the motorway. '*La señorita es loca*,' he'd tell his wife when he got home. For some reason that cheered her slightly.

She'd told Luis that she would make her own way to the villa, but he'd shaken his head. 'I should never hear the end of it from María if I allowed you to,' he said. 'If this is your plan, argue it with her. I want nothing to do with it.'

She was pleased now that she'd accepted a lift. She had to make an appearance for María's sake. If she'd taken a bus and then a taxi to the villa it would have been too easy to turn back. This way she was committed, and driving like Carlos did it would only take about forty minutes to get there.

They came off the motorway and Emma took a deep breath. Already the countryside began to look familiar. It was strange how much of it she remembered, though she'd only spent a week here. It was as if each of those seven days was highlighted in her memory.

They left the main road, travelled along a

smaller one for a few miles and then they were on the narrow lane that led to the villa. The wrought-iron gates guarding the entrance had been left open for guests, and as they passed through Emma felt her chest constrict.

Everything looked exactly the same. She didn't know what she'd expected, but she had a vague notion that after Don Rafael's death things would change. The flower beds were as well tended, the bushes as carefully trimmed, and the gravel drive had been freshly raked. She looked away as they passed the new stable block. Thankfully it wasn't in sight as the car crunched to a halt outside the main entrance.

'Welcome home, *señorita*,' smiled Carlos as he opened the door for her. She was already shaking as she took his hand to climb out of the car, but his joke finished her off. How had he known that was what it felt like? And why had he been so cruel?

She stumbled up the main steps. Although it was early there were plenty of people milling around. María was in the entrance hall, hugging a woman almost as wide as herself. Emma couldn't face her yet. She opened the door immediately on her right, closed it quietly behind her, and rested her cheek on the carved wooden panel. It felt as if someone had ripped out her heart and was stamping on it.

Away from prying glances, Emma allowed her tears to flow freely. Somehow or other she'd have to gain control of her emotions, go back out there and meet people. It would require an Oscar-standard performance, calling on all her resources.

She glanced around the room but didn't recognize it. Then she recalled it was Luis's study and he'd never shown her inside. He mustn't allow the maids to come in either, she thought wryly, glancing at the clutter on the huge walnut desk that dominated one corner. Behind it was an enormous bookcase of the same wood, where books and files were piled seemingly at random. A fax machine, computer, and other office paraphernalia stood silently along the adjacent wall, and a leather chesterfield sofa and chair groaned under a pile of papers in the centre of the room.

Emma walked over to the desk and sat down in the burgundy leather high-backed chair behind it. Opposite, the red velvet curtains were closed, but she could picture the view from the window. It would be pleasant working here. Luis would be able to see everyone who approached the villa, as well as the rolling hills and acres of vines in the distance.

Emma closed her eyes and leaned back in the chair. It was a good idea coming into a room that held no associations for her. If it wasn't for the musky fragrance that seemed to permeate everything and which was so uniquely Luis she could have been anywhere.

She stirred herself with a sigh; she must think about joining the party soon. She dug in her bag, pulled out a small mirror and surveyed her face. It was an easy matter to wipe away the smudged mascara, but not to disguise the puffy eyes and mottled pink of her complexion.

Five more minutes, she decided, snapping the mirror shut. It was then that a familiar image caught her eye. Not one, but half a dozen of them, she realized, picking up a silver photo frame that was half covered by a pile of memos. How strange. She checked the others. Yes, they were all of her. She recalled the day perfectly: Luis had taken a camera with him when they'd gone riding one morning. He'd wanted some photographs of Hierro, he'd said. She'd had no idea until this moment that he'd taken any of her.

'Emma.' The voice was soft and gentle but it made her jump, and she dropped the photograph guiltily. She'd been so intent on staring at it that she hadn't heard him come in.

'They've brightened many a dull day,' he said in the same gentle tones.

Emma pushed the significance of the photos to the back of her mind. It was far too confusing.

'How on earth do you ever find anything you need in here?' she challenged instead.

'I know exactly where everything is.'

'I thought I'd do a bit of industrial espionage. Nobody would notice, the place already looks as though it's been burgled, but you came in before I found anything – '

'Stop it, Emma! Why do you do this? I can see that you're upset. Carlos is mortified that he might have been the cause of it.'

Emma gulped as she remembered the chauffeur's words. 'I don't understand. I like Carlos. I thought he liked me. Why should he want to hurt me?'

'That is the last thing he would want to do.'

'Then why should he say, "Welcome, home, *señorita*"? He must have known how happy I was here when your grandfather was alive. Don Rafael made me feel that it really was my home.'

Luis picked up some papers from his desk, shuffled them, and then tossed them back. He thrust his hands into his pockets, walked over to the window, then changed his mind and came back.

'It is my fault.' Dark soulful eyes locked on hers. 'Normally I keep my own counsel, but this thing between us was too big. After my grandfather's death when you refused to talk to me I thought I'd go crazy. I had to tell someone of my feelings. Carlos and I are old friends; I am godfather to his children and I would trust him with my life. I told him that I would never give up hope of you coming back to the villa one day as my wife.'

'Then you are crazy.'

Luis turned away from her and bowed his

head. 'Why do you hate me so much, Emma? I know that you want me with your body. Why can't you want me with your mind?'

'You know the reason.'

'The fire?'

'If that's what you want to think.'

'I'm sorry, Emma, I'd have given anything for you not to have been there and suffered what you did. But it happened. I can't alter the fact, although I do take full responsibility for bringing you to Sevilla and putting you in such danger.'

Emma leapt to her feet and faced Luis, her eyes blazing. 'Why do you always harp on about the fire? María was the same the other day. Why can't you just be honest with yourself? Accept that you were a complete swine for what you did afterwards. Maybe then we might have some hope of a future. But you've never admitted it, have you? It doesn't fit the idea you have of yourself so you've blanked it out. I don't hate you any more, Luis, but I can't forgive you. You tried to wipe out what you did to me with offers of money and, God help you, you couldn't understand why I wouldn't take it.'

Luis looked punch drunk. 'Are we talking about the same thing here, Emma? The reason I tried to give you money was because I felt so guilty about the damage to your head. The doctors intimated that you may need plastic surgery. I knew you couldn't afford it, and I didn't want it to be a factor in your decision.'

'It wasn't. The hospital told me I was a borderline case. They reckoned the scar would hardly be noticeable after a few years, so I decided not to go ahead. I couldn't face it, to be honest.' She touched the silvery furrow running across her forehead. The hospital had probably been over-optimistic but she didn't regret her decision, and she'd grown used to seeing herself with a fringe now.

'María told me you didn't blame me any longer for the fire,' said Luis flatly.

'Aargh!' Emma let out a scream, picked up a handful of papers and tossed them across the room. 'It's like trying to have a conversation with an answering machine,' she shouted.

'Please, Emma, you'll have to explain. I don't understand you.' Luis grabbed her arms but she shook him off.

'OK, buster, I'll make it nice and simple, in language even you should understand. When I first saw you I hated you. I hated everything about you: your money, your lifestyle, your attitude, everything. You were a spoiled brat masquerading as a man. Plain enough for you?'

Luis nodded. The expression in his eyes almost made her waver, but she forced herself to continue.

'Every now and again I'd catch a glimpse of a nicer Luis underneath and I told myself you were all right really, you couldn't help growing up spoiled. If your parents hadn't died you'd be different. Then you started being nice to me, and sucker that I am I fell in love with you. You could have had me any time you wanted that week, Luis, if you hadn't been conducting that amusing little experiment of yours.'

Luis groaned. 'I'm sorry,' he murmured, not looking at her.

'Your loss, I suppose,' she answered flippantly. 'Now where were we? Oh, yes, the fire, where I killed your grandfather and your favourite horse.'

'*Dios*! Emma, why do you say such things?'

'Because it's the only explanation I can think of for why you should send Ramón to boot me out of the hospital on the day of Don Rafael's funeral.'

Luis's mouth dropped open. 'I would never be capable of such a thing.'

Emma sighed and walked towards the door. 'It's not worth discussing it. You need psychiatric help, Luis. You can't just blank something like that out. It's not healthy.'

Luis grabbed her arm and pulled her roughly back. 'You will explain yourself, Emma.'

'I just have. And that's why I wouldn't answer any of your letters or speak to you. I loved you, Luis. I'd probably have stayed in Sevilla with you if you'd asked me to, and tossed away my degree, so it's probably as well that you turned on me and brought me to my senses. You destroyed any hope of a future together for us. It's too late now. I'll never trust you again.'

'Let me get this straight. The reason for your behaviour towards me stems from the fact that you believe I sent Ramón to the hospital to make you leave the country?' Luis's voice was deathly cold; icicles must have been forming on his tongue.

'It happened, Luis. It's not a figment of my imagination.'

'All right, let me rephrase it. You believed I was capable of such an act?'

Emma nodded.

Luis rose to his feet. Emma noticed with a shock that his eyes were misty with repressed tears. 'I don't know what to say, Emma. I really don't. I begin to think there is no hope for us, that I'll never shatter this image you hold of me.' He turned towards the door, his shoulders hunched.

'I phoned you, you bastard,' she shouted after him. Was she going mad? Could he deny everything as though it hadn't happened?'

'Did I speak to you?' Luis frowned, then raked his hands through his hair. She guessed he was questioning his own sanity.

Emma shook her head. 'The woman who answered the phone went off to find you and came back with a message.'

'And what did I say?' The conversation was taking on a surreal quality.

'That you didn't want to speak to me. You'd

already sent your message with Ramón.'

'I see.' He gritted his teeth in the semblance of a smile. 'I underestimated him. A dangerous mistake. No wonder he was so eager to leave the country; he must have realized that time was running out for him. With you working for me in Herrero's he must have known you'd tell me eventually.'

'One of us is definitely mad,' she murmured.

'No, we're not.' He gripped her hands and the hint of a smile sparkled in his eyes. 'Both of us know or guess only half the story, that's the trouble. Will you listen while I try to guess my part?'

'All right.'

With one hand he swept the pile of papers off the sofa. With the other he pulled her down beside him.

'People came from all over the country to attend Grandfather's funeral,' he began. 'Ramón must have gambled that his absence among the crowd would go unnoticed, and it did. Most of the staff was also present, and there were only a skeleton staff and caterers left at the villa. Ramón came to the hospital, persuaded you to leave, and even had the foresight to tell his girlfriend here what message to relay if you phoned.'

'Girlfriend? I didn't realize he had a girlfriend.'

'One of the maids.' Luis gritted his teeth. 'The

same maid who informed me when I returned that you'd rung and ordered your clothes to be delivered to the hospital. She'd done as you asked because she knew that you were my fiancée and she didn't want to get into trouble. After that I behaved exactly as Ramón knew I would.'

He gripped her arm and looked at her with such pain in his eyes that she felt her whole being reach out to comfort him. She squeezed his hand and smiled at him to go on.

'I'm sorry, *chica*. I never questioned anything. My brain was blurred . . . I had just buried Grandfather . . . I was already in a highly emotional state. I left immediately for the hospital. Ramón drove me, insisting that I was in no fit state to go by myself. At the time I was grateful for his help.' He laughed bitterly and shook his head in self-disgust.

'Of course you had already gone, but Ramón suggested that if I acted quickly and rang the airport there might be a chance of catching you before your plane left. While I was doing this he went supposedly to find the doctor in charge of your case. The doctor was unavailable but he said that he'd spoken to a nurse who confirmed that you'd discharged yourself. She'd also given him a letter which you'd left for me.'

'A letter? What on earth did it say?'

Luis pursed his lips. 'I prefer not to repeat it. Suffice it to say I was left in little doubt that you hated me and blamed me for your disfigurement.'

'Didn't you know what my handwriting was like?'

He shrugged. 'It looked like the writing of someone whose hands were bandaged, as yours were.'

Emma rested her head in her hands. 'I don't get it, Luis. I knew he couldn't stand me, but why go to such lengths?'

'Revenge,' said Luis shortly.

'Revenge? I never did anything to him. I called him names, but I didn't think he'd heard.'

Luis took both her hands and kissed them. 'You are so sweet, *guapa*. I love you.'

Emma felt a warm glow spread slowly across her being. 'Why revenge?' she asked. She had to know everything. She couldn't let herself be distracted yet.

Luis sighed. 'I suppose it must go back to the helicopter crash. Mother and Father were good friends with Ramón's parents. They were on their way to a wine festival when the pilot had a stroke and crashed the helicopter into the Sierra Morena. Nobody survived. It was a tragic waste, but no one could be blamed.' He paused for a moment.

'Grandfather made sure that Ramón and his sister were well taken care of. I learned only recently that Ramón has never forgiven our family. I suppose what happened with Carmelita was the final straw.'

Emma looked at him blankly.

Luis sighed and rapped the back of his hand against the arm of the sofa. 'This is where I am not so very proud of my actions,' he said eventually. 'Before you met me my relationship with Ramón had grown strained. Staff were upset by his high-handed attitude to them, and I'd already had occasion to warn him about it. Possibly I was not as forceful as I should have been because I'd known Ramón all my life. I felt a close bond with him because of the way we'd both lost our parents. I didn't realize he expected this bond to be an even closer one.'

'Carmelita?' she whispered.

'Carmelita,' he agreed. 'Unfortunately I laughed in his face when he told me of it.' He got up and stalked around the room, eventually coming to rest at his desk. He perched on the corner and raked his fingers through his hair. 'I was fond of her, I'd have bought her anything she wanted,' he muttered, 'but thinking that she could be the one I would choose to spend the rest of my life with, to have my children . . . the idea was ludicrous.'

'It obviously wasn't to her or Ramón,' said Emma harshly. She disliked Carmelita intensely but she couldn't help feeling for her at this moment. 'You messed her about and then I suppose you did your usual trick of throwing money around and thinking that would solve everything.'

'I told you I wasn't very proud of myself,' said Luis miserably. 'I can only explain how it happened, and hope that you can forgive me.'

'I suppose things are looking up,' she said. 'You used to demand that I forgive you before.'

'Yet you say you fell in love with me even so. Then I am right to hope – '

'Tell me about Carmelita.' This was the most Luis had ever discussed his personal life with her. If there was to be any hope for them she had to know it all.

Luis sighed and rammed his hands into the pockets of his trousers. 'Carmelita and I were both wild as children. We lacked parental discipline, and the staff couldn't control us. As long as we didn't come to any physical harm Grandfather didn't seem to care what we got up to. Often we'd steal food from the kitchen, take the horses and camp out in a little hut on the bank of the Guadalquivir. We thought it was such an adventure, that nobody knew where we were, but of course they did. María told me later that one of the security guards was dispatched after us. He had to stay outside all night and ensure that we returned safely the next day.'

'I bet he loved you.'

Luis shook his head slowly. 'Never will I allow any child of mine to be as obnoxious as I was.'

Emma smiled. 'It sounds fun, though.'

He nodded. 'It was, and as we grew older we discovered a new type of fun we could have together. Carmelita seemed completely happy with the arrangement, and it continued after she left home. She would visit me when she was in Sevilla, we would play, and she would go away clutching a necklace, a ring, or whatever took her fancy in the jeweller's shop the next day.'

'You treated her like a prostitute,' said Emma bluntly.

Luis groaned. 'No. At least if I did I didn't mean to. She wanted the jewellery so I gave it to her. Why not? She'd made me happy. It wasn't until my argument with you that I realized the harm I was doing, and how much I was hurting Grandfather. You were right, Emma: he might have been old but he wasn't stupid. He knew exactly what was going on.'

'So you gave her the push like you told me?'

'Not exactly. At first I tried to be nice, do it gently, but the woman was so thick-skinned she thought I was joking. Then she started calling you names. That annoyed me and I'm afraid that I was rather blunt with her. According to Ramón, she was deeply hurt. It must have been then that he began plotting revenge; they are very close.'

Emma frowned. 'I can understand them being upset, but I just can't understand anyone going to all those lengths to get back at someone.'

'Of course you can't, *guapa*.' He reached

371

across and stroked softly down her cheek. 'That's why his plan worked.'

'And you had no idea until now that that was why I left the country?'

Luis shook his head. 'Your letter led me to believe you hated me because of the fire, your first words when you saw me again were that you hated me, and you've told me often enough since. I thought the trauma had created a mental block. Even though you sometimes gave signs of liking me, that always cut in when we got too close.'

'I'm sure I must have said something about it.'

'If you did then I misinterpreted it, and remember you didn't speak to me at all until you started work at Herrero's. Thinking back, I vaguely recall your mother shouting something similar at me, but she was in such a state hardly anything she said made sense. I thought about it afterwards and came to the conclusion that you'd had to give some reason for your abrupt departure from Spain, and came up with that one.'

'Talk about a tangled web.'

Luis took her hands and pulled her gently to her feet. 'I think we've both been guilty of taking two and two and adding it up to nine.' He wrapped his arms around her waist and drew her towards him.

'I thought it was five,' she murmured as he kissed her hair.

'I think we're both the type of people who

have to outdo anyone else. Other people make five; we make nine.'

She smiled happily. So she could trust Luis. She should have listened to her heart all along; it would have saved her so much pain. Then she grimaced as she thought about how horrible she'd been to him. And then he kissed her and she forgot everything.

'I want to keep you here with me. I don't want to let you go again. I'm afraid if I do the nightmare will replay itself and you'll tell me you hate me again.' He rested his forehead on hers and hugged her tightly. Her body clung to his like glue.

'I'm sorry, Luis. I don't know how you can still like me. I've been a complete bitch to you.'

'You are the only woman I have ever wanted with all my soul, Emma. It wasn't just you who fell in love that first week.'

Emma frowned. Her brain had turned to the texture of molten honey and it was difficult to think clearly, but she knew something didn't add up here.

'Before Don Rafael took ill you were all set to send me away,' she said slowly.

Luis shrugged, then smiled. 'Can't you think why? I needed time alone to gather my wits. You were so very different from any other woman I had ever met. There is an English expression that describes my state perfectly – you blew my mind, *guapa*.'

'It doesn't have *guapa* on the end of it,' she grinned.

'It does now.' He lowered his head and began a slow and thorough exploration of her mouth with his lips and tongue.

'Whatever you say,' she purred, when he paused for air.

'It was a completely new sensation for me. I had never felt like this with Amanda, but I thought perhaps her rejection had somehow sensitized my emotions. I needed to put some distance between us so that I could analyze my feelings.'

'I can understand that, but it hurt that you could get rid of me so easily. You were so cold with all your talk of experiments.'

Luis groaned. 'How can I explain? I was desperate to make love to you. Have you any idea what it would do to any man to have you lying in their bed? To wake up every morning with your limbs entangled in theirs? I was out of my mind with desire, and I must have been out of my mind for setting it up in the first place.'

'So you tested yourself? To see whether you could last out the week? It was an experiment.'

'It was more than that, *guapa*. I couldn't allow myself to give in to my needs. You were so pure, so innocent, I was afraid of destroying that which you held so precious. In the scrambled depths of my brain I still had some concept of honour. I'd promised not to take advantage of you, and I knew that if we made love that first week, no matter how wonderful it was, you would never trust me again.'

'Is that why you made love to me on my birthday, because you thought I wasn't pure any more?'

Luis shook his head. 'The thought of you with Brad ripped me apart, but I had to blot it out of my mind. We'd been apart almost a year; I had to accept you'd lose your virginity in that time. What could I have done? Come over to England and kidnapped you? No. I made love to you, Emma, because the time seemed right. We seemed close, and there seemed the possibility that you didn't hate or blame me any more. I wanted to put our relationship on a deeper level, and I seized the moment. I should have known that nothing where you are involved ever works out quite as expected.'

'I'm afraid I'm not that good at acting the sophisticated mistress,' she smiled wryly.

'Thank goodness for that. I want you as my wife, Emma, not as a mistress.'

Emma felt a sliver of doubt puncture her happiness. 'I'm not so sure,' she said, hugging herself and staring down at the floor.

'About what? Tell me, *guapa*.' He lifted her chin slowly and stared deeply into her eyes. She was shocked to see the dismay and doubt that flooded his own. 'I don't mean to rush you. We can wait a little while if you're happier with that.

Or do you mean you're not sure about marriage itself?'

He saw the answer in her eyes and he took his hands away. He leaned back on the chesterfield, closed his eyes and clenched his fists. 'The most important thing ever to happen in my life and I've mishandled it every step of the way,' he ground out.

'I think I have to share a large part of that blame.' Emma reached out and hesitantly touched his arm.

Immediately his eyes opened. 'Do you think you could maybe learn to love me a little bit in time?' he asked, his voice thick with emotion.

'It's not that, Luis.' She took his hand. 'I love you quite a big bit already.'

'Then why?' He looked totally confused.

Emma sighed. This was so difficult, it hurt so much, but she had to listen to her head. 'I told you a long time ago I'd never marry you, Luis,' she said.

'I remember.' His eyes clouded with pain. 'Would you believe me if I told you that the man I was then has gone forever?'

Emma slowly shook her head. 'It seems like it sometimes, but it can't be, Luis, it's just words.'

'Not just words.' He took her hand and stroked soothingly over its surface with his thumb. 'What do you think hasn't changed?'

Emma felt the reassuring motion of his touch, and closed her eyes. With each stroke she felt her resistance melting, but she had to be strong. She pulled her hand away.

'How can I defend myself if you won't answer me?' he asked.

'Emma took a deep breath to strengthen her resolution. 'I can't cope with infidelity. Some people seem to, but I couldn't. I love you too much; it would kill me.' She looked up at Luis, but instead of the grim acceptance she expected to read on his face she saw the trace of a smile.

'But I'd make damn sure I took you with me,' she flared.

'It's a deal.' He extended his hand for her to shake.

'It's not funny.'

'Not funny at all,' he agreed.

'So what's with all the smiling, then?'

'Relief that you said what you did and nothing more serious.'

'To me, Luis, that is the most serious obstacle between us.' She wanted to shout at him and hit him, but somehow she kept her voice calm.

'Good,' he said, and this time, out of frustration, she did take a swipe at him. He grabbed her arm and easily restrained her.

'Listen to me, Emma. Since the moment I fell in love with you I have never thought of any other woman in a sexual way. I made a conscious vow to myself that I would remain faithful to you. At first I suspected it might prove difficult, but in the event it proved to be one of the easiest tasks I have ever set myself.'

Emma slowly shook her head. 'I don't believe you. My tutor used to buy Spanish magazines for us to read. You were always in them, Luis, it was awful.'

'I'm sorry. I wish you hadn't seen them. They tell such lies.'

'Photographs! Luis.'

He sighed. 'I didn't say I've lived like a hermit this past year, Emma. There were functions I had to attend, you've seen yourself how many there are. Sometimes I would escort an old friend and sometimes I would meet friends there. I believe that every woman I have ever kissed in greeting has at one time or another been reported as my mistress in the press.'

'But why? You're not exactly royalty, are you?'

He laughed softly. 'Thank you for putting me in my place, *guapa*, it is one of the things I find so refreshing about you. What I find more difficult and shaming is confronting the man I was in the past.' He got up and moved to the window, parted the curtains and stared out into the blackness as he spoke.

'When I was eighteen I came into the legacy left by my parents. I'd always had enough money but this was wealth beyond my comprehension. I could do whatever I wanted, and I was of an age when no one could stop me. I would go to the airport and travel on a whim to Paris, London, the South of France, wherever the fancy took me. I quickly developed a large circle of "friends", in inverted commas, and lived a wild and profligate existence for about a year. That was how long it took me to become bored with my lifestyle and want something different. Luckily Quevedo's offered itself and I found satisfaction in learning all aspects of my family's business.'

He turned and glanced across at her. 'You don't say anything?'

'I'm listening.' She smiled at him to go on.

He gave a deep sigh. 'Unfortunately during this period of excess the press were given a field day. At the time their exaggerated reporting of events amused me and I did nothing to stem the rumours. With hindsight, as with most of the events in my life, this was a mistake. The press portrayed me as a playboy at eighteen, and playboy I will probably remain to them when I am a white-haired grandfather of eighty.'

'So you reckon you started leading an exemplary life at the age of nineteen?'

Again the soft laugh that had such a disturbing effect on her heartbeat. 'No, *chica*, but I did calm down. I started working for a living and developed longer term relationships with the opposite sex. Until I met you, love never entered into it. All I can say in my defence is that if I'd met you sooner my life would have been different. You mean everything to me, Emma.

My first thirty years were a mess. With you by my side, the next thirty will be completely different.'

Emma studied the dark, compelling eyes gazing at her. It was a shock to realize that this rich, arrogant man whom she'd thought in need of nothing or no one was in fact so very much in need of her.

'You swear that what you're telling me about other women is the truth?' she asked.

'I swear it, Emma, on the graves of my mother and father. Since the day I fell in love with you I have neither touched nor wished to touch another woman. And I thank God for his mercy in this age of AIDS that my body is free from any disease.'

Emma smiled. His voice and manner were so serious that she had to believe him.

He took her in his arms and hugged her tightly. 'Will you marry me, Emma? Please say yes.'

'Maybe. I'm not sure. It's all such a rush.' She buried her head against his chest, seeking the reassuring slow thud of his heart. All the obstacles to their happiness had been swept away and she couldn't quite come to terms with it yet.

'Emma. My sweet, lovely Emma.' His hand smoothed her hair and pressed her more closely against him. 'Come to my bed, *guapa*. Let me show you how much I adore you.'

'María?' Belatedly it occurred to Emma that

she was at the villa because of her, and the woman must be wondering where on earth she was.

'María knows that you are here, Emma. It will please her infinitely more seeing you come down to breakfast tomorrow than simply seeing you at her party tonight.' He lifted her face and pressed his lips to hers. Her mouth gave him the answer he sought.

Like naughty schoolchildren they opened the study door, waited until there was no one on the main staircase, then raced upstairs. The noise of music and laughter followed them upwards. The party was obviously a roaring success, but Emma wasn't disappointed that she was missing it.

Luis opened his bedroom door and led her over to the huge bed that dominated the room. 'It mocks me every night how empty it is without you in it,' he said softly.

Emma gazed around the room. Entering it hadn't wrought the disturbing effect on her that entering the villa had. She felt calm and happy. It felt right coming back to this room with the man she loved. She smiled at him and lifted up her face to be kissed.

He kissed her forehead, her eyes, her cheeks, her nose, before pressing his full warm lips against hers. She admired his restraint: the thoroughness of his kiss spoke of his desire, yet he undressed her as gently and carefully as if she were a priceless doll. He showed no such care for his own clothes, which were ripped from his body and flung to one side in a matter of seconds.

At last they stood together naked, and she was almost overwhelmed by her own desire. His own urgent maleness pressed insistently against her and she found herself trembling with the intensity of her longing for him.

'I would never hurt you for the world, Emma,' said Luis, misinterpreting her reaction.

'I know. Oh, I feel so stupid.' She twined her hands around his neck and held on as her body shook uncontrollably. 'I can't help it, Luis. I want you so much.'

'So I see.' The low deep chuckle that gurgled in his throat only served to increase her reaction. 'Have I ever told you how much I love you, Emma?' he said, pulling her down on to the bed.

'Not for a few minutes.' Her words ended with a gasp as he lowered his head and took the swollen bud of one breast in his mouth while he massaged the other between his thumb and forefinger.

'Not a day will pass when I don't say those words to you, I promise,' he whispered against her body. His fingers trailed downwards, smoothing over the firm mound of her stomach and pressing tantalizingly against the golden hairs that hid her feminity. Her body stopped shaking and became rigid. It felt as taut and unyielding as an overstretched violin string.

'Relax, *guapa*.' His fingers slipped lower, discovered the sensitive nub of her sexuality, and caressed it expertly. Words failed her as the sensation held her in its thrall. Luis had ignited the touchpaper of her desire. It was burning too brightly now to dampen or extinguish, and moments later she climaxed in a series of involuntary spasms. She gripped his body, drove her nails down his back, and sank her teeth into his shoulder. During it all he told her how much he loved her, and at the end of it he hugged and rocked her gently against him.

'I'm sorry,' she said, when her vocal cords would function again.

'Why should you be sorry?' He looked at her, genuinely perplexed.

'For being selfish,' she murmured. 'I'm sure you didn't mean that to happen so quickly and without you.'

'It wasn't selfish.' He smiled and kissed the tip of her nose. 'You must learn to take love, *guapa*. I have so much of it to give you. And the night certainly isn't over yet.' His lips found hers and his kiss was full of promise.

'Didn't you think it was odd, the way I was trembling? I bet other women don't behave like that.'

'I can't remember, and I care less. I've already told you, *guapa*, since I met you other women have ceased to exist for me. With you I feel new again. Your maidenly trembling was delightful.

I feel privileged to have been the one to cause it.'

Emma snuggled into him happily. Maybe what he was telling her wasn't the complete truth, but she could live with fibs like this.

'I do love you, Luis,' she sighed.

'And I you, *guapa*.' He buried his face into her neck, and she felt a warm tingle spread through her as he kissed its delicate hollow. He didn't linger there, however, but continued a painfully sweet trail down to her breasts where her nipples responded instantly to the flicking motion of his tongue against them.

Emma lay back on the bed and felt desire for him ripple over her like the warm waters of the Mediterranean. She looked down at the dark head suckling her breast and ran her fingers through the silken strands of his hair. How could she ever have denied what was between them? A savage need coursed through her being as he bit gently on her nipple and sucked it into his mouth. Her fingers tightened their hold and dug into his scalp as she pressed him closer and moaned his name.

His mouth left her breast but she kept her fingers entwined in his hair as his head moved lower, his warm tongue lapping over the gentle curve of her stomach. It was an intoxicating feeling being tasted in this way by her lover, and unconsciously she stirred below him. He continued his exploration, but although every fibre of her being ached with the intensity of the experience she pulled him away. She wanted more. This time she didn't want to travel alone. Luis had to be with her, inside her, part of her. She almost lost control and succumbed to the intolerable tension within her as she thought how much she desired him.

'Make love to me.' It was a request, a moan, a command. Emma sat up and pulled him frantically towards her. He smiled, and his dark, dilated pupils reflected the longing she knew was in her own. Moments later he was above her. It wasn't soon enough. Her nails clawed his flesh, urging him downwards. She felt she would lose consciousness if he delayed any longer.

'I'm all yours,' he whispered, and then slowly, gloriously, sensationally he was. Their bodies moved together effortlessly in a timeless primeval rhythm. Each thrust sent sparks of fulfilment ricocheting to the innermost reaches of her being. He was a magician. No man could conjure up such pleasure as Luis was giving her. Her fingers slid across the hard contours of his back in silent adoration.

Above her Luis gazed into the blue depths of her eyes and smiled. Could he read her mind? Did he know how much she loved him? He controlled her completely now. His body dictated the pace and she was content to follow him. For now she was the inexperienced acolyte, but it wouldn't always be so.

Deftly, he brought her to the very edge of

existence. Emma strained against him, desperate now to transcend its boundaries, and he hastened his pace, sensitive to her wishes. Together, they reached the outermost limits of experience. It was almost too much. She cried out and thrashed desperately against him, until her body was rocked by one final orgasmic crescendo and she was delivered safely to the opposite shore.

A century might have passed before Emma opened her eyes again. Her brain had no conception of time. Every atom of sensation had been squeezed from her body, and she floated languid and lifeless on a dense cushioned mattress of nothingness. As consciousness drifted back she attempted to move her hand. She was so deeply relaxed that it took all her willpower to twitch one finger. With a blissful sigh she recalled exactly why she was experiencing such mind-numbing inertia, then focused all her will on turning her head to gaze at the cause of it.

Luis was sprawled across the bed, a thin film of perspiration glistening on his back. One leg was still resting over her, as if it had been too much of an effort to remove it as he'd finally rolled off her. She could tell by its heaviness that he was as deeply relaxed as she was. Joy radiated through her as she realized that it meant she'd been able to give him as much pleasure as he'd given her.

How she loved this man! She could gaze at his

powerful masculine profile forever. Her eyes luxuriated in his nakedness, but as they travelled over the bronzed perfection of his body it was on his face that they lingered longest. Her heart swelled to accommodate another surge of love as she saw Luis as very few people had ever seen him – vulnerable without his public mask, but so much more precious without it.

This was who she was in love with. He wasn't the remote, aloof figure that she'd imagined, he wasn't a magician, though his lovemaking was a magical mystical experience, he was simply a man with normal human needs and desires. They'd been raised in different circumstances, the workings of their brains were often a mystery to each other, but their souls had experienced instant recognition.

Emma reached across and stroked lovingly down Luis's back. He would never hurt her again, she realized. He needed her too much. Without her he was incomplete, just as she was without him.

'Emma.' He stirred under her touch and turned to face her. 'What do you do to me, *guapa*?' He gathered her in his arms and kissed her. 'No woman should have such power over any man.'

Emma smiled as she recalled thinking similar sentiments, but she kept her thoughts to herself. 'Ask me again, Luis,' she commanded instead.

He didn't ask what. Their thought processes

were becoming more attuned and he was beginning to understand her. 'Must I go on my knees?' he asked.

'Of course.' That would be something for posterity, though unfortunately she probably wouldn't be able to share it with anyone. She could hardly regale their grandchildren with the story of how Don Luis sank to his knees and proposed, stark naked, to their grandmother after the most glorious, fantastic lovemaking known to man.

'Emma. My love. My life. Marry me and make me the happiest man on this planet.'

Emma savoured the moment. Beneath Luis's stern, harsh exterior beat the heart of a true romantic. It was hidden, one had to mine deep before catching the faintest glimmer of it, but like pure gold it repaid the effort of excavation. She was ecstatically happy, but the humour of the scene hadn't escaped her.

'Yeah, OK,' she said, then sank back, giggling, as a look of bemusement filtered over Luis's expression.

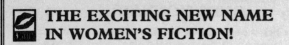 # THE EXCITING NEW NAME IN WOMEN'S FICTION!

PLEASE HELP ME TO HELP YOU!

Dear *Scarlet* Reader,

As Editor of *Scarlet* Books I want to make sure that the books I offer you every month are up to the high standards *Scarlet* readers expect. And to do that I need to know a little more about you and your reading likes and dislikes. So please spare a few minutes to fill in the short questionnaire on the following pages and send it to me.

Looking forward to hearing from you,

Sally Cooper

Editor-in-Chief, *Scarlet*

Note: further offers which might be of interest may be sent to you by other, carefully selected, companies. If you do not want to receive them, please write to Robinson Publishing Ltd, 7 Kensington Church Court, London W8 4SP, UK.

QUESTIONNAIRE

Please tick the appropriate boxes to indicate your answers

1 Where did you get this Scarlet title?

Bought in supermarket ☐

Bought at my local bookstore ☐ Bought at chain bookstore ☐

Bought at book exchange or used bookstore ☐

Borrowed from a friend ☐

Other (please indicate) _____

2 Did you enjoy reading it?

A lot ☐   A little ☐   Not at all ☐

3 What did you particularly like about this book?

Believable characters ☐   Easy to read ☐

Good value for money ☐   Enjoyable locations ☐

Interesting story ☐   Modern setting ☐

Other _____

4 What did you particularly dislike about this book?

_____

5 Would you buy another Scarlet book?

Yes ☐   No ☐

6 What other kinds of book do you enjoy reading?

Horror ☐   Puzzle books ☐   Historical fiction ☐

General fiction ☐   Crime/Detective ☐   Cookery ☐

Other (please indicate) _____

7 Which magazines do you enjoy reading?

1. _____

2. _____

3. _____

And now a little about you –

8 How old are you?

Under 25 ☐   25–34 ☐   35–44 ☐

45–54 ☐   55–64 ☐   over 65 ☐

cont.

9 What is your marital status?

Single ☐   Married/living with partner   ☐

Widowed ☐   Separated/divorced   ☐

10 What is your current occupation?

Employed full-time ☐   Employed part-time   ☐

Student ☐   Housewife full-time   ☐

Unemployed ☐   Retired   ☐

11 Do you have children? If so, how many and how old are they?

_____

_____

12 What is your annual household income?

under $15,000	☐	or	£10,000	☐
$15–25,000	☐	or	£10–20,000	☐
$25–35,000	☐	or	£20–30,000	☐
$35–50,000	☐	or	£30–40,000	☐
over $50,000	☐	or	£40,000	☐

Miss/Mrs/Ms _____

Address _____

_____

_____

Thank you for completing this questionnaire. Now tear it out – put it in an envelope and send it, before 31 August 1998, to:

Sally Cooper, Editor-in-Chief

USA/Can. address	*UK address/No stamp required*
SCARLET c/o London Bridge	SCARLET
85 River Rock Drive	FREEPOST LON 3335
Suite 202	LONDON W8 4BR
Buffalo	*Please use block capitals for*
NY 14207	*address*
USA	

DADEC/2/98

Scarlet titles coming next month:

RETURN TO OPAL REACH Clarissa Garland
When Skye Taylor meets Jarrah Kaine she doesn't *plan* to
end up pregnant and living with him at Opal Reach. Life on
the Australian cattle station is very different to Skye's
glamorous life in New Zealand. Perhaps they might have
made it work though, had the reasons behind their hasty
marriage still existed . . .

THE NAME OF THE GAME Julie Garratt
Maggie Brand has been in love with Rafe Thorne for years,
but he doesn't even know that she exists. Now he's set to
marry fragile Tamsin, so Maggie still doesn't stand a chance
. . . or does she?

SUMMER OF SECRETS Kathryn Bellamy
Linked to *Game, Set & Match* and *Mixed Doubles*
To avoid a scandal, Saul Lancaster and Ginny Sinclair
manage to persuade his friends that they are very much a
couple. All around them relationships are in trouble, so a
pretend romance suddenly seems a very good idea!

HIDDEN EMBERS Angie Gaynor
Cliff Foreman might love Lynne Castle. He might even be
prepared to marry her to give her unborn child a name. But
he *knows* the child can't possibly be his! So why does Lynne
keep insisting he's the father?

JOIN THE CLUB!

Why not join the _Scarlet_ Reader's Club – you can have four exciting new reads delivered to your door every month for only £9.99, plus TWO FREE BOOKS WITH YOUR FIRST MONTH'S ORDER!

Fill in the form below and tick your two free books from those listed:

1. *Never Say Never* by Tina Leonard ☐
2. *The Sins of Sarah* by Anne Styles ☐
3. *Wicked in Silk* by Andrea Young ☐
4. *Wild Lady* by Liz Fielding ☐
5. *Starstruck* by Lianne Conway ☐
6. *This Time Forever* by Vickie Moore ☐
7. *It Takes Two* by Tina Leonard ☐
8. *The Mistress* by Angela Drake ☐
9. *Come Home Forever* by Jan McDaniel ☐
10. *Deception* by Sophie Weston ☐
11. *Fire and Ice* by Maxine Barry ☐
12. *Caribbean Flame* by Maxine Barry ☐

ORDER FORM

SEND NO MONEY NOW. Just complete and send to SCARLET READERS' CLUB, FREEPOST, LON 3335, Salisbury SP5 5YW

Yes, I want to join the **SCARLET READERS' CLUB*** and have the convenience of 4 exciting new novels delivered directly to my door every month! Please send me my first shipment now for the unbelievable price of £9.99, plus my TWO special offer books absolutely free. I understand that I will be invoiced for this shipment and FOUR further *Scarlet* titles at £9.99 (including postage and packing) every month unless I cancel my order in writing. I am over 18.

Signed ....

Name (IN BLOCK CAPITALS) ....

Address (IN BLOCK CAPITALS) ....

....

Town .... **Post Code** ....

As a result of this offer your name and address may be passed on to other carefully selected companies. If you do not wish this, please tick this box☐.

*Please note this offer applies to UK only.

Did You Know?

There are over 120 NEW romance novels published each month in the US & Canada?

♥ *Romantic Times Magazine* is **THE ONLY SOURCE** that tells you what they are and where to find them—even if you live abroad!

♥ *Each issue* reviews **ALL** 120 titles, saving you time and money at the bookstores!

♥ Lists *mail-order* book stores who service international customers!

ROMANTIC TIMES MAGAZINE
~ *Established 1981* ~

Order a <u>SAMPLE COPY</u> Now!

FOR UNITED STATES & CANADA ORDERS:
$2.00 United States & Canada (U.S FUNDS ONLY)
CALL 1-800-989-8816*

* 800 NUMBER FOR US CREDIT CARD ORDERS ONLY
♥ **BY MAIL:** Send <u>US funds Only</u>. Make check payable to:
Romantic Times Magazine, 55 Bergen Street, Brooklyn, NY 11201 USA
♥ **TEL.:** 718-237-1097   ♥ **FAX:** 718-624-4231

VISA • M/C • AMEX • DISCOVER ACCEPTED FOR US, CANADA & UK ORDERS!

FOR UNITED KINGDOM ORDERS: (Credit Card Orders Accepted!)
£2.00 Sterling—Check made payable to Robinson Publishing Ltd.
♥ **BY MAIL:** Check to above **DRAWN ON A UK BANK** to: Robinson Publishing Ltd., 7 Kensington Church Court, London W8 4SP England

♥ E-MAIL CREDIT CARD ORDERS: RTmag1@aol.com
♥ VISIT OUR WEB SITE: http://www.rt-online.com